CALL GAME

**GRAHAM ELDER
AND
LAURA CODY**

Black Rose Writing | Texas

ISBN: 978-1-68513-667-3
LIBRARY OF CONGRESS CONTROL NUMBER: 2025936754
PUBLISHED BY BLACK ROSE WRITING
www.blackrosewriting.com

Printed in the United States of America
Suggested Retail Price (SRP) $21.95

Call Game is printed in Minion Pro

*As a planet-friendly publisher, Black Rose Writing does its best to eliminate unnecessary waste to reduce paper usage and energy costs, while never compromising the reading experience. As a result, the final word count vs. page count may not meet common expectations.

In memory of Dr. Susan Cowdery, our dear friend and colleague who was the epitome of resilience, courage, and grace in the face of terminal cancer.

PRAISE FOR
CALL GAME

"An exceptional debut novel full of intrigue, surprising twists, and medical stories portraying the drama found every day in the hospital."
–Gary Gerlacher, Bestselling Author of the *AJ Docker Series*

"Combines fascinating true-life medical situations and a final twist I did not see coming to offer a suspenseful serial killer thriller that pulled me in and did not release me until the last page. I highly recommend this book."
–Scott Eveloff, MD, author of *Do Not Resuscitate*

"Grabs hold from the very first chapter and doesn't let go. With sharp dialogue, vivid characters, and a steadily mounting sense of dread, *Call Game* keeps the tension high all the way to its haunting and explosive conclusion. A gripping, genre-bending read that I highly recommend."
–Julia Shraybman, author of *Lucky 6*

"Should come with a warning not to read before bedtime … to call it gripping would be an understatement … I have lost 2 nights' sleep reading it and just finished the book now … 6:15 am … well done!! 5 stars!!!"
–John Clement, author of *Musings of the Wandering Whisky Whisperer*

"This book is a read-in-one-evening thriller that you can't put down! Think *Sherlock Holmes* meets *Grey's Anatomy.* Awesome read!"
–Dr. Brynlea Barbeau, MD (GP)

"Anyone who has worked a night shift where it feels like nothing can go right will love this book."
–Dr. Emily Cook, MD (Anesthesiologist)

"A night on call at the Northern Michigan hospital reminded me of some of my long on-call nights at the state hospital, except there no one was trying to kill me!"
–Dr. John Heintzman, MD (Psychiatrist)

"Fast-paced, captivating, and full of unexpected turns. An addictive read from start to finish!"
–Hannah Murray, RN

"Yanks you right into the action of a trauma bay. Addicting combination of mystery, adrenaline, and medicine."
–Mary Grannary, Medical Student

CALL
GAME

CHAPTER 1

Rylan

The wind pushed and heaved like a farmyard workhorse, a beast on a plow with the brute force of its shoulders laying into the harness. Rylan almost felt herself lifted through the portico of the ambulance bay and carried through the sliding doors of the emergency room entrance, a few early November snowflakes stealing their way alongside her. The familiar scent of alcohol and chlorhexidine instantly tickled her nose and settled in the back of her throat. After almost five years of orthopedic surgical residency, she now found the smell comforting, a welcome home present, like grandma's hot apple pie.

She pulled back the hood of her parka and quickly surveyed the scene. The action, as expected, was in the trauma bay. She raced over and took inventory – one nurse starting an O neg blood transfusion, one nurse documenting, and Mike, the ER doc, running the ATLS algorithm, having already intubated the patient. Sizing up the patient, she came to a disheartening conclusion – he wasn't going to make it. But, hey, crazier things had happened. She ditched her parka, grabbed a set of gloves and a visor, and went to work.

"Seriously?" Mike shook his head, peering at Rylan over his visor. "White?"

Rylan looked down at her white blouse. She had come straight from dinner at a nearby Thai restaurant. Another "datus interruptus," a phenomenon all too familiar to the chief orthopedic resident. In this case, though, she didn't much mind. Dude was boring as all hell. Someone tossed her an impermeable scrub gown, and she donned it reflexively.

Approaching the bedside, she performed a quick head-to-toe scan. "What's the damage, Mike?"

"For you? So far, just the open tibia. I checked his pelvis, and it seems fine."

Her eyes darted to the victim's right tibia, where a pool of well-oxygenated, bright red blood was forming on the gurney sheets, and a jagged, pearly white shard of bone was pointing towards the ceiling. She shook her head in dismay, realizing she was going to greet Thanksgiving morning with big, purple bags under her eyes. "Well, I always say sleep is overrated."

She looked up and noticed Mike shaking his head at her as he threaded a central line through the patient's left subclavian vein. "You guys kill me. You hit fifth year, and everything you see is calculated in terms of sleep hours lost."

Rylan gave Mike a sassy smile, then grabbed a bottle of warmed saline and poured it sloppily over the tibia, drenching the bed in the process. "Anyone give him a shot of orthocillin and tetanus?" she asked, grabbing a sterile brush and scrubbing the bits of dirt, asphalt, and black leather off the bone.

"Pretty sure osteomyelitis and lockjaw are the least of his worries at the moment," Mike said, squeezing an IV bag until his knuckles turned white.

A nurse to her right nodded. "I gave him both. A second unit of O neg going in."

Rylan threw the brush into a corner sink, backhanded. *Nice shot.* She then put one sterile gloved hand on the bone fragment and another around the ankle. With a combination of traction and pressure, the shard of bone disappeared beneath the skin with a grotesque slurping sound. A final farewell, it launched a large tear-shaped droplet of blood into the air straight towards Rylan's face. She expertly dodged the blood bullet with a twist of her neck. *Easy.* She smiled.

Mike smiled back. "Nice dodge. Your blouse didn't make it, though."

Rylan tucked her chin in and glanced downward, barely able to see the errant collar of her blouse protruding from the top of the scrub gown. She saw enough, though. "Motherfucker!!" She stamped her foot. "This was my date night blouse."

"Did we yank you from a hot date?"

"More like tepid. Let's just say, I'm not entirely unhappy to be here."

"Right. Gotcha." Mike looked over the vital sign readings on a monitor and frowned. "Check his pelvis again, Rylan. I may have missed something. He's got at least 4L of Ringers on board, a unit of blood, and I'm still having trouble keeping his pressure up."

Rylan moved her hands to either side of the patient's pelvis, over the iliac wings, and pushed. At first, there was no give, then she pushed a little harder, and they opened wide. *Shit.* "Mike. He's got a fucking unstable open-book pelvis. This should've been the priority." She gave Mike an evil glare.

"Hey, it seemed stable to me. That's why you're the specialist, right?"

The chief of security poked her head into the trauma bay. "They found a wallet at the scene. Guy's name is Brad. He's twenty-eight years old and has two young kids – a boy and a girl." She held up a wallet-sized photo, waving it in the air like a red cape at a bullfight.

"Thanks, Helen. Thanks a lot," Mike snapped. "Any more good news? It's not like we can try any harder."

"Chill out, Mike," Rylan said. "We'll save this guy." She wasn't sure she believed it, but she wanted to. She turned to one of the cupboards, grabbed a bed sheet, and folded it lengthwise. She passed it under the patient's legs. "Helen. A little help here?"

"Not really in my wheelhouse, Dr. Fraser." A short pause. "But, since it's you …"

Helen grabbed the other side of the sheet, and together, from the end of the bed, they shimmied the sheet up under the patient's legs and under his buttocks. Rylan took hold of Helen's end and pulled tight, tying a gigantic square knot on the front of the patient's pelvis in the process.

"You wrappin' up a present for the OR?" Helen asked.

"Something like that. His pelvis is broken and wide open, allowing a ton of blood to accumulate back there. In fact, we call this an *open-book fracture*, and the idea is to close the book by wrapping the sheet tightly around his pelvis. Normally, we would have special binder devices designed for this, but I guess Northern Michigan General Hospital is a little too strapped for that."

"That's better," Mike said, pointing to the monitor. "His BP is stabilizing, and his pulse is coming down a little."

"Well. Learn something new every day." Helen smiled. "I guess my job is done here. I have to make rounds. Rylan? Up for a midnight coffee?"

"Sure," Rylan said, "unless I'm up to my ass in … what's his name? … Brad?"

"You've got my cell number."

"On speed dial." Rylan smiled and patted the cell phone in the rear pocket of her black slacks. She gave Helen a cursory wave then quickly slapped a plaster splint on Brad's lower leg. When she was done, she turned her attention back to Mike. "Hey, where's that dickwad general surgery resident, anyway? Isn't he supposed to be leading this trauma team?"

"Ahem."

Rylan stiffened upon hearing an exaggerated throat-clearing behind her.

"Dickwad?

"Oh. Hey, Todd." Rylan smiled wryly at Mike and rolled her eyes. "Didn't really mean that. I'm pissed my R3 hasn't shown up. Apparently, he never answered his –"

"Forget it," Todd interrupted, placing his hands on the patient's abdomen. "I've been called worse." He worked his hands over the four quadrants, pushing deeply into the tissues of the patient's abdomen. "Belly's like a rock. He needs a CT, Mike."

"No kidding? CT? Great plan, Todd. Brilliant. You're the man. I'll get right on it."

"Spare me the attitude. I'm calling my staff to get the OR ready. He'll likely need a laparotomy."

"How about if we stabilize him first?" Mike said, raising his eyebrows.

Rylan backed away, giving Mike a cautious wave of her hand. "I'll let you boys discuss things. I have to call my staff. Not to mention find out where my R3 is," she said, referring to the third-year resident who was sharing the night's call with her. This last part she mumbled to herself as she left the trauma bay and scooted to the main desk in the emergency room where she greeted the ward clerk behind the desk. "Hey, Carla, did my R3 call back?"

Carla, a brunette with bright, green-framed glasses and a strangely deep, baritone voice, said he had not. "However, I *did* find this when I came back from break." She held up a pager with an envelope folded into the clip. "It's addressed to you."

Rylan plucked the pager from Carla's outstretched palm, unclipped the envelope – noting her full name (Dr. Rylan Fraser) written in black ink on the outside – and opened it. She unfolded the paper tucked inside and quickly scanned the contents. Carla looked on, her inquisitive eyes glued to Rylan's face. "So? Where is the little shit?"

Rylan shook her head, crumpled the paper, and tossed a three-pointer into a nearby trash can. "He's taking the weekend off to visit his sick grandmother in Detroit. WTF. I'm pretty sure his grandmother passed away last year. Asshole. He's left me solo for the entire Thanksgiving Day weekend."

"Asshole," Carla repeated, looking back to her computer screen.

Rylan played with the pager, tossing it from one hand to the other, mentally reorganizing her entire weekend to a soundtrack of expletives she managed, heroically, to keep in her head and off her lips.

She looked up from the pager and was startled to see someone she did not recognize standing only a few feet away in front of Carla's desk. He smiled at her, and she smiled back, taking in his wavy black hair, sharp-cut jaw, and thin, solid build. He was wearing an unbuttoned Armani black suit jacket over an open-collar shirt tucked into a pair of jeans. He turned to Carla and said, "Hi. I'm Dr. Bennett. Paul Bennett. I'm just coming on staff, and I was told to pick up some sort of emergency psych pager here. Does that make any sense to you?"

Carla gazed into his eyes, seemingly awestruck, before yammering, "Umm, yeah, Dr. Bennett. I have an envelope for you from admin right here. You're on staff? Like, permanent staff?"

"I am. Just moved up from Toledo this week." He leaned forward and dropped his voice. "To tell you the truth, I'm a little nervous. You know, new job, new town, new people?"

"Umm, yeah. Sure."

Without further words of reassurance forthcoming from Carla, he turned to Rylan. He was about to ask something but paused, mouth half open, and stared. Wordlessly, he lifted his hand towards her, and for a second, Rylan thought he was going to touch her cheek. Instead, he pointed an index finger at her neck and said, "I believe you have something on the collar of your blouse."

Rylan blushed and stammered, "Blood. Yeah, blood bullet. We were just in the middle of a trauma … my new blouse." For Chrissakes, she was worse than Carla.

"Hope you can save it," Dr. Bennett said. He smiled kindly and turned back to Carla. "Also, I was on the psych ward just now, and someone named – Dr. Curran? – left a message on my phone about a suicidal patient here in the ER that needs my attention. Presumably, I would be contacted for such a thing on this pager." He held the new black pager in front of him. "Fairly archaic, isn't it? I haven't used one of these since residency. What's wrong with my phone?"

Rylan, holding the R3 pager in her hand, explained, "There's been a high turnover of psych docs recently, as well as some high-profile psych cases in the ER. The powers that be felt a pager would be a more consistent way for the ER staff to reach out for psych help." Rylan, herself, as the chief orthopedic resident, was only reachable by her phone. Junior residents carried the pagers. She could tell Dr. Bennett felt the pager was demeaning, and she didn't blame him.

"Right," he said, clipping the pager to his belt. "Not sure I'm going to like this. Where can I find this Dr. Curran?"

Both Rylan and Carla were about to point towards the trauma bay when Mike appeared at the entrance, walking towards them with his hands in the air, clearly frustrated. "Rylan, Todd the Dickwad is taking my barely stable patient to CT then straight to the OR. He thinks our patient might have a bowel rupture. He wouldn't know a bowel rupture if it shit on him."

"Mike," Rylan said firmly, her eyes pointing towards Dr. Bennett, "This is our new psychiatrist, Dr. Paul Bennett. You called him?"

An almost audible clicking sounded as Mike shifted gears. He ripped his blood-soaked gown off and dumped it, along with his gloves, in a nearby trash bin. He thrust his hand out to Dr. Bennett and said, "Welcome to Northern Michigan General Hospital, Paul. I'm Mike Curran, ER staff. Your services are sorely needed." They shook hands, and Mike dragged Dr. Bennett towards the lockdown room, all the while apologizing for his earlier profanities.

Rylan, still standing at the desk holding the R3 pager, suddenly registered what Mike had said. "Wait. What do you mean Dickwad is taking our patient to the OR? I haven't even called my attending yet. FUCK!"

CHAPTER 2

Paul

Paul followed Mike through a labyrinth of ramshackle corridors lined with empty gurneys, nearly running to keep up. Mike moved like a man powered by a tiny motor, and Paul quickly pegged him as a Type A, alpha male – a fast thinker, fast mover, and fast talker. Right now, he was fast-talking about the budget cuts and staffing issues that had necessitated the dissolution of the hospital's psychiatric residency program a few years earlier. Now Paul understood the archaic little pager clipped to his waistband, scratching at his stomach with every step. No residents meant he'd be the first one called for any psychiatric issue throughout the night. *And* throughout the holiday tomorrow. *And* throughout the rest of the long weekend. No wonder the people in HR had been so anxious to get Paul Bennett to sign on the dotted line and get started ASAP. It was going to be a *long* weekend. The emergency room was hopping, and the snow was really coming down outside. Paul hadn't expected to spend the whole night at the hospital, but now he was thinking it might be a smart move to ask about a call room. If he could get a word in, that is. He opened his mouth to say something as he trailed Mike through a door which, quite literally, hit Paul in the ass.

"Watch those doors. They're heavy, and they close fast."

"Yeah, thanks," Paul grumbled.

Mike grinned. "Triage is over there," he said, waving to a woman in beige scrubs taking a patient's blood pressure, "and the pediatric waiting room is back there."

Paul nodded, and Mike went on. "Psych is this way, through the double doors." Mike bent and waved his ID card at a scanner attached to an outer door. "Hopefully, your ID card has been activated. You'll need it each time you come in. The unit is locked."

Paul unclipped his ID from the lapel of his jacket and tested it. It worked, no problem, but Paul wished it hadn't because just as he and Mike entered the psych ER, he was spit upon. Literally spit upon. A big wad of frothy, yellow-tinged spit hit him square in the chest and spawned little baby spit-wads that splashed up to his chin and down to his shoes.

The revulsion was sharp and immediate. The humiliation of being spat on upon entrance to his new place of work was bad enough, but Paul had germ issues – and everyone knew the human mouth was beyond filthy.

"What the hell?!" Mike demanded, but he was largely ignored as a nurse and a few large men in latex gloves tried to coax a very resistant, scraggly old man out of the open hall and into a room.

"Hiram there is a spitter," the nurse said, shielding her face with a clipboard.

"Jesus, that's disgusting." Mike looked down the front of his lab coat and checked for errant droplets. "Is his name actually Hiram?"

"We can't get a name out of him yet, but that's what was on the soggy label stuck to his shoe."

"That explains why it smells like a distillery in here. Give him ten of Haldol, and he can sleep it off. Just let me know if his vitals are unstable."

"Will do."

"This, by the way, is Dr. Bennett, the new psychiatrist," Mike said, clapping Paul on the back and nudging him toward the nursing station.

"Not the kind of welcome you're used to, I'll bet," he said as he guided him through a glass door.

The station was empty except for a clerk who was busy with the phones. Paul saw her wave to Mike while picking up a ringing line, "Psych ER."

"That's Nadia," Mike said. "Be nice to her, and she'll be nice to you. Cross her, and she'll make your life hell."

As Paul wondered what constituted "crossing," Mike handed him a couple of alcohol wipes. "For the … you know," he said, pointing a finger at Paul's chin.

Paul accepted the wipe and went to work scrubbing. He tried to be nonchalant about it, like a little spit was no big deal, but inside he was screaming for a shower and change of clothes. He was self-aware enough to know that he had a bona fide hang-up in his distaste for secretions and body fluids. This hang-up had even cost him a relationship or two when a partner found his irrepressible need to shower within minutes of an intimate encounter insulting.

While Paul was scrubbing a red spot on his chin raw, Mike clapped his hands once and directed Paul's attention to the dry-erase board beside Nadia. "The top name," he said, "that's who I want you to see."

"Jane Doe?"

Mike nodded. "Brought in by ambulance from the parking lot of a local Mickey D's. She was causing a disturbance, so the manager called 911. No ID on her whatsoever, and we can't get a word of sense out of her. Seems young, though. I'm guessing fifteen or sixteen."

"Tox screen?"

"Negative. Vitals stable, no obvious signs of trauma. Medically cleared but definitely not safe to leave in her current state. Plus," Mike said, "without an identity or an age, we have nowhere to send her and no one to contact. Social workers have tried, but she's … been difficult."

"Give her anything?"

"Almost."

"Almost?"

"When she got here, she was thrashing about and screaming like a wild thing. We drew up a B52," Mike said, referring to a potent cocktail of antipsychotic and sedative medication given sometimes in emergencies, "but when she saw the needle, she went still and shouted, 'No meds, no meds!' so we held off. Since then, magically, the agitation has ceased. But I think she's hallucinating and responding to internal stimuli."

Paul scratched at his chin. "Fifteen or sixteen, that's young."

"Hey, that's just a guess. She could be older. We've made a police report in case anyone out there is looking for her, and the social workers have called child services, but I can't see anyone getting to her tonight. Not with the storm coming."

"Can I see her?"

"Right this way." With a theatrical flourish of his arm, Mike pointed Paul to a small room. The door was open, and a plastic chair was perched across the threshold. On the chair sat a woman. She looked up when she saw Mike approaching. "Hi, Dr. Curran."

"Hi, Marie. This is Dr. Bennett from psychiatry."

She smiled at Paul.

"Marie is the one-to-one aide."

Paul looked past Marie into the room. A mattress on the floor was occupied by a young woman in hospital pajamas lying on her back staring at the ceiling. Her palms were pressed together over her chest, as if in prayer, and her lips were moving non-stop, although little more than a faint murmur could be heard.

Mike took a few steps into the room, maintaining a safe distance. He cleared his throat. "Ahem. Um, we met earlier … not sure if you remember?"

The patient on the mattress gave no indication she'd heard him.

"Anyway," Mike said, "I'm back with another doctor who'd like to speak with you."

The girl's lips continued moving. Quiet, inaudible words. After a moment, she turned her dark, penetrating eyes to her visitors. They wandered disinterestedly over Mike and landed on Paul. "Are you one of them?" she asked.

"Yes, I'm one of the doctors –"

"No!" she shouted, causing both Paul and Mike to step back. In an instant, she was sitting bolt upright on the mattress. "Are you one of *them*?" Her eyes ping-ponged frantically from left to right and back again. With white knuckles, she twisted and squeezed her hospital nightgown in her lap as though wringing a wet washcloth dry.

"Okay, then, I'll let you take it from here," Mike said in an only-too-happy-to-go voice, clapping Paul on the back. "When you're done, look for Sandy. She's the head nurse on duty for psych down here tonight, and she can get you hooked up with a computer to do your charting."

Paul nodded. His young patient had gone immobile and fixed a flat, unnerving stare on him.

"I'm heading back to the trauma bay, but I'll be in and out. Let me know if you need anything." Mike jotted his cell number on a sticky and handed it to Paul before he walked off.

Paul focused on those unsettling eyes. He scooted further from Marie and approached the mattress. The young woman watched him approach, and her lips started working again, producing that indecipherable murmur. Then her eyes did a slow drift into the right corner of the room where they lingered with interest. Paul followed her gaze to the empty corner and saw nothing there. His patient nodded slowly – in response to what, Paul was unsure – then turned her attention back to Paul. "Are you one of them?" she asked again, this time with a preternatural calmness that bordered on spooky.

"I'm the psychiatrist," Paul said, enunciating each word with gentle clarity.

"You're the *psychiatrist*?" she repeated, her voice rising strangely on the last word. "Oh, *wonderful*."

Paul stole a glance at the aid by the door who raised her eyebrows and shrugged. He swallowed hard and turned back to his patient. Using the most nonthreatening body posture and tone he could muster, he said, "You're in the right place. You're safe here."

The girl closed her eyes and appeared to shudder with rapturous delight. She lifted her face toward the ceiling and smiled widely, showcasing a set of slightly crooked teeth that glowed in the room's dim light. "Good," she said. The tension in her body seemed to melt away, and her hands and lips went still. She relaxed into a cross-legged posture on the mattress and gazed at Paul, waiting.

"Can we talk for a bit?" Paul asked.

The girl nodded, and her arms opened in welcome, like those of an enlightened monk.

Paul addressed the aide at the door. "Marie, I think we'll be okay now."

Marie left to take a break, and Paul pulled the vacated chair into the middle of the room and sat down. He found Jane Doe staring at him with a strange, expectant look on her face. Carefully, Paul said a few opening words. These words seemed to satisfy Jane Doe, and the two fell into conversation.

When Paul exited the room twenty minutes later, two things were clear – Jane Doe was more disturbed than even he had anticipated, and she was definitely not leaving the hospital that night.

CHAPTER 3

Rylan

"Dr. Huang?"

"What?"

"It's Dr. Fraser, Rylan Fraser."

"What do you want?"

Rylan took a deep, calming breath. She was the on-call surgical resident, and Dr. Huang was the on-call surgical attending. What the hell did he think she wanted? *Oh, your godliness, I just wanted to know whether you'd prefer apple or pumpkin pie for Thanksgiving dessert tomorrow.* Truly, she wanted nothing at all from this megalomaniacal narcissist, but he was the boss, and he needed to know. She cleared her throat and got to it. "We have a twenty-eight-year-old male with an open tibia fracture, an open book pelvic fracture, and an abdominal injury. Gen Surg is taking him straight to the OR for a laparotomy after he gets a head-to-toe CT scan."

"I see." A short pause. "What do you want to do, Dr. Fraser?"

She spewed her rehearsed answer quickly, "Given that he appears systemically very unstable, I thought a damage control approach would be best –"

"Yes, yes, I understand, Dr. Fraser, but what specifically do YOU want to do?"

"Ex-fix tibia and pelvis with tibia wash out."

"Have you done this before?"

Slight hesitation. "Yes." She had assisted her chief resident last year in applying a tibial external fixator on a woman who had jumped off a bridge. She remembered it was like playing with a Meccano set. Easy peasy. She had never, however, seen a pelvic external fixator applied other than in teaching videos and textbooks.

"Hmm," Dr. Huang responded, "I doubt it. Prepare the patient. He'll be in CT for a while, so there's time. I'll be along shortly."

The line went dead, and Rylan muttered under her breath, "Condescending asshole."

She stepped out of the emergency room and took flight to the elevators, her unzipped parka flapping like wings. As she passed the main security desk situated near the entrance, she heard Helen comment, "Someone not treating you right, Rylan?"

Rylan put the brakes on and whiplashed her head to face Helen, who stood no more than five feet tall and carried some extra weight around the midsection that she described as "absolutely necessary to the fulfillment of my job since I need to be able to throw a little weight around this place." *Wink, wink.*

"Damn," Rylan said. "The sterile walls have ears around here."

"Nothing gets by me, darling. You know that."

"That was my attending, not the easiest guy to work with. I think I'm going to need some moral support tonight. Can I call you later?"

Helen chuckled. "Anytime, darlin'. I'm here all night."

"You may live to regret those words. Remember, I've got you on speed –" Her R3 pager erupted with a tinny, annoying version of Twinkle Twinkle Little Star. *Seriously?* She scowled at it, unclipped it from her waistband, and made a move like she was going to throw it into a nearby trash can. "I hate this pager. And Twinkle Twinkle Little Star irritates the hell out of me."

Helen grinned. "Off you go," she said, making a little sweeping motion with her hand.

Rylan groaned and started walking toward the elevators. "See ya later," she called over her shoulder.

Rylan pressed the up button on a nearby elevator with one hand while she grabbed her phone from her jacket pocket with the other and punched in the number from the pager. She was heading to the OR but planned to stop by her locker to drop off her parka and backpack, as well as get her lab coat, remembering that, among a million other particularities, Dr. Huang freaked if you didn't wear a lab coat outside the surgical suites. The call connected as she stepped onto an empty elevator and pressed the third floor. It was fast approaching seven p.m. on a long holiday weekend, and there wouldn't be many people around, so she'd at least be able to make good time getting from point A to point B throughout the hospital. Her call connected to a busy signal. "Who the heck pages someone then uses the same phone to call out? Stupid …"

She was listening to the rumblings of the decades-old elevator, staring at her phone when it rang.

She toggled the green answer button and said, "Hi, it's Dr. Fraser."

There was a long pause, and she was about to hang up, thinking the elevator was interfering with the signal, but then she heard, "Congratulations, Dr. Fraser. First woman ever to win the Charles M. Washburne top resident award." It was a man's voice, one she didn't recognize.

"Umm. Thanks?" The award had been bestowed weeks earlier, and her colleagues and mentors in the orthopedic department had already honored Rylan with a celebratory brunch, so she was at a loss regarding who was on the other end of the line now. The elevator arrived abruptly at the third floor, and the door squelched open. "Who is this?" she asked.

"Let's have some fun …." Click.

Rylan stared at her screen. *What the f–?*

The door to the elevator began to close. She thrust one foot into the gap, and her sneaker got crushed by the thick, metal doors. In normal elevators in normal places, an electric eye would sense the obstacle and prevent the doors from closing. But not here in Northern Michigan

General. Here, one was required to risk life and limb to escape an elevator whose doors had committed to closing. Those fainter-of-heart were compelled to ride to the next floor then take the stairs, but not Rylan. Rylan was a fighter, and by God, she was getting out of this elevator now. On her own terms. She stepped forward, wedged her whole body into the door space, and wriggled her shoulders to create room for her head (*like delivering a baby: first the head, then the upper shoulder, then the lower ...*). An alarm sounded, and Rylan felt sweat break out on her forehead. "Freaking ... Ugh ... Ancient ..." The door squeezed tighter. "Argh ... piece of garbage elevator ...."

Finally, she pushed through and stumbled out the other side, accidentally launching her phone down the hallway. The door slammed behind her like a mousetrap as she lost her footing and pirouetted forward. She caught herself on the opposite wall and stood bent at the waist, huffing and puffing. She looked left and right, happy to see her woman-against-machine moment had gone unnoticed. She stood up tall, patted her hair, and rubbed a sore shoulder. Her stupid pager twinkled loud and annoying, pulling her back into the moment. She'd have to tend to her bruised shoulders (and ego) later. Down the corridor, she retrieved her phone and dialed up the latest page on the fly.

"Surgical ward, Linda speaking," a voice on the phone answered.

"Hi, Linda. It's Dr. Fraser. Someone paged?"

"Oooh, yeah. Hang on."

Barely a second passed before an anxious voice came on the line. "Dr. Fraser, you have to get up here, stat. Mr. P. is pissed and wants to leave AMA."

Damn. There's always something. She looked longingly down the hallway to the surgical changing rooms, fingering the collar of her blouse where the blood bullet had pinged her. "Okay. Tell him to hold his horses. I'm coming."

Rylan totally did not feel like dealing with Mr. P right now. Or ever, really. And she was running short on time. She spotted the door to the stairwell, hit the latch, and leaned into it. She ran up the stairs three at a time, and on each landing, her pager went off. By the time she reached the sixth floor, she had accumulated six more pages. She was definitely losing ground in her race to save lives.

She burst through the stairwell door, gritted her teeth, and walked the length of the hall, rapid-fire answering one page after another.

"No more narcotics for Mrs. Potter, only Tylenol."

"Mr. Kettering's BP is low? Give him a bolus of 500cc Ringers."

"A sleeping pill? She's so gorked she can barely stand up. How's she ever going to be discharged home?"

"Put a splint on it and send him to the fracture clinic."

"A note for work? Seriously? We can deal with that at her follow-up appointment."

"What do you mean he passed out and fell in the toilet? Of course he needs an X-ray of his hip."

Incredibly, as she pulled into the nursing station, she had answered and dealt with – mostly – all six calls from every part of the hospital. If she'd been carrying a six-gun, she would have blown smoke off the barrel.

"All right. Who's got Mr. P?"

Mr. P was her "personal" patient and had been admitted forty-eight hours earlier with a nasty case of arm cellulitis and an abscess the size of an orange near his elbow where he had been shooting up. Track marks covered his entire body. She had taken him directly to the OR to incise and drain the abscess. She'd been completely on her own for that procedure as it was deemed a resident case. Likely something to do with his lack of insurance and his reputation for being a wicked nasty son-of-a-bitch. His wound was left partially open so that it could continue to drain. He was now on IV antibiotics, getting the wound packing changed daily. He was not a nice man and carried a posse full of attitude that instantly irritated every cell in Rylan's butt.

"He's all mine," a young nurse named Darlene said. "Come quickly."

Rylan left her backpack and parka at the nursing station and followed Darlene to Mr. P's private room. He was on full isolation precautions because he was growing MRSA, a type of bacteria that was not sensitive to standard penicillin-based antibiotics and required big guns like Vancomycin to treat.

Rylan was preparing to don gloves and a gown – contact precautions – when Mr. P suddenly appeared in the doorway. He was twenty-eight years old, very large, and completely bald. His massive body and face were covered in pockmarks from longstanding meth use, and he had grown to embrace them, going by the name of "Pockface." He even managed to work some indescribable tattoos around them. He was wearing a blue hospital gown and holding an IV pole with a small machine attached that dispensed his Vancomycin.

He looked from Rylan to Darlene. "This is who you bring me? Another nurse? I want to speak to a fucking doctor."

"Mr. P," Rylan said, "I *am* a doctor. Dr. Fraser. Not only am I a doctor, I'm the surgeon who performed your operation. What's wrong? Why do you want to leave?"

He tilted his chin to the left and clenched his jaw on a toothpick sticking out of his mouth. "I don't remember you, Doc. Guess you didn't make much of an impression." He shifted the toothpick to the other side of his mouth. "Listen, I've got business to attend to, so I need to get out of this place. And I need stronger painkillers."

"Well, which is it? Do you want to leave? Or do you want stronger painkillers? You can't have both."

Mr. P. stood to his full height, and Rylan was at eye level with a mouth full of crooked, chipped, brown teeth. There were a few empty spots in the lot, too, where the tortured toothpick rolled in and out. His breath was horrid, a mixture of stale cigarette and cannabis smoke laced with some kind of dairy product. Her nose wrinkled – she couldn't help it – but she stood her ground.

Mr. P smiled a smarmy smile. "How about you script me some oxys and a PO antibiotic equivalent to the Vanco, and I'll get out of your hair?"

Mr. P was a lot of things, but he wasn't stupid. He'd been in and out of the hospital many times and knew the system. Rylan also remembered hearing that he had worked his way through his first two years of law school before drugs dragged him down. "Can't do it, Mr. P. Infectious disease says you need at least a week of IV Vanco before we can transition you to PO antibiotics. Also, your wound packing needs to be changed regularly until it stops draining. You might even need a second trip to the OR."

His eyes narrowed, and his free hand tightened into a fist that he raised in front of Rylan's face and shook. His mouth opened wide, but before he could utter a word, Rylan closed her hand gently but firmly around his fist. There was no point in fighting. She flicked away the comment about how forgettable she was, swallowed her pride, and ignored his breath. She was the doctor here, and it was her job above all else to do no harm. "Look," she said, her voice calm, "I know it's rough. Just give it some more time. How about if we play it day by day? I'll speak with ID about converting you to PO antibiotics sooner. We'll check your dressing tomorrow morning and see where we stand."

He dropped his arm slowly, let out a big, nasty breath, and chewed the toothpick while weighing his options. "Fine. For now. But if we don't make progress soon, *you* are going to seriously regret my being here."

Rylan was quite sure she was well beyond regretting his being here.

Mr. P looked at Darlene. "I'll be back. Going for a smoke."

He trudged down the hallway towards the elevators, wheeling his IV pole next to him, his tattooed asscheeks alternately peeking out from the split in the back of his hospital gown with each step.

"But," Darlene yelled out, "there's a storm outside. And you're on isolation precautions!"

Mr. P responded with an upraised middle finger.

"Let him go, Darlene," Rylan said. "Let's take the small victories where we can get them. At least he's coming back."

"That may be a victory for you …." Darlene sighed.

"Yeah," Rylan said, placing a hand on Darlene's shoulder. "He's definitely a challenge. Listen, I gotta prep for a big surgical case. Can you document our discussion?"

"Sure. And good luck with your MVC."

Rylan marveled at how fast word spread in the hospital. "Thanks. If all goes well, you'll get to meet him here eventually."

Rylan picked up her backpack and parka at the nursing station and headed back down to the third floor. This time, she got as far as the front of the changing room door when her cursed pager twinkled again. She looked at the door and was about to swipe her ID over the scanner to gain entrance when she shook her head and dropped her pack to the floor.

"The way this night's been going …" She dialed the number on the pager. "It's Dr. Fraser. Someone paged?"

"Hey, it's Mike. Got one I need help with stat in the ER."

"I'm kind of busy right now."

"I know, I know, but this seventeen-year-old kid has a dislocated shoulder with a dead arm, and I can't get it back in."

"How dead?"

"All the way dead."

CHAPTER 4

Paul

"I'm gonna sue you, and I'm gonna sue this whole hospital!"

Paul took a deep, steadying breath. The woman before him was about five-foot-two, mid-sixties, her head surrounded by a halo of brightly-dyed red hair. Her voice was a tremulous staccato that tore through the psych ER with all the acoustic elegance of an angry barn owl.

"Don't you touch me! Don't you dare touch me, you quack! That's assault and battery! I'm going to have your face plastered across television sets from here to Texas! You'll be in jail!"

Paul looked over her shoulder where two psych techs and a nurse stood at the ready, observing the scene with a sort of detached professionalism. "Please, ma'am," Paul tried, taking a step back from the agitated patient, "I am not going to touch you. I just want you to walk into the exam room here so we can talk."

"You sick pervert! I know what men like you want!"

Paul sighed and turned to the nurse who was shifting impatiently from foot to foot while trying to suppress a tired smile. She cleared her throat. "The note from triage says Mrs. Fitzgibbons stopped her lithium three months ago."

Paul nodded and turned back to his patient. "Mrs. Fitzgibbons, we can give you some medication –"

"DO I LOOK LIKE SOMEONE WHO NEEDS MEDICATION?"

Paul considered his response. "Well –"

"Poison! Poison is what that is! You're trying to poison me! You listen to me, mister –"

"Actually, I'm a doctor. My name is –"

"You listen to me, mister! I have connections to all the news networks! My ex-husband owns CBS!"

Paul looked again at the nurse. She shook her head.

"Look, Mrs. Fitzgibbons," Paul tried again, "the police brought you here –"

"For no reason!"

"They brought you here, and now we have to get to the bottom of things. So, I suggest –"

"You let me go right now! Give me back my phone. I'm calling the governor. He takes my calls, you know!"

The nurse shook her head again.

Paul made a final, half-hearted attempt to usher Mrs. Fitzgibbons into the exam room, knowing before he started that it was a lost cause. Finally, he gave a verbal order for STAT meds. Mrs. Fitzgibbons refused to take them orally and ranted some more about toxins, so the nurse calmly drew up a syringe. Paul backed into the enclosed nursing station where Mrs. Fitzgibbons' shouts were diminished a few decibels when the door clicked shut. With a swipe of his ID card, he unlocked the electronic record and began entering orders.

Sandy, the charge nurse, appeared at his elbow. "Dr. Bennett, the escort is here to bring Jane Doe upstairs."

Paul looked through the glass partition and spotted the young woman he'd interviewed earlier being assisted into a wheelchair. She had a glassy look in her eyes, and her head lolled to the left once she was seated in the chair. She seemed to instantly fall asleep. "Did she take any medication?" Paul asked.

"No, not a thing," Sandy replied. "Poor thing is probably just worn out."

"Where's she being taken?"

"There's a bed for her on psych. They're putting her in a single room right outside the nurse's station. Any special instructions for transport?"

"No," Paul answered, watching as a blanket was neatly folded across Jane Doe's lap. She seemed to be out cold. "I don't suppose anyone has called looking for her?"

Sandy shook her head. "Hopefully, they'll be able to sort it out in the morning." She left the station to confer with the transportation escort. Paul observed the exchange that ended with the escort wheeling Jane through the locked door and out of the psychiatric ER. *Good*, he thought. *She's on her way.*

He turned one hundred and eighty degrees to view Mrs. Fitzgibbons, now in a face-off against a syringe. The psych ER was basically a big square with small exam rooms tucked along the perimeter. In the center of the square was a smaller, glassed-in square from which all parts of the ER were viewable. This was the nurse's station, which Paul quickly learned to refer to as "the fish tank."

"Are you the new psychiatrist?"

A tall man of about thirty with an athletic build and crop of strawberry curls entered the fish tank, hand outstretched for a friendly shake. "I'm Kevin, one of the nurses."

Paul shook his hand and formally introduced himself. Kevin had a firm grip and disarming smile that probably served him well with patients. A smattering of freckles crossed the bridge of his nose, underscoring the overall appearance of a young boy stretched to the size of a full-grown man. "There's a message for you from that one's outpatient psychiatrist," he said, pointing a finger toward Mrs. Fitzgibbons. Paul followed the finger to where the woman was verbally tussling with ER staff, though the actual words were muffled by the thick glass walls of the fish tank. "Said she has bipolar disorder, stable for decades on lithium. Had a very supportive husband who kept her on her meds."

"I guess the key word in that sentence is *had,*" Paul said.

"Right," Kevin continued, "the husband died last year, and the doctor said she's been all over the place with her moods. She hasn't shown up to meetings for a few months, so he assumed she stopped her lithium. In recent days, she's been leaving all sorts of bizarre messages on his machine. He called for a mobile outreach team to assess her. And here she is."

Paul looked anew at Mrs. Fitzgibbons. Take away her puffed-up bluster, and she was really just a tiny wisp of a thing. She was berating a nurse offering to give her a needle "the easy way," but it seemed a lot of the fight had gone out of her – which might have had something to do with the four gloved technicians standing behind the nurse. Mrs. Fitzgibbons finally dropped her shoulders and shuffled into a little exam room where she was helped onto a cot. It seemed, in the end, she'd opted for the easy way after all. She squeezed her eyes shut, and the needle slipped into the sparse meat of her left deltoid.

"Anyway," Kevin continued, "the doctor left a name and number, so you can call him back for more info." He handed Paul a scrap of paper.

Paul tucked the paper into a pocket. "I'm going to duck out for a minute and try to get a call room. I'll be right back."

"Sure thing," Kevin said.

Paul turned to go, then halted and turned back to Kevin. "Do you know where I should go?"

Kevin chuckled and provided Paul with directions to the security kiosk in the main lobby.

Paul navigated his way easily to the kiosk which he found staffed by a portly middle-aged woman sporting a gray bob haircut that framed a set of piercing blue eyes. The type of eyes that not much got by, Paul thought. He presented his ID and managed to snag one of the last available call rooms.

"It's really coming down outside," Helen, the head of security, said, repeating what Paul was hearing all over the hospital. She handed Paul a little chrome key with a tiny sticker bearing a room number. "All of the on-call docs are staying in house rather than risk the roads. You got here just in time." As Paul inspected the little key and prepared to ask where call room 241 was located, the PA system crackled to life. Helen squinted her eyes and tilted her head upward as though God, Himself, was speaking from the heavens.

CODE ORANGE 4th FLOOR

CODE ORANGE 4th FLOOR

Quickly, Helen wrangled a walkie-talkie from her belt. Paul could hear a grumbly voice report that a patient en route to the psychiatry unit jumped ship during transport.

Jane Doe!

Paul tugged his chin with a hand. "That's one of mine," he said. Helen put up a finger, telling Paul to wait a minute, trying to hear the last of the report. "On my way," she said into the talkie.

"Can you come with me, Dr ... Bennett?" she asked, looking down at the room assignment log sheet where she'd just entered the new psychiatrist's name. "You know what the patient looks like. Maybe we can cut her off before she gets very far." She called for another security guard to man the kiosk, and she and Paul took off at a rapid clip for the elevators.

"Would it make more sense to take the stairs?" Paul asked.

"It might ... but I'm not as young as I used to be," Helen said, jabbing at the elevator call button.

On the fourth floor, a knot of people buzzed in the hallway outside the locked psych unit. Paul recognized the escort who picked up Jane Doe from the ER, looking contrite and maybe a little sick.

"What happened?" Helen asked.

The escort anxiously rubbed at the scruff on the back of his neck. "We got out of the elevator and rolled toward the unit. She was asleep the whole time. About halfway to the unit, a blanket slipped off her lap and got tangled in the wheel. I bent to fix it, and I swear she pushed me over. By the time I got up, she was long gone."

Helen gave him a look of disbelief. "Right. Which way?"

The distraught escort pointed, and Helen followed the finger with her eyes. "I imagine she'll try to find a way out." Helen got back on her talkie and gave orders to the security team to space out, specifying various locations. "We are looking for a young girl, about…?" She looked at Paul.

"About 15 or so," he said.

"… in hospital pajamas and…" Again, she looked expectantly at Paul.

"She's small, slim, with brown hair."

Helen repeated the description into the talkie. She looked at the wheelchair the patient had been in moments before. A pouch on the back of the chair contained a plastic bag with Jane Doe's personal effects. "It looks like she left everything behind. Tell me, Dr. Bennett, is this patient dangerous?"

Paul shook his head. "Hard to say. The whole time I was with her in the ER, she was calm. Psychotic, but calm."

"Did you think she was suicidal?"

"She denied it, but she was talking about dead people."

Helen threw one hand into the air and raised the talkie back to her mouth with the other. "Find her. Now!" she barked into the device. She returned the walkie-talkie to her belt and turned to the small, assembled crowd. "Okay, everyone, that's it. Please get back to your stations. We'll find her and bring her back. We're on it." As the onlookers started to move along, Helen looked at Paul, and her proud demeanor faded just a bit. "This is probably not the best first impression for you."

Paul waved off the comment with a smile. "Hey, things happen."

"We'll find her, don't you worry." Her sharp, blue eyes gleamed with such reassuring intensity that Paul couldn't possibly doubt her. She continued, "I know you have other things to do. Go back to the ER or wherever you need to go, and we'll notify you ASAP when she's found."

Paul walked off, his head swinging left and right, wondering where Jane Doe could have run off to. And, even more concerning, what she might get up to. Paul Bennett had a history of things going less than well with young, female patients. Lost in thought, the psychiatrist ran his fingers along an old, frayed newspaper clipping he kept in his jacket pocket as he made his way back to the ER.

CHAPTER 5

Jane Doe

The girl they called Jane Doe was riding high on an epic wave of exhilaration. She'd done it, pulled it off without a hitch. Escaped from her handler in the blink of an eye, soaring down the hall with the speed of a peregrine falcon and the silence of a butterfly. The pair of rubber-soled socks those witch nurses had jammed on her feet in the ER made for the ideal getaway vehicle. No slip, no sound.

She hid in a dark conference room undergoing renovation, wedged into the space formed by a large whiteboard leaning against a wall, praying that the rapid bass-drum thump of her heart didn't alert the entire floor to her position. She had to bite the back of her hand to suppress a self-congratulatory peal of laughter when she heard the call for "Code Orange" over the PA system. She had no idea what Code Orange meant, but she sensed that it was about her, and she loved that. Just loved it. If it meant that people would be looking for her, though, she'd need to stay on her game.

Elevator doors opened out in the hall, and she heard walkie-talkie static. Security. She willed herself to stay calm. *Deep, centering breaths – in through the mouth, out through the nose.*

A long moment passed. Someone came by and turned on the lights. "Hello, hello, anyone here?" The walkie-talkie crackled, as she held her breath. To get caught now would be so anticlimactic. Plus, she'd be looking at the business end of a syringe for sure. *Stay calm, girl. Stay calm.* After a few seconds, the lights went off. Jane Doe frowned, caught somewhere between elated and insulted by the realization only a half-assed effort was being made to locate her. If this was a "Code Orange," it was pretty lame.

The talkie crackled down the hall, and bits and pieces of conversation floated by her ears.

"… probably took stairway A to the ground floor…"

"… need to guard all the exits…"

The girl they called Jane Doe rolled her eyes. If they thought she was planning to run out into a blizzard in nothing more than a flimsy hospital gown and socks, then they really did think she was crazy. Already, her bare legs were cold as ice. She shimmied a little in the tight space to pull her knees to her chest and tuck them under the gown, wishing she'd nabbed the blanket when she made her break. Not only did the hospital pajamas offer no warmth whatsoever, but wearing them was like having a bullseye on her back.

She was pondering the likelihood of finding some actual clothing when she became aware of movement in the hall outside – rolling and clanging with the irksome squeal of rusty wheels. Her whole body tensed as the sounds grew louder and closer. Then, someone stepped into the room. She knew because the squealing stopped, and she could hear heavy breathing.

Shit.

A rustle. A click. The smell of lighter fluid. This had to be a bad joke. Some asshole had chosen this room of all rooms to light up.

She pursed her lips tightly together and screamed in her head. *Get out! This is my room, asshole!* Security would almost certainly be back any second, drawn by the stink of cigarette smoke, and then they would both get busted. This was bad. Really bad. Murderous rage bad. Jane wriggled low-and-slow to peek from behind the whiteboard.

Silhouetted against the hallway light, she could make out the profile of a tall man with hunched shoulders, an IV pole, and the orange tip of a lit cigarette dangling from his mouth. He was inhaling and exhaling hands-free. He probably thought he was pretty cool, this gigantic dumbass. He was wrong. Jane Doe was here to do a job, and this smoking douchebag would ruin everything. She wondered whether she could use the tie on her hospital pajamas to strangle him from behind but quickly reconsidered. Jane Doe was, after all, barely ninety-five pounds soaking wet. It was one of the reasons she was always mistaken for a kid. And one of the reasons she was always underestimated. The smoking dumbass was at least double her size – but, then again, he was sick, and she wasn't. At least, she assumed he was sick since he was attached to an IV. Sick meant weak. Probably. She watched Mr. Shit-for-Brains angrily rip the cigarette from his lips, slam it to the floor, and roll over it with his IV pole. He began making some sort of weird humming sound and muttering. Jane strained to make out the words. "Bitch" came out pretty clear, and, for a moment, she wondered if he'd spotted her. But he was facing the opposite direction. No, he wasn't talking to her at all, he was conversing with some bitch inside his head. His next phrase almost made Jane feel sorry for that bitch: "… not the only one who's gonna suffer here tonight."

Things were getting interesting. Jane was of half a mind to ask her irate visitor what he meant, but the raw, frenetic energy that engulfed him was like an invisible force field preventing her. Sick or not, he didn't look weak. Actually, he looked downright scary. Jane turtled her head down behind the whiteboard and shimmied out of sight.

A few more ramblings, a disgusting hock followed by a nauseating splat, and soon the squeaky wheels were rolling again. Out the door. Gone.

She counted to one hundred, extricated herself from her hiding spot, stretched her stiff limbs, and tiptoed to the door. In the hall, she saw no one and could hardly believe her luck. *Don't get too cocky*, she admonished herself. After all, there was still work to do, and much could go wrong.

The girl they called Jane Doe stepped into the hall. Her socked feet made no sound on the shiny hospital linoleum as she darted along the corridor and disappeared behind the heavy door of stairway A.

CHAPTER 6

Rylan

This is bad. Really bad.

"No pulse?" Rylan asked.

"Nothing. Not even by Doppler."

"And you tried reducing the shoulder at least twice?"

"Three times, and it hasn't budged."

"Okay, Mike, I'm on my way. Prep him for another conscious sedation. I'll be right there."

A dead arm with no pulse meant either the head of the humerus was resting on the artery, or the artery was ruptured. She was hoping dearly for the former since she was fairly sure there was no vascular surgeon on call. Typically, these kinds of cases were shipped out to a bigger hospital nearby, except, given the weather, she really didn't want to think about it.

A stream of sweat trickled between her shoulder blades, and she wished she had an extra moment to ditch her parka and lighten her load, but the clock was ticking on the dead arm, and there were no moments to spare. She picked up her pack once again and ran to the hallway, automatically pressing the elevator button for the millionth time tonight before she backed away, recalling her last ride from hell. "No way."

Just as the elevator bell sounded, she bounded into the stairwell and down the three flights, centrifuging herself around each stairwell corner by holding on to the metal railing post. When she arrived at the bottom, she was just dizzy enough to need a second to recalibrate. As soon as she lost the tilt to her vision, she went straight to the trauma bay, the same room that her MVC victim was in earlier this evening.

"We have to stop meeting like this," Mike said. He had already drawn up a syringe of Propofol, or milk of amnesia, as it was commonly referred to in the ER.

"Yeah, I agree. Listen, can you give him succs also?"

"Mmm, that's getting a little out of my comfort zone," Mike replied.

"You've already tried three times." Rylan was now looking at an X-ray of the patient's dislocated shoulder on the computer screen. "The proximal humerus looks incarcerated in the axilla. We need full paralysis to even have a chance at reducing this."

"Okay," Mike relented. "Guess I'll just have to bag him for a while afterward."

A nurse drew up a syringe of succinylcholine, a short-acting paralytic drug, and passed it to Mike.

"Sure *you* don't want to give this?" he asked the nurse. She put both her hands in the air and backed away.

"It's all me, then." He administered the Propofol followed by the succinylcholine.

While he was doing that, Rylan examined the patient. The poor kid was squirming all over, writhing in pain. She checked for his radial pulse and found nothing, noting that the hand was now dusky and mottled. *Yeah, this is really bad.* By the time she pulled her fingers away, the anesthetic agents had kicked in, and he was unconscious. No small mercy, that.

"I told you. No pulse."

"How long ago was the injury?" Rylan asked.

"Four hours. Playing basketball. Took him forever to get here. Had to wait for his mother to pick him up at school. He's had multiple dislocations of the other shoulder in the past. They didn't think there was any urgency until he told them he couldn't feel anything in his hand."

"Damn, he could lose his arm. Or his life if that artery is ruptured." Rylan allowed herself a gaze into the smooth face of her young, sleeping patient. The game she was about to play had very high stakes. She prepped herself to maneuver the arm.

"Hadn't thought of that, a ruptured artery." Mike paused his pressure on the second syringe. "You sure it wouldn't be better to attempt a transfer out? We have no vascular surgeons available."

Rylan examined the patient's axilla and chest wall. "I don't see any acute hematoma or bruising. That's a good sign. If we do nothing, he has a one hundred percent chance of getting compartment syndromes and losing his arm function. Maybe even losing his whole arm. There's a very small chance he has a ruptured artery, and the dislocated humeral head is blocking any potential bleed. I think the benefits outweigh the risks."

"Alright, I trust your judgment. Let's do it," Mike said and pushed the remainder of the medication through the IV. He picked up the patient's arm and let it go. It fell limply to the bed. "He's all yours."

Rylan grabbed the arm by the wrist and placed her other hand in the patient's armpit. Expecting the worst, she summoned every ounce of strength to lever on the arm. To her surprise, it popped back into the joint effortlessly. She could almost swear she heard a sucking sound, a *beautiful* sucking sound, as the humeral head found its way back into the socket. She held her breath as she manipulated the arm around with normal range of motion.

"Hey, I think it's back in."

She checked the radial pulse. All eyes in the room were on her. There was a long, tense pause. Then, she smiled. "Bounding pulse."

"Yessss!" Mike exclaimed, elated, pumping his fist. "Score one for the good guys. No lost limbs or dead teens on our watch. Good work, Rylan. You're a superstar."

A warmth overcame Rylan from head to toe, and she felt her face flush. She recalled words her father once said to her after she graduated med school. "It's the little victories, stacked one on top of the other, that propel us to greater heights." This felt like a propelling little victory.

"Mike, can you put him in a sling and watch him for a few hours? Keep an eye on his neurovascular status before sending him home. He can follow up in the fracture clinic."

"Sure thing. Thanks again for the bailout."

She gave Mike a mock curtsy and then flashed him a sly smile. "The pleasure was all *yours*."

She then bounced away, heading back to the elevators. She would have to take one eventually, and there was no way she had enough adrenaline left to climb three flights. She just needed to avoid the middle one, the death trap. She was about to say something to Helen at the security desk when her pager sang again. She sighed, already on the descent after her little victory.

She waved to Helen. With a feeling of déjà vu, she stabbed the elevator button and answered the page. "Hi, it's Dr. Fraser. Someone paged?"

A voice spoke urgently. "Mr. Kettering in room 617, a post-op hip fracture from five days ago, isn't doing well. His temp is up, and his blood pressure is dropping, now 80/40, pulse is increasing at 120, and his breathing is rapid and labored."

"I wasn't told about the temperature earlier," she said, irritated. "And he didn't respond to the Ringer's bolus?"

"No."

Rylan immediately thought of a blood clot to the lungs, a potentially terminal event. At five days post-op, this was a definite possibility. She shook her head in dismay. Mr. Kettering was her patient, and his surgery had gone smoothly, as had his post-op recovery, until now.

This night is just getting better and better.

"Okay, do an ECG and chest X-ray. Restart an IV, draw the usual blood work, and I'll be right there." The elevator on the right opened.

She stepped in and then serial-jabbed at the "close door" button – which, she was quite sure, was permanently disconnected. While she waited for the elevator to do something, her thoughts turned back to

Brad, the motorcycle victim with the two young kids. She mentally rehearsed step by step the surgical procedures she would have to do. Assuming Dr. Huang would let her do anything. Of course, if he couldn't make it in because of the weather, she would definitely get to do something. In fact, she would have to do everything. On the one hand, she was excited to prove herself; on the other, she was scared shitless. The door finally closed.

The elevator passed the third floor, and she thought about the OR suites where the action was going to be, where she needed to be. A potentially dying patient on the ward, however, took precedence.

Within minutes, she was walking the halls of the sixth-floor surgical ward, bee-lining it to room 617 and the ailing hip fracture patient. She expected a frenzy of activity at the bedside, but, instead, when she arrived, she saw only the patient with a blanket pulled over his head – the universal hospital sign of failure. A deceased patient.

"What the hell?"

She pulled the blanket down just far enough to confirm that it was, in fact, Mr. Kettering and that he was, in fact, deceased – which, judging by the cold, pale skin of his face and the lack of respirations, he clearly was. Although Rylan had seen many deceased patients, she still hadn't quite gotten used to it and found it eerie as all hell. She had liked Mr. Kettering, something about the way he smiled at her when she rounded on him in the early pre-dawn hours seemed to brighten her day and lift her spirits. He may have been having problems with pain and mobility and age, but he still made the effort to smile at Rylan every day to let her know she was *seen* by him. Really seen. In some ways, he reminded her of her father, the legendary orthopedic spine surgeon Patrick Fraser, who made his name at Detroit's Henry Ford Hospital, operating on some of the most famous people in the country. Even when he was fully immersed in a hellish work schedule, he always had a way of smiling at her that told her she was more important than everything else he was doing.

She felt a tap on her shoulder and jumped just a little, pulled from her inner thoughts.

"Dr. Fraser. Sorry."

Rylan turned her head to face a young nurse. "Amanda, what's going on here? When did Mr. Kettering pass?"

"Not long after you dealt with Mr. P going AMA."

That made no sense, given her last phone conversation.

"I knew you were busy in emerg, and, given that he was a DNR, I didn't want to bother you. Since you're back, though, there's a big bed crunch, and we need someone to pronounce him and fill out the paperwork, so we can move him off the floor and down to the morgue."

"You, or somebody else, didn't page me earlier, like a few minutes ago, to tell me Mr. Kettering wasn't doing well?"

Amanda shook her head. "Like I said, Mr. Kettering passed almost a half hour ago. Maybe you were paged for another patient? On another floor? A name mix-up?"

This time, Rylan shook her head. She hadn't mixed anything up. There was no doubt the call concerned Mr. Kettering. She scratched her chin and replayed the exchange on the phone. "Listen, are there any male nurses working tonight?"

"No," Amanda responded. "It's an all-girls show tonight on the surgical ward."

"Did Mr. P come back?"

Amanda's lips tightened into a straight line. "A few minutes ago."

Rylan looked down the hall towards Mr. P's room. He was standing at the door, his hand on the IV pole, glaring at her. She tried to reconcile the ground-glass quality of his voice with the one on the phone. He wouldn't pull a sick stunt like this. Would he?

The sound of heavy winter boots clomping down the hallway derailed her train of thought. She found herself staring at a strange little man with short-cropped gray hair wearing a long overcoat and sporting a deerstalker Sherlock Holmes type hat. He was carrying a small black doctor's bag, the kind you would see in an old black-and-white movie, and he was flying down the hall, taking lengthy strides that reminded Rylan of the John Cleese Ministry of Silly Walks skit. She raised her eyebrows and asked Amanda, "Who is *that*?"

Amanda turned her head to follow Rylan's line of sight and smiled. "Yeah. I believe that's a new internist. He's probably following up on some consults. A little… eccentric."

Rylan shook her head. "D'ya think? Internists are so strange, sometimes."

Amanda nodded her head in agreement and then asked gently, "You'll do the paperwork?"

Rylan's mind circled back once again to that strange call. Unraveling the mystery would have to wait. She checked her watch. Her patient would be getting out of the CT scanner shortly. She looked back to Mr. Kettering, appreciating this was all a formality but a necessary one. "Of course, I'll do the paperwork. Pass me your stethoscope." Amanda passed a stethoscope from her neck to Rylan's, who then positioned the earpieces and placed the diaphragm on Mr. Kettering's chest over his heart. She listened but heard no heartbeat and no respirations. She then palpated the carotid artery with her index and middle fingers at his neck but felt no pulse. Finally, she raised his eyelids and flicked the beam of a small penlight over each pupil, noting no reaction. The pupils were fixed and dilated. She looked at her watch and made her declaration. "Official time of death, 1910 hrs."

Rylan pulled the blanket back over Mr. Kettering's head and followed Amanda to the nursing station. "Gimme a second. I just need to call CT." Todd the Dickwad, the general surgery chief resident, answered immediately. Other than the fractured pelvis and tibia, there were no other orthopedic injuries. There was, however, a splenic rupture, and the patient was destabilizing rapidly. Unfortunately, there was already a case being done in the OR, and it would be an hour before there was operative time available. Because of the storm, there was no way to get a second OR team in quickly enough. Rylan feared Brad had picked a lousy night to have his accident. He was being brought to the Intensive Care Unit in the interim. Hopefully, they'd be able to stabilize him before the showdown in the OR.

She sat down at a computer in a smallish room behind the nursing station and swiped her ID card to activate the electronic medical records system. She toggled the mouse until she found Mr. Kettering's file. She scanned his most recent bloodwork as well as an ECG from a few days ago. Everything looked completely normal, or at least as normal as one would expect for a nonagenarian following emergency surgery five days earlier. Her cell vibrated.

"Hello, Dr. Fraser here."

"Roads closed. Impossible for me to get to hospital. Keep the trauma patient in the ICU until I can get there. Do you understand, Miss Fraser? You are not to take him to the operating room unless I am there. Is that clear?"

"Dr. Huang?"

"Who else would it be, Miss Fraser?"

It could be anyone, you condescending asswipe. "What if … what if general surgery takes him to the OR? His spleen is ruptured, and his pressure is dropping. They may not have a choice –"

"THERE IS ALWAYS A CHOICE," he bellowed. "I will discuss with the gen surg staff. Miss Fraser, you do NOT have my permission to operate on the patient." Click.

"*Miss* Fraser? How about *Dr.* Fraser you piece-of-shit chauvinist pig?" Rylan said into her dead phone, eyes glaring.

"Sounds like someone has a problem?"

She looked up from her cell and straight into the eyes of Dr. Bennett.

CHAPTER 7

Paul

The pretty doctor with the blood-stained collar was muttering curses under her breath when Paul arrived on the floor, looking likc she was about to chuck a cell phone down the hall. When her eyes met Paul's, she froze for an instant, a doe in headlights, and seemed to reboot. "Oh," she said. "Hi."

"Hi." Paul looked from her face to the cell phone and back. "You okay?"

"Fine." She sighed, slipping the cell phone into the pocket of the down parka she had yet to take off. "Totally fine." She attempted a smile. "You're the new psychiatrist I met in the ER, right?"

Paul nodded. "I didn't catch your name, though. You're …"

"Rylan. Chief ortho resident." She straightened as she said this and extended a hand. "I think you may have gotten lost. This is a surgical unit. Psych is on the fourth floor."

Paul pulled a small sticky pad from his pocket and glanced at the top page where he'd chicken-scratched a room number after answering his beeper. "Pretty sure they said the sixth floor."

"I guess someone needs a consult." She frowned. "Usually, that would be handled in the daytime, though. Only emergencies at night."

"The caller said severe depression and suicidal ideation," Paul said. He looked up and down the hall, squinting to make out the numbers on the rooms. "I'm looking for 617."

"Oh, that-a-way," Rylan said, pointing. Then, she quickly drew back her finger. "Wait, not 617."

"*Not* 617?" Paul crinkled his brow and gaped at her like she was a little batty, then consulted his sticky note again. "That's what I wrote down."

"The patient in 617 is deceased," Rylan said.

Paul's jaw dropped. "What? I don't understand." He shifted uneasily. "I just received the call –"

"It wasn't a suicide." Rylan tugged a thick clump of auburn hair back off her forehead and met Paul's eye. "This is weird." She glanced in the direction of Room 617 and took a deep breath. "The patient in that room was my patient, Mr. Kettering. I repaired a hip fracture on him last weekend, and he was recovering nicely. About twenty minutes ago, I got a page saying he spiked a fever, and his pressure was dropping, so I came up."

"Okay."

"And he was deceased."

"Gee, I'm sorry."

She nodded. "But what's even stranger is that the nurse said he died a half hour earlier."

"A half-hour?" Paul looked down at the sticky in his hand as though willing the markings there to rearrange themselves into another number. "I agree that makes no sense. And I must've written the wrong room because, clearly, I don't belong here. Let me find a nurse –"

"Over here." Rylan cocked her head and indicated for him to follow. She took a few steps along the counter that separated the nurse's station from the corridor. A heavy-set woman in lavender scrubs with stiff honey-colored hair and funky cat-eye glasses sat behind the counter scanning information on a computer screen. She looked up when they approached.

"Hello, Dr. Fraser," she said.

"Hi, Linda. This is Dr. Bennett from psychiatry. He said he was paged to the unit."

"Paged *here*?" Linda scrunched her face in confusion. She swiveled her chair around and called out, "Someone page psych?"

A chorus of "no's" rang out. Paul followed their origins to a nurse pushing a blood pressure machine, another retrieving blankets from a closet, and a third a few doors down, jotting something on a clipboard outside a patient's room. They all glanced at him disinterestedly and turned back to their tasks.

Linda shrugged. "Someone must've gotten their signals crossed. She paused and looked at Rylan as if the matter with Dr. Bennett was settled. "Did you see your hip fracture?"

Rylan gave a glum nod. "What happened?"

"We really don't know. His vitals were strong. He wasn't complaining of anything unusual. Then, suddenly, we found him unconscious with no vitals."

"I received a page that he'd spiked a fever and become unstable."

Linda pushed her glasses up her nose and tapped the computer screen. "That's not right. Last set of vitals was fine. Look." She made a beckoning motion with her hand, and Rylan came up beside her to peer at the screen. "See? One minute he was okay, the next he was dead."

From the other side of the desk, Paul watched Rylan's clear green eyes flit methodically about the screen. "I really don't get it."

Linda covered the younger woman's hand with her own for a brief moment. "I know, neither do we," she said. Then, gently added, "While you're here, can you do the paperwork, so we can get him down to the morgue? Maybe they can get us some answers."

Rylan took a deep breath and let it out heavily. "Already on it." She dropped onto a wheeled chair behind Linda and pulled up to a small desk.

Paul recognized his cue to go. "Well," he said, "I'm certainly not needed here. I'll head back to the ER. Nice to meet you, Linda."

"Yup, so long, doc."

"Rylan." Paul gave a small wave and turned to go.

"Hold on!" Rylan called out.

Paul turned back.

Rylan opened her mouth to speak. "Um." She looked flustered, like she had surprised herself by calling out to him. "If you're not in a really big hurry, you can wait here. For a minute. Once I fill this out, I can show you around. A little. At least point out the highlights, like where the psych unit is and where the cafeteria is. If you want." She was talking fast, and her cheeks had turned a bright shade of pink. "Or not. I just… whatever. I'm sure you're busy. So am I. I just …"

Paul grinned. "That would be great."

The nurse, Linda, looked from Rylan to Paul, then smiled smugly, readjusted the cat-glasses, and focused back on her computer screen. "Who could say no to our famous Dr. Fraser?" she said, tapping on the keys.

"Oh, please," Rylan said, burying her pink cheeks in her hands.

"Famous?" Paul asked.

"No!" Rylan shouted.

"Yes," Linda insisted. "Our very own Dr. Rylan Fraser won the Charles M. Washburne prize for outstanding orthopedic resident, beating out all other orthopedic residents across the system, including –"

"Linda, stop!" Rylan shouted. She was dismissively waving one hand and covering her face with the other, but Paul could just make out a smile behind the fingers.

"Including," Linda continued, dropping her voice to a whisper appropriate for divulging scandal, "*all* the boys." Her broad cheeks widened to a big smile. "Oh no" – she shook her head without moving a single hair – "it's not an all-boys game anymore! This juggernaut is single-handedly shattering the glass ceiling to tiny little pieces."

"Wow," Paul said, looking over at Rylan who was pretending to pay no attention. "I'm impressed."

"This here is a celebrity," Linda continued, jutting her chin in Rylan's direction. "Her picture was in the papers. They called her a *new and rising star in orthopedics*. They said she was unstoppable." She made a vocal flourish on the last word and repeated it for emphasis. "*Un-stoppable!*"

"They obviously don't know me very well," Rylan said.

"Modest, too." Linda winked. "Don't tell me you didn't see the story in the local paper, Dr. Bennett."

"Regrettably, I did not see it as I'm brand new in town. But I can Google as well as anyone else," Paul said, retrieving a cell phone from his pocket. He swiped a finger around on the screen. "Got it! *Young Surgeon Makes Hometown Proud.*"

"Oh, please. It's just a silly little article," Rylan mumbled in protest as she filled out the rote forms before her.

Paul scratched his head and studied his phone. "It's a good picture," he said, turning the screen on his phone to Linda.

"Right?" Linda agreed.

Rylan rose from the desk, rolling her eyes and doing a poor job of smothering a smile. "I'm done here." She came around the counter and stood next to Paul. "Ready?"

"Let's go."

They said goodbye to Linda and started toward the elevators. Halfway down the corridor, Rylan stopped short, took a step backward, and gaped through an open doorway. Paul followed her lead and peeked into the room. All he saw was an empty bed with ruffled bed sheets. Rylan stepped into the room and checked the bathroom – also empty. "Where the hell is he?" she muttered.

"What's wrong?" Paul asked. "Whose room is this?"

"A nasty motherfucker named Pockface who –"

Paul's eyebrows shot upward of their own accord. Rylan raised a hand apologetically to her mouth. "I'm sorry. I swear like a sailor, but I'm trying to break the habit. I didn't mean to call him a mother –"

Paul shook his head. "Pockface?"

"Yeah." Rylan bobbed her head up and down like an overeager child trying just a little too hard to convince an adult she was telling the truth. "That's what everyone calls him. In the hospital and outside. It's what he calls himself. Anyway, he's supposed to be on MRSA precautions, but he spends less time in his room than a kid at Disney World." She looked up and down the hallway, probably hoping her patient would materialize so she could deliver a good tongue-lashing. Her gaze locked on something or someone behind Paul, and he thought, *Okay, here it comes*, but instead, she gently poked Paul's shoulder and said, "Excuse me, just a minute."

Paul turned to watch Rylan cut diagonally across the hall and approach a doctor – at least he assumed it was a doctor. The guy was wearing a white lab coat and carrying a scuffed leather physician's bag, the kind doctors used to carry on home visits when home visits were a real thing. Balancing the bag caused him to hobble a little as he walked, something exacerbated by the thick soles on his heavy-duty winter boots that, Paul estimated, added about two inches to his height. Paul watched Rylan approach the man, arm extended in front of her. "Hello," she said, "I'm Rylan Fraser, chief ortho resident."

The doctor did not take her hand but merely nodded and returned his gaze to a room number he seemed to be matching to a handwritten list he held in his hand. Rylan dropped her hand to her side. "I just wanted to introduce myself since I'm on the floor a lot."

The man gave Rylan a sideways glance and twisted the ID card on the breast pocket of his lab coat between his thumb and forefinger, so the face was visible to Rylan, almost. "Dr. Upslinger," he grunted.

Paul saw Rylan squint to read the ID, but Upslinger let it drop back onto his chest too quickly. Rylan frowned and looked quizzically back to his face. "Are you a locum?" she asked.

Upslinger rolled up the paper he was holding into the shape of a telescope and slipped it into his breast pocket. "Yes," he said, finally turning to face Rylan. "Several staff physicians called out due to the weather. I anticipate a busy night. Now, you will excuse me." The way he said it, Paul noted, was more demand than polite farewell. Rylan stepped back, her expression openly befuddled, and Dr. Upslinger walked past her down the hall. When he was a good distance away, Rylan made eye contact with Paul and bent her arms, palms up in a *what-was-that?* kind of gesture. Paul shrugged as Rylan rejoined him, and they continued toward the elevators. "It wasn't me, was it?" Rylan asked.

"It wasn't you."

"Good." As they waited for the elevator, Rylan seemed to shake off the strange encounter and shift gears. "So," she said, "you just moved to town? Where're you from?"

"Wisconsin, originally, but working in Toledo up until just recently."

"Toledo. Never been there."

"It's not exactly a bucket list city."

Rylan laughed. The elevator came, and they stepped on together. She punched the button for the fourth floor. "What made you leave – that is, if you don't mind me asking?"

Paul watched the lights on the control panel, saying nothing. *Five* lit up, then *four*. The door opened.

"Well," Rylan said into the awkward silence, "this is the floor where the psychiatry unit is – in case you haven't seen it yet. The unit, itself, is locked, so you'll need your card to swipe in." She stepped out of the elevator and pointed.

Paul nodded. He had already been here, of course, when Jane Doe escaped, but he wanted the tour – and the company – so he didn't say anything and followed suit, joining her on the fourth floor.

"The rest of the floor is mostly administrative offices, but the Occupational and Physical Therapy Departments are located in the D wing. I actually pop onto the floor fairly often to see my post-op patients in PT."

"So, we could conceivably run into one another in the elevators?" Paul tilted his head to one side and looked at Rylan inquisitively.

Rylan flushed. A happy flush, it seemed to Paul. "It's entirely conceivable."

"Good," Paul said, his lips curving into a grin. The two stood facing one another in the dim light of an empty hall that lacked the usual bustle and beeps of a typical hospital unit. The small crowd that had gathered after Jane Doe's escape was long gone.

Rylan's eyes broke away, and she looked at the floor. "Listen, I'm sorry if I was being too personal when I asked why you moved."

"Too personal?" Paul was genuinely surprised by the suggestion. "Not at all. I was just trying to figure out the best words to explain what happened."

"What happened?"

"I needed a new start." Paul shrugged and looked down at his shoes.

Rylan nodded slowly. "New starts are good." She thrust both hands into the pockets of her parka and rocked forward and back on the soles of her sneakers, like an anxious child. "Is there a reason *why* you needed a new start?"

Paul raised his eyes, took a deep breath, and exhaled. "I felt there was."

"Personal or professional?" Rylan asked. As soon as the question was out of her mouth, she bonked herself in the head with one hand. "Sorry. There I go again with the overly personal questions. I can't help it. I'm a surgeon. You know, cut to the chase and all that."

Paul's fingertips brushed the newspaper clipping in his pocket. "Professional."

"Oh, okay," Rylan said. She examined Paul's face for a moment, and he expected a follow-up question. Instead, she said, "I hope you find what you're looking for here."

"I think I will."

Rylan smiled and clapped her hands together once. "Okay, next stop, the cafeteria. You need to know where caffeine and sugar are available on long shifts. Come. Let's do the stairs this time."

Paul followed Rylan through the heavy door that led to the stairwell, and they began to descend. Rylan was giving Paul the scoop on cafeteria food (the deli and frozen yogurt were okay, but the soups and wilted salad bar were to be avoided) when the ring of a cell phone startled them both. Rylan answered without breaking stride. She exchanged a few words with the caller and hung up. "I'm sorry, but it's the OR, and I gotta run."

Paul saw she wasn't kidding. Without another word, Rylan jumped a few stairs onto the landing, pulled open the third-floor door, and bustled through, parka swishing in time. "Maybe I'll see you later," she called with the door closing behind her.

"Hope so," Paul said as it clicked shut.

CHAPTER 8

Rylan

"Goddamnit! What am I going to do? That, that stupid … dickwad!"

Rylan was closing on Mach 1 as she rounded a hallway corner on her way – finally – to the changing room. There was no stopping her now. Her patient was crashing and being brought from the ICU to the OR. She had about ten minutes at best. She called Dr. Huang repeatedly, but all she got in return was a frustrating "beep, beep, beep" every time.

Rylan skidded to a halt before the operating room desk and tapped an impatient toe, waiting for the sour-looking charge nurse to glance up from a clipboard she was perusing. "Hey, Donna. Is my patient here yet?"

"If you mean Dr. Huang's patient," Donna replied curtly, not bothering to look up, "not yet."

"Oh. Where is he?"

"Dr. Huang?"

"You know where Dr. Huang is?" Rylan asked.

"How the hell would I know where that impertinent jackass is?"

"He hasn't called in?"

"Hell no. He just arrives whenever the hell he wants to."

"And my patient?"

"Do I look like air traffic control to you? Probably on his way, stuck in some shitty elevator between floors."

Rylan agreed this was highly likely. "Can you call me when the patient gets here? Also, call me if Dr. Huang –"

"So now I must look like a messenger service to you," she grumbled. "Damn chief residents. Every one of 'em thinks the rest of the world exists only to serve them. Especially the award-winning ones." Donna gave Rylan a subtle wink.

"Sorry, Donna. I didn't mean it like that. It's just I'm on my own this holiday weekend, and this patient's in really bad shape, and right now, I don't even have staff support."

Donna took a deep breath, squared off in front of Rylan, and placed a hand on each of her shoulders. "Hon, the first thing you need to do is get into some scrubs. That's step one, alright? But before you do that, you need to tell me what kind of toys you need. Gen surg has already booked their case, and you need to do the same. So?"

"So?"

"So, what equipment do you want?"

"Well, I don't know. I can't reach Dr. Huang. He said the roads were closed and didn't think he could make it in."

"Honey. Once upon a time, residents really ran the show here. We would be lucky if a staff man ever showed his face after hours. Nowadays, your generation is coddled like kittens. You don't brush your teeth unless you talk to your staff. Lord, I don't know how you'll ever be able to survive in the real world when you're through here."

"But Dr. Huang probably won't make it…"

"Rylan, do you know what to do?"

"Yes, I think so."

"Think so?"

Rylan paused and took a deep breath." I know exactly what to do. I need the large ex-fix set and everything for a washout. We need to stabilize his pelvis as priority one and then clean out and ex-fix his open tibia fracture."

"Alright."

"Alright. I guess I'll go get my scrubs on."

The OR elevator bell rang.

"That's a good plan because here comes your patient."

An ICU fellow named Sean – a sweet catch who, regrettably, after a few sparkling dates last year, found another pond to swim in before Rylan could reel him in – was pulling their patient out of the elevator on a stretcher. A respiratory technician was squeezing an Ambu bag, forcing air mixed with oxygen down the patient's endotracheal tube. Sean was not only pulling the bed but also squeezing a bag of packed red blood cells with his other hand, trying to force the blood through the patient's IV. He paused for a second, letting the momentum of the bed carry it forward, while he administered one medication after another via syringe into a second IV. For a second, he appeared to have three or four arms keeping the patient alive. He yelled out, "Ready or not, here we come!"

"Not," Rylan said, just a little whisper. She pushed her shoulders back and gave a resigned sigh. "Gotta get changed."

Donna moved shockingly fast for a woman of her size, helping Sean and the respiratory technician wheel the patient into the operating room. Dickwad was right behind them, shouting orders no one was listening to. Rylan darted off to the changing room. She grabbed a pair of scrubs on her way in and stood in front of her locker, staring coldly at the padlock, a very old padlock with a very old combination. She hadn't actually locked her locker in months, normally keeping the lock partially closed to allow quick access. She kept very little in it other than her prescription surgical glasses, a pair of stained Birkenstocks, her lab coat, and a few custom-made scrub caps. Certainly, nothing anyone would steal. Unfortunately, someone had tried to be a Dudley Do-Right and completely closed the lock for her.

"Damn it. What's the number, what's the number, what's the number?"

The locker room was deserted. She spun around, tearing off her sweltering parka in the process. She threw it to the floor and plopped into a chair, trying to remember. "I wrote it down somewhere."

She searched her phone with no success. She emptied the meager contents of her backpack onto a chair, hoping there might be a piece of paper with some numbers scrawled on it. Nothing. She stared at the locker door, biting her lower lip, deep in thought. She heard the tick-tock of the clock mounted above the door only a few feet from her locker. She turned to look at it, and her eyes flowed from the clock to the edge of the door frame. She stepped closer and remembered. Written in pencil along each edge were two tiny digits. She read the first number – 28 – with an arrow pointing up. She pushed her backpack off the chair and stood on it, looking at the upper horizontal edge of the doorframe and the second number – 32 – with an arrow pointing to the right. She got off the chair and traced the right side of the door frame with her index finger until she saw a final number. Or rather, didn't see the number. The cleaners had been through and smudged it beyond recognition.

"No, no, this isn't happening!" Perspiration soaked her armpits as she recited the numbers she had, hoping to trigger something: "28-32-?, 28-32-?"

Nothing. She punched the locker once with an open palm and stopped to think out loud.

"Alright. The only important thing in my locker are my glasses. I can still see without them, mostly. The X-ray monitors may be a problem, but I'll have to adapt."

She quickly changed into her scrubs, put booties over her Nikes, and donned a standard, off-the-shelf scrub cap. She stuffed her parka and backpack into a random empty locker and drawled to the empty room, "Here's hoping there's no thievery in these parts tonight."

She ran out of the changing room and back to the OR desk. Deserted. They were all already inside getting the patient ready. She spotted a landline and tried Dr. Huang again. Maybe it was her phone that was the problem? This time, she was kind of hoping he didn't answer. She had this. Didn't she? Busy signal. She smiled nervously, slammed the phone down, and headed to theater one with a determined stride.

She picked up a surgical mask with a face shield protector from the scrub sink area, pushed through the doors to theater one, and took stock. The patient had already been transferred to the surgical table, and the anesthetist was doing his bit. Since the patient was already intubated, it was really a question of administering various medications to eliminate awareness and kill pain. In addition, he was starting an arterial line to allow moment-to-moment monitoring of blood pressure. Given the amount of anesthesia work that still needed to be done, it looked like Rylan had a few minutes to get her shit together.

"Rylan, what's the plan?" The chief general surgery resident was standing in front of a wall-mounted computer screen, scrolling through something. Rylan could just see the screen and did a double-take. *Is he browsing running shoes on eBay?*

"Hey, Dick – …Todd. I was going to ask you the same thing." Rylan looked around, and besides the scrub nurse, Larry, who was prepping instruments in the sterile field, and Donna, who was unfolding instrument after instrument and passing them to Larry, there was no one else in the room.

"Where's your staff?" Rylan asked. Todd's attention was still focused on the monitor screen.

"He said he'd be in later after all the ortho garbage was disposed of. My R3 resident will be along as well. Where's your staff? Isn't Dr. Huang on tonight? He's a real hardass, right?"

This last statement required no answer. Dr. Huang was a legendary, grade-A asshole, and Todd knew it. Even through his mask, Rylan could make out his *sucks-for-you* grin.

"He said he'd be in later, and I should get the ball rolling."

Todd finally turned away from his shopping spree to face Rylan. "Really? I heard Dr. Huang never leaves residents on their own. He's the master control freak."

"Well, the weather's bad out there with the snowstorm and –"

"Right. And you are the award-winning resident of the year." Todd chuckled and gave her a mocking bow.

"You're such a dick –"

A strong British accent interrupted her retort. "Alright, my little lovebirds. The patient is suitably anessss - thetized." Dr. English, in keeping with his moniker, was the most "English" person Rylan had ever met, and he had a slithery way of always elongating the "s" in anessss - thetized. He hovered somewhere in the seventies to eighties age range – no one could be certain – and was so old school that many thought he predated the invention of actual anesthesia. "So, one or both of you, get to work, NOW."

"Wait, Dr. English, my staff –"

"NOOOOOWWWWW."

Rylan looked at Todd and made a command decision. "Okay, Todd, I'm going to scrub in and ex-fix his pelvis. When I'm done, you and your staff can take over and work the belly while I deal with his tibia."

Todd took a small half-step backward, eyes widened by her assertiveness. At first, he simply nodded his head, but then he said, "You have no staff."

"And this guy's got no time."

Rylan ran out the doors to the scrub sink and performed a one-minute version of a five-minute scrub. With her hands held high and her elbows far away from her body, she entered the operating room, leaving a trail of soapsuds on the floor behind her. As she approached the sterile field, she called out, "Donna, can you call for X-ray?"

"Already done. They'll be here shortly."

Larry passed her a towel to dry her hands, and once she was dry, they began their glove and gowning pas de deux. First, the gown, tied and Velcroed in back by Donna, finishing up with a little tug at the waist to get rid of the folded creases. Then, three pairs of gloves, one over the other. Snug to the point of cutting off circulation, however, more gloves meant more protection against accidental needle sticks or cuts from jagged bone edges.

"Hey, Larry, how's your night going?"

"Rather be at home watching my recording of the Patriots game."

"C'mon, Larry. You know you love this."

"As long as it's ortho, I'm good. It's that bowel stuff that turns my stomach. Pun intended."

Rylan laughed. Larry was the regular ortho scrub for elective surgery and had been for a couple of decades. He'd done more orthopedics than probably the whole ortho department combined. His eyes smiled as he said, "Glad to see it's you on call tonight."

"Well, that makes one of us."

"Haven't worked with you for a while. Congrats on the award. I guess I'm working with a big shot now."

"Still the same ole me, Larry."

"Just don't let it go to your head. Your exams are around the corner, and you'll need all the room up there you can get."

"Ugh, don't remind me."

"Is your fearless leader joining us?"

"Dr. Huang? To be honest, I don't think so. Weather's bad."

"Who needs that blowhard, anyway? You got this."

"Hope you're right. Okay, prep stick."

Larry passed Rylan a self-contained sponge stick that leaked Chlorhexidine, and she painted the patient's pelvic area liberally to disinfect the skin.

"What about the tibia?" Larry asked.

"We'll take care of that while gen surg is doing the laparotomy."

Rylan then covered the rest of the body with paper-like drapes, leaving only the pelvis exposed. While she did this, Larry placed a sterile cover over the fluoroscopy machine, which looked like a big "C", one end emitting the X-ray and the other side receiving it.

"Scalpel. Come in with X-ray." The X-ray technician flashed a picture of the pelvis, which appeared on a monitor. Rylan made a stab wound with her scalpel just over the bony rim of the pelvis. The patient was quite slim, and the landmarks were easy to find. Larry passed her a power drill with a thick threaded wire attached. She positioned the tip of the wire through the stab wound on the crest of the pelvic bone and then looked up at the X-ray monitor. What she saw was nothing but a big black-and-white blur. She squinted furiously with minimal improvement.

"Rylan, where are your glasses?"

As she turned to look at Larry, all power went out in the operating room. It was out for less than a few seconds, but it was long enough to wreak havoc with anything in the OR that had a computer chip in it, like the X-ray machine. Rylan looked up at the monitor, and even with her lousy vision, she could tell that the screen was a black hole. She looked back at Larry who gave a little shrug.

"Well, guess you didn't need that anyway."

"Yeah," she mumbled in response, "didn't really need it."

FUUUUUUCK. Not only have I never done this before, but now I don't have X-ray.

The X-ray tech said, "I'll have to completely reboot. Could take twenty minutes."

Dr. English poked his head over the drape. His mask was hanging loosely under his chin, and she could see little torpedoes of spit flying high into the air as he yelled, "This bloke doesn't have twenty seconds, let alone twenty minutes. GET ON WITH IT."

Adrenaline spiked through Rylan's body, and she prayed the OR's incessant melody of pings and dings drowned out the stallion galloping inside her chest. *Twenty seconds. I can do this.*

Her fingers moved faster than she thought possible, and within minutes, she had drilled one pin into the right side of the pelvis and another into the left.

"Bloody hell!" Dr. English yelled. "Pressure's dropping. I can't get the blood in fast enough. We're losing him."

Rylan attached a clamp on one side and did the same for the other. Next, she attached a cylindrical carbon bar to each clamp in a Meccano-set fashion and pulled the two rods together, effectively closing the pelvis, like a book. Finally, she clamped the two rods together, held her breath, and stared at the drape separating the sterile field from Dr. English. He poked his head above the drape. This time, she could only see his eyes. "Better."

Rylan released her breath and finished tightening all the clamps.

"Gonna call you *Lightning Woman* from now on," Larry said from behind so that only she could hear.

"I have no idea how I did what I just did, but I think it worked."

"Okay, enough dicking around, Rylan," Todd said. "It's our turn."

Todd was scrubbed with his hands in the air, dripping. Another resident Rylan didn't recognize, a newbie, was standing behind him in a similar posture, looking green as a spring pea.

Rylan backed away from the table to stand next to Larry, allowing Todd and his minion to gown and glove. They quickly went to work performing a laparotomy while Rylan addressed the open tibia fracture. As Larry was now busy helping Todd, Rylan prepped and draped the leg with Donna's help and delivered the fractured bone ends into the outside world. She pulled a small swath of denim material out of the wound, along with a couple of pieces of gravel. She irrigated the wound with saline and then, somewhat like she did for the pelvis fracture, applied pins above and below the tibia fracture and secured them with carbon bars. She sutured the wound closed, applied a dressing, and took a step back to assess her work.

Pretty damn good, she thought.

"Fuck," she heard Todd mutter under his mask, a mask that was now covered in blood. She crowded in, seeing the large open abdominal wound, and made eye contact with Larry who subtly shook his head from side to side. Things were not going well.

"Not good?" she asked.

"Not good. Spleen crushed. Have to resect," Todd said. A pumper arced through the air onto and over Rylan's face shield, smacking her in the forehead and dribbling down between her eyes. Todd quickly clamped the bleeder as Rylan instinctively closed her eyes and turned her head away from the surgical field. When she opened them, she realized something. "Hey, where's your staff man?" she asked.

"Stuck in a ditch somewhere, apparently. Storm is bad. A couple feet of snow already."

"Well, that's just great. Listen, need me to stay and help?" Rylan asked, even though she could barely see through her blood-smeared face shield. Larry was nodding his head hopefully.

"No, we're good here," Todd said. They looked anything but "good."

Rylan shrugged her shoulders and made apology-eyes at Larry. This was gen surg territory, and she was not about to stick her nose in where it didn't belong, especially when she was already so far over the line with Dr. Huang not being here. She backed away and ditched her gown and gloves into a trash bin.

On her way to the door, she yelled thanks to Larry and Donna. "Call me if you need help transferring the patient."

All eyes remained focused on the patient's open abdominal wound. No one responded to Rylan, and she took that as her cue to exit stage left. She stopped at the scrub sink, removed her blood-soaked mask and face shield, and then wet some paper towels to clean the blood from her forehead and between her eyes. She looked at herself in the mirror and took stock. Her eyes were tired but triumphant. She had just stopped a patient from bleeding out and dying right there on the table. And she did it by herself. *Screw you, Dr. Huang.*

Her stomach gurgled loudly. *Mmm,* she thought, *time for a celebratory ice cream.* She looked up at the clock over the scrub sink which read midnight. Midnight?

Twelve.

28-32-12!

But first, a quick trip to her locker.

CHAPTER 9

Paul

Paul sat nursing a cup of bad coffee behind a shiny Formica table with a perfect view of the cafeteria entrance. The hour was late, the overhead fluorescent lights were dimmed, and a majority of the tables were unoccupied. A smattering of bleary-eyed hospital workers hunched over tables, nibbling day-old blueberry muffins and playing with their phones. A few looked up when the newcomer entered but rapidly turned their attention back to YouTube or Tinder or whatever it was that held it at this hour of the night.

Paul smiled and waved Rylan over, studying her over the lip of his coffee cup as she strode toward the table. The parka was gone, replaced by blue scrubs a little too long in the legs. They bunched around a pair of cringy, stained Birkenstocks and dragged on the floor behind her heels. Her hair was pulled into a crooked ponytail with a few frizzy tendrils curling about her forehead, peeking from under a light blue scrub cap decked out in cute little broken femur bones. She looked tired but also happy. Really happy. Too happy for a hospital cafeteria at midnight. It was the kind of look that people get after running a marathon or reaching a mountain summit. The afterglow of victory.

She stopped across the table and smiled down at Paul. "I see you found the cafeteria just fine without me. I guess this tour guide owes you a refund."

"It wasn't too hard. Just follow the aroma of stale coffee." He sipped from his cup and grimaced. "This stuff is really awful."

"My advice: always use at least four sugar packets per cup. And lots of milk." She dropped onto a chair opposite him. "So, what have you been up to for the last few hours?"

"I'm guessing nothing as exciting as you. You look like you just stepped off the world's best roller coaster – and are getting on line to go again."

Rylan laughed. "Something like that." She leaned forward and lowered her head. "Between you and me, I just did a pretty complicated procedure that I've never done on my own before. I was running on pure adrenalin, trying to beat the clock and not screw up."

"And?" Paul asked, even though he could read the outcome on her face.

"It went fuckin' awesome!" Rylan banged her fist on the table, and her hand immediately flew to her mouth. "Sorry. I swear too much."

"After I get my refund, I'll lodge a complaint with the tour manager."

Rylan folded her arms over her chest and pretended to anxiously bite her nails. "Aw, do you have to? I can't afford to lose another job."

"You should've thought of that before you launched an f-bomb, my dear." Paul wagged an emphatic finger. "Now, you need something you can fall back on, something nice-and-stress-free that doesn't require any sweet talking. Something like, I don't know… surgery?"

"Be a surgeon? Please, I'd need to have my head examined!"

"Well, I know just the guy."

A smile flashed across Rylan's face. "Hmm, I may ask for his name," she said. They grinned goofily at one another. Finally, Rylan cocked her head to one side. "Really, how has your night been going?"

The playful look dissolved from Paul's face. He cleared his throat and swirled his coffee cup in agitated circles. "I've had a few, let's say, 'feisty' patients in the ER and one escapee, so…" He shrugged his shoulders and attempted a weary grin.

"You look wiped out."

Paul observed Rylan staring into his face with an intensity he found disconcerting. He dropped his gaze to the depths of his stale coffee.

"Is something wrong?"

"No." Paul slouched back into his chair, and his shoulders drooped. "Yes." He rubbed the bridge of his nose, then sighed. "There was a patient down there – the one that escaped – who just messed with my head a little."

"Aren't you supposed to be the one messing with the heads?" Rylan gave a weak laugh.

Paul tried to smile but found he couldn't. "She reminded me of someone."

"Another patient?"

Paul pulled a crumpled newspaper article from his pocket and laid the folded paper on the table. He looked around to be sure no one was watching. "Remember when you asked why I moved here?"

Rylan looked at the paper. "You said it was professional."

"Right." He slowly unfolded the clipping. "This is the reason." He turned the article so she could read it.

Rylan dropped an index finger onto the paper and slid it her way. She looked down and read the headline: *Troubled teen, 17, latest suicide on Y-Bridge*. There was a photo with the article, and she gently traced her thumb over a young woman's high school senior portrait. Then, she looked back up at Paul and waited.

"My patient," he said.

Rylan nodded.

"Kayla Jennings. Seventeen years old, nice parents, and nice home. A golden girl – an A student, lots of friends, the whole deal. At least until she turned sixteen or so."

"What happened?"

"It was gradual at first. Moodiness, social withdrawal, falling grades. Initially, her parents attributed it to the trials and tribulations of being a teenage girl in the age of the internet. They thought it might be emotional immaturity or raging hormones. Maybe even drugs. I became involved after an incident in the high school bathroom."

Rylan frowned. "What kind of incident?"

"Change of periods at the high school. Without a word, Kayla entered the second-floor girls' bathroom with a black Sharpie in hand. She drew a series of complex markings and diagrams across the walls, along the stalls, over the sink. She paid no attention to the giggling girls who wandered in to steal a smoke, ignored the crowd of gawkers that eventually crammed the lavatory, gave no response to the teacher who ordered her to stop. By the time security got there, she was squatting in the center of the floor, enclosed in a circle drawn by her own hand, urinating with her eyes closed."

"Drugs?"

Paul shook his head. "Her parents took her for a mandatory psych eval. Tox was negative. She was ultimately diagnosed with first-break psychosis and assigned to yours truly for follow-up."

Rylan's big green eyes searched his face. "You work with patients that young?"

"I did a child and adolescent fellowship through Case Western before taking the position in Toledo. Most of the kids I dealt with were anxious, attention-seeking, attention-deficient, or just pissed off, but Kayla was a little different. She was a great girl… bright and insightful, but also very unlucky."

"Unlucky, how?"

"Significant psychotic symptoms at a young age are a bad prognostic indicator. And her symptoms were bad." Paul closed his eyes for a moment, then fixed his eyes on the table. "We tried various meds, alone and in combination. Watched her gain weight. Watched the bright light in her eyes dim to a dull haze. The worst part about it was that she was self-aware. At least on some level, she knew what people were saying about her, how they were looking at her. She knew she'd become an outsider, and she hated it. Like anyone would."

Paul paused, elbows on the table. He dropped his head into his hands and raked his fingers through his hair. The next part of the story would be rough to say out loud. "On the night of the senior prom – which she wasn't attending – she waited until her parents were asleep, and the house was dark. Then, quietly, she slipped out with her mom's car keys in hand. She drove forty-five minutes to a bridge in Akron, a bridge known as *The Suicide Bridge*." Paul swallowed hard and continued, not looking up. "Her remains were discovered in a backyard the next morning – by a six-year-old letting the family dog out while the mom made pancakes in the kitchen. There were parts of her everywhere.

Rylan covered her mouth with her hand. "I'm so sorry."

Paul nodded slowly, hands balled into tight fists on the table.

"You can't blame yourself."

Everyone said the same thing. Paul disagreed but was in no mood for debate.

For a while, Rylan said nothing else. She picked at a loose thread on her scrub shirt and looked around at the other tables in the cafeteria. Paul figured she was looking to make a getaway. She'd come in riding high. Last thing she'd want is to get caught in the thick emotional sludge of some other doc's failure. Paul crushed his empty coffee cup in his hand and began to stand.

"We all lose people." The words shot quickly out of Rylan's mouth, like the flick of a lizard's tongue. Paul didn't really want to have this conversation, but his legs stopped taking orders from his brain and held him in place. Rylan dropped her voice and continued. "I know it may be different in psych, but still… it hurts. It hurts every one of us. My father – he's kind of a surgical legend, actually the reason I went into the field – always told me we can't fix everyone, and to think we can, is just plain narcissism. We try, always try, but we have to accept our limitations." Paul could feel her eyes searching his face, willing him to look at her. He didn't want to look at her, though. He didn't want to see another person spewing out a tired line of sanctimonious bullshit that was supposed to make him magically feel better. But he did look, and, when he did, he was surprised by the depth of sincerity he saw overflowing Rylan's pretty eyes. "Easier said than done, I know," she said with a sad smile. And she looked like she really did know.

Paul sank slowly back into his seat. Rylan reached out and circled his left wrist with her fingers, giving a gentle squeeze. The physical touch was an unexpected jolt to his system, and he sat wordlessly, processing the sensation. Then, barely a whisper, "Thank you."

Rylan dropped her head and stared at the table. "So, is that why you left Toledo?"

Paul sighed. "I wasn't running away, at least not entirely, if that's what you're thinking. Truth is, I'd been thinking about a change for a while."

Rylan raised her face to look at Paul. "And you chose *Northern Michigan*? What about Florida? Or So Cal?" Her tone was cautious, testing the waters, seeing if it was safe to steer the conversation in a different direction. Lighten things up a little.

Paul played along. "Sunshine is overrated."

"Really? You say this in a blizzard." She pointed at a window whited-out by snow.

Paul followed her finger and gazed at the window. He felt his face relax and thought at least one side of his mouth was trying to smile. He didn't fight it. "I couldn't move that far. My mother is on her own in Wisconsin, and I don't like to be more than a few hours' drive."

"A good son."

"Right. And a good Packers fan."

Rylan leaned across the table, so her face was only about a foot from Paul's. "Last Sunday. Packers. Seahawks. 27-17!" She thumped a triumphant fist on the table.

Now, both sides of his mouth were definitely smiling. "You like football?"

Rylan began to say, "Hell, yeah!" when *Twinkle Twinkle Little Star* erupted from her pager.

"Catchy," Paul said.

"Crappy," Rylan grumbled, tapping the callback number into her phone. She turned away and spoke to someone. Paul couldn't make out all the words, but he recognized the tone of annoyed resignation. "All right, all right, I'm on my way," she grumbled. Rylan dropped the phone back into her pocket and turned to Paul. "Duty calls," she said, rolling her eyes. "You should try to catch a few zzz's."

"Yeah, good idea," Paul said as Rylan got up to go. "And Rylan…"

She looked at him.

"Thanks."

For one electric moment, their eyes locked. Then, Rylan gave an overhead wave, smiled, and walked away.

CHAPTER 10

Rylan

Rylan could not suppress the sultry little smile on her face. She moved at a languid pace, climbing one step at a time, thinking back to her tête-à-tête with Dr. Paul Bennett. A wonderfully intense conversation interrupted by a stupid consult from the Fast Track in the ER regarding a 70-year-old benefactor to the hospital – who apparently had just donated seven zeros – with insomnia, a jacked-up Hummer with gigantic tires made for heavy snow, and acute tennis elbow. Nice enough fellow, but definitely a little wacky in that super-rich person way. She gave him a cortisone injection with a long-acting freezing which seemed to solve his problem – at least for the time being, until the freezing wore off and the steroids kicked in over the next few days.

Having dealt with the VIP, she was headed for the ICU to check on Brad, the trauma victim, now fully equipped with his own portable Sputnik satellite system on his right leg and pelvis, courtesy of one Dr. Rylan Fraser. Hopefully, Dickwad hadn't screwed up his belly too much, and he would be well enough to have his tibia washed out again and definitively repaired with a rod and screws in a couple of days. An intramedullary nail was a procedure Rylan enjoyed doing and could always use a little more practice with.

She checked the time on her phone – 12:55AM – and thought about circling back to the ER after she rounded on Brad to see Helen. She wondered whether her friend had met the hospital's newest psychiatrist and whether she had a take on him yet. Helen was good at reading people. In fact, too good. She'd take one look at the goofy grin on Rylan's face and raise a knowing eyebrow. Then Rylan would start gushing like an eighth-grader and –

She was actually blushing when her pager twinkled mercilessly off the concrete walls of the stairwell and dragged her back to reality. Rylan waited until she was on the next landing, checked her pager, and then slowly pecked the four-digit number into her phone, trying to delay the inevitable bad news. The thing about a medical pager was that it never brought good news, only bad. Always bad.

"Hi, it's Dr. Fraser. You paged?"

"Dr. Fraser, we need you on the surgical ward. It's Mrs. Potter in room 606. She's not doing well."

"What's going on?"

Her question was met with silence.

"Hello? Anyone there?"

She heard a clicking sound and then a busy signal.

"Did you just hang up on me?" she asked incredulously, staring at the phone in her hand. "Shit."

She bolted, bounding three steps at a time with jaguar speed from the second to the sixth floor. When she pushed open the heavy fire door, she was sucking wind so hard, she needed to crouch for a second to catch her breath. Then, she speed-walked to the nursing station and yelled, "Who paged for Mrs. Potter?"

Two nurses, Amanda and Darlene, were charting on computers at the back. Linda, with her funky cat-glasses, was doing some old-fashioned paperwork at the front desk. All three looked up at Rylan with blank faces and then looked at each other. Linda spoke first. "Rylan, you know I've been here all night. No one's paged you for Mrs. Potter that I'm aware of."

"Come on, I was just paged minutes ago. Are there any other nurses on the floor?"

"Just us. Skeleton crew tonight between the holiday and the snowstorm." Linda swiveled to face Rylan head-on. "You know, this is sounding a lot like the same confusion that happened with Mr. Kettering earlier this evening."

"But –" Rylan stopped. Linda was absolutely right. "Crap. What room's Mrs. Potter in?"

"Room 606," Darlene answered, a nurse who had been working on the surgical ward for many years. "She's my patient. She was fine when I checked on her thirty minutes ago. In fact, she was talking about how excited she is to be going home tomorrow and wondering if she could get her IV out."

"Follow me," Rylan said, darting down the hallway.

Room 606 was a four-person room, but only Mrs. Potter was there. Everyone else had been discharged home before the long weekend. When Rylan entered, it was dark with the only illumination coming from the crack under the bathroom door. She walked directly to the foot of Mrs. Potter's bed and stood completely still. Darlene was right behind her. Mrs. Potter had undergone an elective knee replacement two days earlier. Rylan had performed the majority of the procedure under the supervision of her staff. Everything had gone exceptionally well, and she had done the procedure skin-to-skin with minimal help. Rylan had rounded on her yesterday and earlier this morning, and Mrs. Potter was following a routine postoperative recovery.

Rylan listened intently, trying to hear beyond the sounds of her pounding heartbeat. Through the shadows, she could just make out Mrs. Potter's face with the sheet pulled to just below her chin. She was lying on her back. There didn't appear to be anything amiss. There was no moaning or groaning. Really, there were no sounds of any sort. No sounds at all.

"Darlene, turn on the light."

Darlene went to the wall and flicked the switch for the overhead fluorescent lights. Rylan was blinded for a moment, and then she saw

Mrs. Potter's ashen, still face. Rylan pulled the blanket down and placed her fingers on Mrs. Potter's neck.

"No pulse."

Darlene connected a pulse oximeter to Mrs. Potter's index finger and confirmed, "No pulse." She then pulled the alarm button on the wall and ran back into the hall, yelling, "Code Blue! We need the crash cart."

Darlene flattened the bed completely as Rylan started chest compressions, humming the age-old Bee Gees' classic, *Staying Alive,* to maintain proper rhythm. She felt the 72-year-old brittle ribs snap like raw strands of spaghetti from the force of her hand pressure and was reminded of every other time she had worked a code. The crash cart arrived, and Amanda placed an Ambu bag over the patient's face and started ventilating Mrs. Potter with 100% oxygen. Darlene placed defibrillator pads on Mrs. Potter's chest as Dr. Curran from the ER arrived. Everyone looked to the defibrillator monitor simultaneously and saw only a straight line.

Rylan was downloading information as fast as she could talk to Mike, trying to bring him up to speed. She finished with, "You're on the code team as well?"

"Internist couldn't make it through the storm. She asked me to cover."

Rylan wondered why the eccentric doc she'd seen on the floor earlier with the Sherlock Holmes hat couldn't do it. A question for later.

"Damn, you're a one-man team."

Mike shrugged and immediately began ACLS protocol, ordering a cocktail of potentially lifesaving medications. Words swirled in a vortex around the bed.

"Still asystolic."

"Ringer's running wide open."

"EMR indicates she's a full code."

"No response to first dose of Epi."

Finally, Mike yelled, "Stop chest compressions."

Rylan, for the first time in ten minutes, stopped pumping Mrs. Potter's chest and took the opportunity to catch her breath. A river of sweat washed over her own chest, soaking her bra and scrubs. CPR was exhausting work, and while it made sense to alternate with other caregivers, this was Rylan's patient. She was responsible and would absolutely not allow anyone else to die on her watch. She looked up to the monitor.

"No change. Still flatline."

"Defibrillate?"

"Not indicated for asystole," Mike reminded everyone.

He then released a loud breath. "I'm calling it. Time of –"

"NO. FUCKING. WAY," Rylan cried out as she jumped on the bed and straddled Mrs. Potter, restarting chest compressions. "This is my patient," she squeaked out somewhere between an up and a down movement, "and… I, *huff*, AM, *huff*, NOT, *huff*, GIVING UP!"

"Rylan." Mike placed a gentle hand on Rylan's galloping shoulder. "It's time to stop. This patient is not revivable, and you know that."

Rylan heard everything Mike was saying, and she knew it to be true, but she couldn't accept it. She couldn't lose another patient tonight. Another failure. She continued pushing harder and harder, ribs crunching, fragile skin tearing, until Mike said, "Even if we brought her back now, she's been down at least fifteen minutes. That's fifteen minutes her brain has not had oxygen. She would be brain dead."

The science of it all finally penetrated Rylan's emotional walls and made sense to her. There were plenty of things worse than death, and not being allowed to die was one of them. Like her mother years ago. As breast cancer ate her up, organ by organ, and no one would let her go.

Rylan gave a last compression and pushed herself off the bed. Her hands were shaking, and her shoulder-length hair had come loose from her hair tie and was hanging over her face, hiding tears. She backed away from Mrs. Potter's bed, pulled her phone from the rear pocket of her scrub pants, looked at it, and said, "Time of death, 1:15AM."

She turned abruptly and walked out of the room, leaving Mike to perform the formalities. She readjusted her hair into a sloppy ponytail and trudged to the nursing station to complete the death certificate. She also had to call the patient's MRP (Most Responsible Physician), her next of kin, and the coroner – three tasks on her to-do list that she still hadn't completed following Mr. Kettering's passing. The details of the dead always came last on a busy shift.

She wasn't able to reach anyone, although she left messages requesting callbacks. So, that just left the death certificate – *another death certificate*. She plopped into a chair at the now deserted nursing station. Linda was on break, and the other two nurses were busy with Mrs. Potter. Rylan passed her ID badge over the computer scanner, and her monitor sprang to life, listing all of her patients on the screen. She reached for the mouse with an arm made of lead, resonating from the efforts of lengthy CPR. Her whole body sagged into the chair, heavy with sorrow and exhaustion. The adrenaline coursing through her arteries for the past many hours, keeping her going, was spent, and her adrenal glands had run dry. From superhero to dead weight in the blink of an eye. She stared through the screen for a few minutes, her lids growing heavier and heavier, until she leaned forward, rested her forehead on the table, and whispered to herself, "None of it makes any sense."

She snorted a couple of times, briefly losing consciousness, until, "Hey, Fraser, wake up!"

Rylan could just hear it, a word salad attacking her Z sanctuary. It took a few moments before the words made any sense to her. She lifted her head slowly off the table and looked in the direction of the voice. Her right eye refused to open, caked over with a layer of dried tears. She pulled a sleeve across her face and then tried once more to make out the owner of the voice.

"Look, man, I'm done. I need to get the fuck out of here. Just script me the Percs and the antibiotics. Okay?"

Pockface.

"And I need my fucking clothes back, man," he growled.

Rylan was too tired and too dispirited to deal with this now. She was of half a mind to let Pockface walk out the door, find a fix, and pass out in a snowdrift. But that wasn't the doctor half of her mind thinking. Instead, it was the overwrought half, the failure half that had lost two healthy patients over the span of a few hours and wanted nothing more than to stick the hard shell surrounding both halves of that mind into the sand. The doctor half, however, understood that even Pockface deserved compassionate care. Despite his bravado and bluster, he was suffering.

Her best approach, she decided, was a firm and professional one. She took a deep breath. "Look, I know this is hard –"

"I want out! OUT! Do you understand me? No bullshit, man, I'm leaving!" He slammed his hands on the counter, startling her. She reflexively pushed back in her chair, although she was determined to hold her ground. She was not going to let Pockface get the upper hand. Keeping her face neutral and her voice steady, Rylan leaned forward and said, "I am going to ask you to lower your voice so that we can have a rational conversation about this. I am also going to remind you that my name is Dr. Fraser, not 'man,' and I would appreciate you referring to me as such."

Pockface's eyes narrowed. He hunched over and glared at her, his face close enough that Rylan could make out each individual pockmark on his forehead. "Why don't you suck me off? Bitch!"

The doctor part of Rylan's brain wasted no time hopping a portal to a distant dimension, leaving behind a bulging, frayed sack of rage. Rylan rose from her seat with hands curled into fists and prepared to unleash a scathing torrent of profanity that would've made the saltiest sailor blush and Mother Teresa roll over in her grave when a voice yelled from somewhere down the corridor. "Mr. P! Where are you? You are on contact precautions. Get your ass back in your room."

Pockface looked to the hallway and then back at Rylan. "Screw all of you!"

He ripped the IV from his elbow and swung his arm around as he turned to leave, releasing an arc of blood droplets that sprinkled the floor, with one errant droplet smacking Rylan in the chest just above the "V" neck of her scrubs. If it was possible for a human head to spontaneously combust, Rylan's came dangerously close.

Pockface stormed off, knocking his IV pole over in the process. The pole struck the floor, and the machine that was clamped to the pole delivering his antibiotics shattered into multiple pieces of plastic. The one-liter bag of saline hanging off the pole exploded on impact, creating an instant puddle. As Rylan stepped forward to chase after Pockface, her foot slid out from under her, and she landed unceremoniously on her butt. She heard the clang of the large stairwell door closing. "You idiot! There's a huge snowstorm outside and nowhere for you to go!"

She sat for a moment to collect herself, each elbow resting on a bent knee while the derrière of her scrub pants soaked up the saline, making her feel like a toddler with a wet diaper. She realized her pride was hurt more than any body parts, and she was grateful that her father, the great PJ Fraser, was not here to witness his little girl's humiliation. She bit her lip to keep it from quivering.

An open hand appeared from nowhere, dangling in front of her face, offering to lift her up. "Funny place for a sit-down."

CHAPTER 11

Paul

"Why are *you* here?"

Hardly a warm and fuzzy welcome. Paul's initial impulse when he registered the fury in Rylan's eyes was to withdraw his hand and run for the hills. But before he could move, her fingers clasped his, and she rose to her feet. She gave an abashed smile, and her eyes softened. "Let me try that again," she said. "I mean –"

"Well, it's obvious, isn't it?" Paul grinned. "I simply can't keep away."

He was joking, of course, but a funny look came over Rylan's face, and Paul regretted his timing. Her hair had come loose from her ponytail, the collar of her scrub shirt was damp with sweat, and her pants were dripping from the puddle of saline she'd landed in. Paul watched her open her mouth to say something, then falter and close it again. Finally, she asked, "Really?"

Now it was Paul's turn to fumble. He gently extricated his hand from Rylan's and dried it on the leg of his jeans. "While I much prefer my first answer, duty compels the truth." He made a scout's three-finger sign of honor with his newly dried right hand. "I was paged," he admitted, eyes slipping sideways to scan for hand sanitizer.

Rylan's face wrinkled in confusion, a follow-up question perched on her lips, but Paul's wandering eye distracted her. "It's just saline, you know."

"No, it's not." Paul did a visual connect-the-dots between the drops of blood on the floor that led straight to Rylan's collarbone. A little déjà vu from their earlier meeting in the ER. "You've, um, got another spot."

"Shit." Rylan sighed. She snatched a wad of paper towels from behind the nursing station, doused them with sanitizer, sighed once more, and began scrubbing at the spot on her chest. With her free hand, she slid the bottle across the counter toward Paul. When the spot on her chest gleamed an angry red and the air was thoroughly saturated with the sharp tang of isopropyl alcohol, she tossed the towels into a hazard bin and twisted her neck to look down and over her right shoulder. With the fingers of her right hand, she plucked soaked scrubs from her wet backside. "Lovely," she mumbled. "I need to change." She straightened up and faced Paul. She made to excuse herself, then abruptly changed course by shaking her head, the motion seemingly engineered to dislodge the trivial fluff of the last few minutes and re-center that dangling, loose thread. "Wait. Paged *here*?" she asked. "Back to surgery?"

"Um-hmm." He pulled his little yellow sticky pad from his blazer pocket and read, "I was called to see a Mrs. Potter."

"No," Rylan said. She actually stamped a foot, which had the effect of launching a few drops of saline into the air to splatter on Paul's leather Oxfords. "No, no, no, no, no."

Paul looked from the beads of moisture on his shoes to Rylan.

"No," she repeated as if he hadn't heard her the first six times. "*Who* paged you?"

"I didn't get a name," he answered, looking guiltily at the yellow note. He felt like a schoolboy called out for bad behavior. "I'll start asking who the caller is when I get beeped."

"Was it a guy?"

He dropped the sticky note back into his pocket. "Mmm, not sure."

The interrogation continued. "Same voice as last time?"

Paul hesitated, "Maybe," he admitted. His heart rate kicked up a notch. "Maybe it was the same. I'm guessing from this Q and A session that something's not right?"

"Mrs. Potter is deceased."

"And you know this how?"

"I was paged to see her, also."

It was déjà vu. "Why?"

"She was a post-surgical patient of mine. I replaced her knee, and she was recovering just fine. *Just fine.* Then, I got a page saying she was not doing well. Well, not doing well was a bit of an understatement, considering she was already dead as a doornail by the time I got to her." Rylan was talking fast, rambling more to herself than Paul. "Still, we called a code. Didn't you hear the Code Blue announcement?" She didn't wait for Paul's response. Instead, she began to chew rather inelegantly on a gnarled thumbnail, forming her words through clenched teeth. "It's Mr. Kettering all over again!"

Paul took a step back from Rylan. The more he studied her, the more unhinged she appeared, and he became unsure what to make of her – though he knew he didn't ever want to be one of her patients. That much was for sure, post-op complications and all.

"Glory be, what now?"

His musings were interrupted by the arrival of a stout blur in lavender. Linda, the nurse he'd met on this same unit earlier in the night, came barreling down the hall from the commotion outside of what Paul now assumed was the room of the late Mrs. Potter. Her cat-eye glasses were slightly askew, but her caramel-stiff hair was exactly as it had been before, not one strand out of place. She stopped in front of the puddle of saline, careful not to wet the toe of her white sneaker, and warily eyed the tipped IV pole, broken bits of plastic, and droplets of blood that made a ninety-degree arc from counter to computer terminal to wall and continued like a trail of breadcrumbs down the hall in the direction opposite Mrs. Potter's room and off the unit. "Dr. Fraser?"

Rylan stopped chewing her nail and rubbed the back of her hand across her brow. "Pockface left AMA."

"That asshole. I'll call janitorial," she said, reaching for a desk phone beside a computer terminal. She pulled her hand back at the last minute and checked for errant blood droplets on the device. Once the inspection was complete, she dialed an extension, simultaneously asking Rylan, "Security, too? He was on withdrawal and contact precautions."

This just kept getting better and better. "Withdrawal from what?" Paul asked.

"Meth user. Heroin. Whatever else –"

"Opiate withdrawal's no joke," Paul said, worrying over the disappearing blood trail down the corridor.

"Gee, thanks," Rylan snapped. "You know, we *are* capable of managing withdrawal on a surgical unit, Dr. Bennett."

Dr. Bennett? Uh-oh.

Rylan released Paul from her fierce glare and dropped her eyes to the mess on the floor. After a heavy exhale, she said, "Yes, call security, too. They'll need to be alerted in case he ends up somewhere else in the hospital. I can't imagine he's going to get far in this storm."

Linda nodded and made the call. Then she turned her attention to Paul. *Gang-up time.* "Dr. Bennett, I didn't expect to see you again so soon, though it certainly is a pleasure."

Paul noted that her tone and expression indicated she was anything but pleased. "May I ask what brings you back to our unit?"

He shifted uneasily, anticipating she would not like his response. "A page."

"No one here paged psych," Linda said in a way that left no room for contradiction.

Paul took a breath and continued, "To evaluate Mrs. Potter."

Linda squared her shoulders and stared at Paul from behind the lenses of her funky glasses.

Definitely not pleased, Paul decided.

"You're telling me you received another page to this unit to evaluate another dead patient?" She made little quotation marks with her fingers around the word "page."

Paul stared back mutely at Linda, blinked once, and looked at Rylan. Then, Linda looked at Rylan. Rylan, in turn, looked from one to the other and threw her arms up in exasperation. "Don't look at me!"

"Isn't it strange that we have two deaths in one night on two previously healthy patients, and, in each case, Dr. Bennett shows up?"

Those sounded like fighting words. Anger welled inside Paul like floodwaters after a storm surge and erupted in sentences he'd soon regret. "Look, Linda, I don't know what you're implying, but I *have* been paged twice to this unit, and, yes, both times, I've arrived to find deceased patients. So, instead of questioning me, maybe you should be examining the nursing care being provided on your unit because, frankly, it doesn't look so great."

The color drained from Linda's face, and, for a second, Paul thought she was going to take a swing at him. "Who the hell do you –"

"Stop it! Both of you!" Rylan shouted from the sideline. "Dial it back."

Linda glared at Paul, her chest heaving. Paul took his yellow sticky note out of his pocket again and read it, rather unnecessarily, so he would have somewhere to direct his gaze other than at Linda.

Dr. Mike Curran whirl-winded into the nursing station, clipboard in one hand, cell phone in the other. He plunked the clipboard onto the counter. "Code flowsheet for Mrs. Potter's chart," he said to no one in particular, simultaneously answering a call on his cell. "Give a dose of Maalox and repeat the ECG," he ordered into the phone. "I'll be back down in a minute." He stuffed the phone into the pocket of his white lab coat, scanned the vicinity with a sharp, appraising eye, and did a little double take. Paul watched Mike's eyes hopscotch between the puddle on the floor, the blood spatter, the broken equipment, and Rylan. "Dr. Fraser," he said.

"What, Mike?"

"Your butt is wet."

Rylan rolled her eyes.

"Housekeeping is on the way," Linda offered.

"To mop Rylan's butt?" Mike asked.

"Oh, shut up!" Rylan yelled.

"What happened?"

"Pockface," Rylan said.

Paul observed that this answer seemed to satisfy Mike as if the single word provided an entire explanation. Mike nodded. "Left AMA?"

Rylan bobbed her head in the affirmative.

"Asshole," Mike said. His shoulders rose and fell with an indulgent sigh. "That must be about the thirtieth incident of the night. At least that I've heard of so far. This is shaping up to be one for the record books."

Mike's gaze landed on Paul. "Having fun yet?"

There was no way anyone could expect Dr. Paul Bennett to be having "fun" in the current circumstances, but he played along. "Sure," he said, unable to make the word sound anything but grim.

Mike clapped him on the back. "That girl from the ER –" he began.

"Lost in transit," Paul finished.

"I heard." Mike massaged the back of his neck. "Like I said, one for the record books. You picked a hell of a night to come on." He turned his attention back to Rylan. "How'd your surgery on the motorcycle guy go?"

"My part went fine. He was in General Surgery's hands when I scrubbed out."

"Did your staff man make it in?"

"No."

Mike winced. "It's Huang, right? He never lets residents operate without him."

"Well, what was I supposed to do? Let the guy bleed out and die?"

Mike dismissed this with a wave of the hand. "No, you did the right thing. I'm just saying, don't be surprised if he gives you hell, anyway. Huang is the kind of guy who watches God's glorious sunrise over the Grand Canyon and thinks, *I can do better*." He glanced at a text message on his phone. "I need to get back downstairs." He thumped his hand twice on the counter and started toward the elevators. "Hopefully, I *won't* see you later."

Paul watched Dr. Curran's form retreat down the hall. Behind him, Rylan said she would do the necessary incident paperwork, but Linda forbade her from sitting in any of the chairs with her wet bottom.

A moment later, the wet-bottomed surgeon was standing shoulder to shoulder with Paul whose eyes were still trained on Mike, now waiting for the elevator.

"Is he really that interesting?" Rylan asked, following Paul's gaze.

Paul gave a dry, mirthless laugh. The truth was he was watching Mike for no other reason than he was tired and spacey and unsure what to do next. It was clear he had no reason to be on the surgical ward now.

"I need to change," Rylan said.

"Yup." He could feel Rylan trying to make conversation, trying to be friendly, but his head had gone blank, and he had nothing to say.

Rylan tried again. "I think we should tell someone, you know, about the pages we received tonight. Something is definitely not right."

Paul nodded. "Agreed." He turned his head slightly to the left and found Rylan looking up at him.

"Listen, I'm sorry about how I reacted before."

Paul waved a hand, the universal gesture for "forget it." He'd let bygones be bygones.

"And what Linda said, you have to understand that she was just upset."

"I know." Paul forced himself to find his voice. "But I don't think I made the situation any better."

Rylan made a little clucking sound and stole a look over her shoulder where Linda was charting. "Probably not." She dropped her voice and nudged him gently with her elbow. "But, hey, don't worry about it. She's okay."

"Well, that makes one of us," Paul said. He scratched at the five o'clock shadow on his chin and watched Mike step onto the elevator and disappear, thinking it might be a good time to explore the call rooms. He was tired. Really, really tired. An hour of rest might get him back on track. He considered first offering to walk Rylan to the locker room – what with escaped patients and a mysterious disembodied voice on the loose – but had the feeling she'd be more likely to slug him than acquiesce to chivalry. He dropped his weary arms to his sides and opened his mouth to speak, but, instead of the intended farewell, a gasp steamrolled out.

"Hey," Rylan said, "what's up?" She followed his gaze and squinted down the hall. "Paul? What is it?"

Paul stepped forward and cupped a hand over his eyes. "It's her!"

"Who? I don't see anyone."

"The teen from the ER."

"Are you sure? I'll call security."

"No, I got this!" For the first time tonight, Paul had a chance to make something right. He started to run.

"Paul, stop! Ugh, okay… just wait for me!"

CHAPTER 12

Rylan

"Linda! Call security stat and tell them the missing teen from psych is up here," Rylan yelled, as she watched Paul disappear around a corner at the end of the hall.

"What's her name?"

Rylan was mid-step into a catch-up run when she braked, grabbing onto the main desk at the nursing station to keep her balance. "Her name?"

"The teen," Linda said. "They'll want to know who they're chasing after."

"I don't know. How many escaped teens from psych can there be tonight? Just tell Helen and her team to get up here ASAP."

Linda rolled her eyes, snorted, and reached for the phone.

"Thanks," Rylan said, already underway and building speed, her Birkenstocks squeaking rhythmically from her recent foray into the saline puddle.

After she rounded the corner at the end of the hall, she stopped momentarily to listen for some clue as to what direction to take.

There were three options: The first, a steel door leading to a stairwell at the rear of the hospital; the second, a hallway connecting back to the main surgical ward; and the third, a large double door opening on to a section of the hospital where she had never been before, a section that had been closed for renovations for as long as she could remember. Normally at night that section was pitch black, but tonight she saw through the door windows that several ward rooms were lit up. She approached the entrance and noticed that one of the doors, typically locked, was partly ajar.

A tiny chill crept up her spine as she pushed one of the heavy doors open and passed the threshold. Hospitals full of sick and traumatized people didn't bother her, but for some reason, the idea of an empty ward did.

"Hello? Paul? You down here?" An eerie echo responded faintly with her own voice.

Light spilled from the third room on the right, casting an impression of the doorway onto the floor of the corridor. She advanced slowly towards it, unable to shake the uneasy feeling that someone was nearby.

"Paul?" She yelled a little louder this time, her head swiveling from side to side looking for any potential horror-movie-teen-psycho-killers that might be lurking about. When she arrived at the first lit room, she slowly goosenecked her head around the doorjamb and saw an empty four-bed ward with gleaming floors. The smell of fresh wax was overpowering, and she stepped back.

"Hey!"

Startled, Rylan did a clumsy bounce into the wall next to the door and turned to see the figure behind the voice. A scrawny, older man in ragged blue janitorial overalls was glaring at her from an arm's length away. They were at similar eye levels, but he likely would have been much taller than her in his youth, his spine now C-shaped and hunched. A smattering of thin, grey hairs circled his crown. One hand held a wax scraper, the other a mop handle.

"Shit!" Rylan yelled. "You scared the crap out of me. I damned near wet myself." She cringed inwardly at the irony of her own words since her ass, of course, was already drenched in saline.

The man leered at her with narrow, slit eyes, his pupils barely visible. He pointed the scraper at her, a glint of fluorescent light reflecting off the edge. He smiled coolly and said, "Dr. Rylan Fraser, you shouldn't be here. Off limits for maintenance."

Rylan remembered an email that had circulated a week earlier, indicating that they were coming into the flu season, and the administration was being proactive, prepping extra rooms in several wings of the hospital in anticipation of the yearly onslaught.

The staredown continued, and Rylan's heart skipped a beat as she watched the wax scraper waver in front of her face. The fingers holding it were grossly deformed. The knuckles twisted and gnarled, barely able to grip the handle. At first, she thought he had rheumatoid arthritis, but his other hand looked completely normal. *Post traumatic?* she wondered. He took a step closer, and Rylan shrunk into the wall, prepping herself to bolt. But then she rallied, dug deep, and stood tall. She wasn't going to get pushed around by some creepy janitor. "How do you know my name?"

He dropped the hand holding the scraper to his side and stepped back, smiling sardonically. "You and me are old friends."

Rylan's eyebrows shot up. She didn't recognize him. "I'm sorry, but I don't know you."

"Well, I know you."

Rylan and the janitor stood looking at one another for what felt like an interminable moment, neither speaking. Rylan wondered if he had seen one of the articles about her award in the papers. Many local people had, so she guessed it was a possibility.

The janitor finally spoke. "You're not supposed to be in the D wing. What are you doing here?"

She crossed her arms over her chest. "Looking for someone. You didn't see a tallish man with dark hair wearing a black blazer come through here in the last few minutes, did you? Or perhaps a teenager in a hospital gown?"

The janitor tilted his head to the side and eyed her suspiciously. There was a blackness to his pupils that completely creeped Rylan out. "A guy in a black blazer and a teen in a gown?"

Rylan nodded her head.

"No. No one but me here."

Rylan glanced down the hallway and now saw another light coming from a half-open door. She turned back to the janitor and noted for the first time a pair of old earbuds dangling from the front pocket of his overalls. The gears of her mind were spinning.

She pointed to the cleaning closet. "Is that where you were just now?"

He shrugged his shoulders. "I was getting a few things."

"Listening to some tunes?" she asked, pointing her chin at his earbuds.

"A podcast."

Rylan deduced that the janitor was probably in the closet and may not have seen or heard Paul or the teen race by, if indeed they had come this way.

The loud first notes of *Twinkle Twinkle* on Rylan's pager made the janitor jump, and he dropped his wax scraper. He scowled as he bent over to pick it up. Amidst the fading echo of *Little Star* and the dying clatter of the scraper hitting the floor, Rylan said unnecessarily, "My pager."

She checked it and then pulled her cell from the side pocket of her scrub pants and dialed. The janitor had the scraper back in his hand and was staring at her with undisguised loathing. Rylan had no idea what his problem was. For all she knew, maybe she'd come onto the unit as the guy was yanking off in the utility closet. Total weirdo.

"Hello? It's Dr. Fraser. Someone paged?"

There was a crunching sound, like someone chewing on a candy. "Hey, it's Todd."

"Todd? Why didn't you just call me on my cell?"

"Thought there was a better chance of you answering your pager than you answering my phone call."

He isn't wrong about that.

"Plus," he said, "I know how much that pager bugs you."

Asswipe. He isn't wrong about that, either.

"What's up?"

As Rylan continued the conversation, she moved steadily away from the janitor and back down the hallway towards the surgical unit. She made a final eye contact with the janitor, who stood watching her, grim-faced, mop held upright in his right hand, looking uncannily similar to the scary guy from the American Gothic painting. She couldn't get out of there fast enough.

On the phone she heard the crunching sound again, this time with a bit of slurping. *He's so disgusting.* "Don't think our motorcycle guy is doing very well," Todd said. "They're still having difficulty keeping his pressure up. Any chance one of your ex-fix pins went astray through the pelvis? Maybe poked a small hole through an artery or something?"

"What! No. Of course not."

"Okay. Anyway, just thought you should know he's not doing too well. The ICU staff has been trying to contact Huang, but he hasn't answered."

"Contact him? He doesn't even know the guy's had an operation yet."

"Yeah. Wouldn't want to be in your shoes. Anyway, thought you should know. A couple of chief residents looking out for each other. Right?"

Yeah, looking out for me as you throw me under the bus.

"Did you reach *your* staff?"

"Yup. All good. That's why we were wondering if it could be something on your side."

"No. My part was perfect." In spite of her cold, wet scrubs, Rylan was suddenly burning up. She felt sweat at her temples.

"Sure, it was. Still, you should come by the ICU when you get a chance, and you'd better let Huang know ASAP before he finds out through back channels."

"Right. Okay, thanks. I'll drop by the ICU." The part about telling Huang just made her sweat more. What the hell was she supposed to do? Get her parka, trudge into the blizzard in the wee hours of the night, and haul her ass to Huang's house to tell him?

She pushed through the doors and stood on the surgical ward, thinking through in detail the ex-fix procedure she had done on Brad's pelvis, wondering if there was anywhere she could have screwed up. It all happened so fast.

Her pager rang again. She squeezed her eyes shut tightly and released a long sigh. She dialed in the paged number. There was a pause and then a single sentence. "You are needed on the medical ward."

No explanation, no patient name, no description of emergency. "Who is this?" Rylan asked.

Silence.

Rylan sucked in a deep breath and then turned a hard left, opening the door to the rear stairwell. She pounded down the steps to the fifth-floor medical ward, realizing she wasn't just running to a patient in need. She was running because she was scared. Wide-eyed, knee-quivering, chest-thudding scared. She burst through the stairwell door expecting God-knows-what. What she found was something both she and God knew all too well. Death was in the air. She easily zoned in on the room. It was the one with all the lights on, like a pulsating neon sign on the Vegas strip. Medical personnel milled about, not knowing what to do with themselves. A sure sign of failure.

Rylan stopped before the door and tapped a nurse she recognized on the shoulder.

"Millie. What happened?"

"Dr. Fraser," the nurse replied, turning to look Rylan in the face, "this is strange. I was about to call you. We just ran a code on Dr. Whitaker's patient with the septic knee."

Rylan looked past Millie's shoulder into the room. There was that sheet again, pulled over the patient's head.

"Wait," Rylan said, "Mr. Robinson? The 35-year-old man off-service with the septic knee?" Not infrequently, when the surgical ward was full, surgical patients would be offloaded onto other floors for postoperative care.

Millie nodded.

"But he was fine when I rounded on him this morning. On IV antibiotics, recovering nicely from his arthroscopic I & D."

"Dr. Lombroso from the ICU had to run the code because the code team was apparently tied up elsewhere."

The sensation of Mrs. Potter's crumbling ribs suddenly revisited Rylan's fingers, causing her to inhale a short gasp of air. She shook both her hands as if they were wet.

"He wondered if Mr. Robinson had an acute flare-up of sepsis from the knee again. Complete flatline the whole time. We tried everything." Millie dropped her voice. "And I have to tell you, Lombroso was super grumpy and not at all happy being here."

Rylan, who most certainly wasn't happy being here either, walked slowly past Millie into the room and stood next to the deceased patient's bed. First, she respectfully pulled the sheet from the patient's face. She needed to be sure it was her patient. She gazed upon the pale, dead face of Mr. Robinson, a face that seemed to be in mid-sentence saying, "It's not my time yet."

Next, she pulled the sheet from Mr. Robinson's left knee, the infected one. She unwrapped a tensor bandage and pulled off layers of gauze soaked with dried blood from the surgery two days earlier. The knee and leg still had a pinkish color to it from the prep solution used at surgery. Rylan grabbed a small bottle of saline from a nearby table, along with a face cloth, and scrubbed the knee until the prep solution was completely off. She felt Millie's presence over her shoulder.

"It doesn't look infected to me," Millie said.

"No, it doesn't. It looks perfect. Swollen, as you would expect for post-op day two, but no redness or drainage. Certainly not a source of widespread septicemia that would kill a man."

"I guess it wasn't infection that killed him," Millie said.

Rylan turned to look into her eyes. "And no one called me? Or tried to page the R3 ortho resident?"

"There was no time. It all happened very quickly. As I said, I was just about to call you directly. Dr. Whitaker needs to be made aware. He's the responsible attending. And don't forget Mr. Robinson's wife."

With a sick feeling, Rylan remembered that Mr. Robinson had at least two, maybe three kids. Could this night get any worse?

"I'll call them," Rylan said, slapping a wall in place to hold back tears. She never wanted to be on the other end of *that* phone call.

Rylan covered Mr. Robinson's face and knee with the sheet and tiptoed out of the room into the hallway. It was a ubiquitous and uncontrollable habit to tiptoe around the freshly deceased in the hospital, as if they might awaken from their final dreams. She pulled out her cell phone and was scrolling through her contacts when she realized that she hadn't yet phoned her staff attending about the other deceased patients – Mr. Kettering and Mrs. Potter. All three patients belonged to Dr. Whitaker, and he would need to know.

She dialed 911 instead.

CHAPTER 13

The Janitor

Sid Kosinski braced his upper thighs on the edge of the deep metal sink in the janitorial closet before dousing his hands in mineral spirits. The fingers of his deformed right hand were raw from the late-night work, but there was no other way to get errant globs of wax off. Gloves worked to a point to protect his crippled limb, however, there always came a moment when his loss of dexterity and sensation required him to unglove to finish the job.

Electric arcs raced through his fingertips as the spirits made contact with his skin and networked through tendon and bone up his arm to his brain's pain center. He clenched his teeth until his jaw ached. Finally, as the pain eased off, he ran warm water over his hand and used a soft cloth to cleanse it.

Four years earlier, there had been an accident, one that cost him his career as an ironworker at the plant. He was sober now and had never felt healthier, but the chronic pain in his hand was far worse than the daily hangovers had ever been.

He gazed upon his gnarled digits and slowly opened and closed each finger. The hand was hideous, like a prop off the set of some B-list fright-night movie. He barely recognized it as his own. The skin grafts transferred from his front thigh were patchy, meshed, and ugly. It looked – and felt – like an unskilled seamstress had sewed his skin with a thread an inch too short.

Her fault.

It was all her fault.

·   ·   ·   ·   ·

They thought he was sedated, even asleep, but he heard it all.

After the two-ton machine press had trapped his hand, all hell broke loose. His crew extracted him swiftly and wrapped his mangled hand in gauze from the first aid kit and used towels to soak up the blood, which was everywhere. He was transported to Northern Michigan General Hospital in record time. The ER staff was quick to assess the damage, and they called the plastic surgery specialist as soon as they cleaned the debris from the wounds and gave him antibiotics and painkillers. Until that point, everything went smoothly.

Then it all turned sour. A green, first-year orthopedic resident by the name of Rylan Fraser came to assess him in the ER. It was July, and she had just transitioned from medical school to her first residency rotation: a three-month block in plastic surgery. A dark cloud crossed her face as she examined the hand. She told him it looked bad, but that they should be able to fix him up.

What the hell did she know? She was barely a doctor, let alone a specialist. To her credit, she got him to the operating room quickly. Maybe too quickly. Before he even met the actual hand specialist, the anesthesiologist performed a nerve block at his neck. God bless her; the pain disappeared completely. That was the last time in his life Sid didn't have pain.

They washed up his arm and covered him with drapes, blocking his view of whatever they were doing. A man in a mask and bonnet who claimed to be his plastic surgeon stuck his head over the drape and introduced himself – some unpronounceable name. Told him everything was going to be alright. He then looked at the anesthesiologist and nodded. Sid felt warmth course through his veins as the sedation reached for him.

It didn't work, though. Not the way it was supposed to. It gave him a five- or six-beer buzz, but nothing more. He heard everything. And it seemed like just a few minutes into the procedure before the plastic surgeon with the unpronounceable name declared that he had more *important* things to do, and that Sid was a good resident case. He left Fraser all alone to do the job.

•   •   •   •   •

The hand was clean, and the pain was back to baseline now, tolerable. Sid sat on a small stool and fiddled with the rusty clips of an old-fashioned metal lunch box that was on a bench, trying to open it. His right hand slipped, though, and twisted, firing another jolt of pain and setting off the usual cascade of nausea. He pushed the lunch box off the bench in frustration, resulting in a loud, tinny thud as it struck the floor, causing the lid to open and lay his peanut butter and jelly sandwich bare on the linoleum.

"God damn her," he yelled, blanketing the fingers of his good hand around the fingers of his bad, rocking back and forth on the stool.

•   •   •   •   •

Sid returned countless times for follow up after the surgery, but not once did he see the plastic surgeon. Only Fraser. He nicknamed her *the Queen of the King's Guard* because she would never let him see the surgeon – to ask him what went wrong, to ask him why his hand hurt so much, to ask why it was so useless. All he ever got from Fraser was, "Dr. Unpronounceable Name says you're doing as well as can be expected, and it should continue to improve with time."

"How the hell would he know? He's never even seen me."

"Of course he has. He was in the operating room –"

Liar.

"– and he checks your X-rays. He thinks we did a great job fixing you up, given how bad it was."

She actually looked proud of herself. She gave him a goddam Frankenstein hand, and she was proud of herself. No one wants a Frankenstein hand working iron. Too dangerous. Worker's comp eventually settled, arranging housekeeping gigs at various hospitals.

Which Sid hated.

Almost as much as he hated Rylan Fraser.

•   •   •   •   •

When he had calmed, he picked up the sandwich and took a hesitant bite. The sugar rush helped him focus, and he finished the sandwich quickly. He knew the consequence, though. He retrieved a container from his backpack and opened it, revealing a series of syringes and needles. He drew ten units of insulin, lifted his shirt, and injected it into the fat of his belly. In the beginning, after his accident, this had proved difficult. He was a quick learner, though, and mastered the mostly one-handed technique swiftly. He had skill with a needle. At times, he joked to himself that, if the housecleaning job didn't pan out, he could always become a nurse.

Rylan Fraser. Rylan Fraser. Rylan Fraser. The name tumbled around in his brain like an evil wind.

She hadn't recognized him.

But she would.

She owed him that much.

CHAPTER 14

Paul

Paul was unsurprised to find Rylan at the nursing station since they'd been doing this same dance all night. She had her phone to her ear and was squeezing a stress ball with her free hand. The harried expression on her face softened for an instant when she spotted Paul. She opened her eyes wide, and Paul understood the question they held – *Were you paged again?* He nodded, and Rylan flung an arm in the direction of the room Paul had been called to visit. She knew which one. Same dance.

Paul dragged his feet toward room 515 and passed a forlorn-looking crash cart in the hallway. A few staff people meandered about, cleaning up and moving on. Paul peeked into the room and saw a corpse covered by a sheet. Again, he was unsurprised. He glanced around at the stragglers, but no one paid him any mind. There was really no point in asking who had paged him. He knew the response would be another round of vacant eyes and shocked stares. "*What? No one here paged psych.*" He glanced at his watch and calculated the hours until daylight when he could get the hell out of Northern Michigan General Hospital. His first night would be his last. Enough was enough.

He leaned against the wall and turned his head to face the nursing station where he could see Rylan still on the phone. She did not appear to be having fun. No, Rylan was definitely not having a good night. Her patients were dropping like flies, and Paul suspected none of this was doing much for her surgeon's ego. Or future.

He sensed movement to his right and turned to see the strange doctor Rylan had tried to speak to upstairs, the one with the weird name, *Gunslinger* or something. "Excuse me," the man said, "what happened to the patient in this room?"

Paul looked at the guy's ID badge. *Upslinger.* He shook his head. "Don't know. You want to talk to –"

"Psychiatry?" Upslinger asked, noting the department on Paul's ID badge.

Paul understood it was unusual to see a psychiatrist on a medical floor, especially at such an off hour. He started to explain. "I was called –"

"Dr. Paul Bennett," Upslinger read, cutting Paul off.

"Right." Paul nodded and waited for him to continue, but Upslinger said nothing else. He just stared disconcertingly into Paul's face for several seconds until Paul felt like he was playing the who-blinks-first game. "Yes, Paul Bennett. That's me," he said into the awkward silence. He extended a hand to shake, then dropped it as nonchalantly to his side as possible when the other man ignored it.

Gunslinger or Upslinger – *whatever* – studied Paul for another eternal, bizarre moment. Paul wanted him to go away, but he just stood there. Finally, Paul asked, "Were you paged to this room, too?"

"No," Upslinger said. He began to turn away.

Then why the fuck are you here? Paul thought it was a good enough question to ask aloud, so he went for it. "Then why are you here?"

Upslinger, however, was already receding down the hall. Paul noted that no one seemed to pay him any mind, either, which he thought was kind of weird. White coats were usually bombarded with questions when they appeared on a unit. But, then again, everything here was kind of weird. The dead body in room 515 was Exhibit A. Exhibits B and C were upstairs. Paul shook his head. No, that wasn't right. It should be in temporal order. That meant Exhibits A and B were upstairs. Paul was standing outside the room of Exhibit C. Then it occurred to him that A and B were probably already in the morgue and no longer upstairs. He slowly rubbed both eyes. Damn, he was tired.

He made his way back to Rylan who had hung up the phone and dropped her head to the desk, thumping her forehead on the plastic counter.

"Hey," Paul said.

She looked up. "Hey," she returned. "What happened to you? I lost you upstairs. Did you find your patient?"

Paul explained how he'd lost Jane Doe's trail after she disappeared into a stairwell. "I couldn't tell if she'd gone up or down, so I chose down. Wrong choice, I guess."

"So, she's still running around the hospital somewhere?"

"It would appear that way," Paul said wearily. "What happened here?" he asked, indicating the room down the hall.

"Same story. I received a page to come see a patient I'd treated with a septic knee. When I got here, he was already dead — and had been dead for a while before I ever got the page."

Paul stroked his chin. "I was paged to the same bed, something about a delirium."

"That's bullshit," Rylan said. "They wouldn't page psych for that, especially not at this hour," she said.

Paul shrugged. "I knew it sounded strange, but…"

"Yeah, strange," Rylan repeated. "Do you find it strange that every time you get paged to a unit to see a patient, they happen to be dead?" She made little finger quotes around the word strange.

"It hasn't happened every time I've been called to a unit. Just every time you're already there." It didn't come out quite the way he'd intended.

Rylan's nostrils flared. "So, it's me? I'm responsible?"

"No." Paul opened his mouth to say more, then let out his breath in a long sigh and played with the cuffs of his blazer while collecting his thoughts. "I don't think you're *responsible*, but you definitely seem to be somehow *connected* to what's going on, don't you think?"

Rylan dropped her eyes sulkily to the floor.

"And so do I," Paul said. "I have no idea why, but there must be a reason we are both getting paged to these same after-the-fact shitshows. Someone is playing a game. A sick game."

Rylan nodded her head and ran the stress ball along the back of her neck. "So, I called the police," she said.

"Good. And?"

She dropped the hand with the ball to her lap, and Paul saw her knuckles turn white as she squeezed. "Well, the connection sucked, for one. All sorts of static from the storm. Finally, when I was able to get the information across, they sounded thoroughly unimpressed. And then asked me a ton of questions." She mimicked a bored, pissy voice. "Why do you believe crimes have been committed? What signs of foul play are there? Aren't patients in a hospital because they are sick to start with?"

Paul could understand why someone outside the situation might have questions like these, but he suspected Rylan wasn't in a benefit-of-the-doubt kind of mood. He just said, "That's annoying."

Rylan snickered. "A bit. Finally, they agreed to send a car out to have a look, although they don't expect it will be until morning because of the storm and the closed roads."

Paul chewed his lip thoughtfully. "You don't think it really could all just be coincidence, do you?"

"No," Rylan said. "Believe me, I get that things can go unexpectedly sideways at times, but not *three* times in one night. And getting paged by some mysterious voice after the patients are dead with a made-up, bullshit story is ... bullshit. Plus, there's the fact that you keep getting paged to the scene, too. And these are not even psych patients. Someone is cat-and-mousing us."

Paul tapped his fingers on the desk and stole another look at his watch: 2:17AM. He wondered when the roads would get cleared.

"Here, you look like you need this more than I do now," Rylan said, tossing the stress ball to Paul. He caught it in one hand. "Anyway, after I called the police, I also called the administrator-on-call to let him know what was happening here, and he got all up my ass for involving the police."

Paul winced. "I'm sorry."

"Then he called the surgery attending to explain what happened with these cases, and two minutes later, the attending called me with a hundred more questions. Everyone is freaking out, and the implication seems to be that it's all my fault."

"I really am sorry," Paul said. "It's not your fault."

"Damn right it's not my fault." Rylan looked at the ceiling, and her eyes welled with tears that Paul pretended not to notice. She quickly blinked them away.

"Hey," Paul said, trying to steer the subject in another direction, "I found your friend, Mr. Pockface."

"He's not my friend." The look on Rylan's face suggested she'd sooner be friends with Ghengis Khan. "Where did you find him?"

"Smoking in the stairwell between the second and third floors."

"And you're sure it was him? You've never seen Pockface before."

"The name says it all. Anyway, I asked if he needed any help."

Rylan snorted. "What did he say?"

"I'm not going to repeat what he said."

This time, Rylan actually laughed. "He's a real charmer. I knew he couldn't go anywhere in this storm. Did he even have a coat?"

"Not that I saw, just a hoodie. I reported his location to security."

"You mean Helen?"

"That's right. And, while I was there, I told her about all the other stuff. The strange pages, the deceased patients."

"What did she say?"

"Honestly, I don't think she knew what to make of me, my being new and all. But when I mentioned your name, she totally shifted."

A soft smile appeared on Rylan's face. Paul thought it was a tremendous improvement over the scowling of the last ten minutes. "Helen and I are friends."

"Well, she wants you to call her."

Rylan interlaced her fingers at the base of her head and leaned back in her chair. Paul tried not to look directly at her chest which proved a bit of a challenge. "Yeah," Rylan said, stifling a yawn. Paul noted that just the mention of Helen's name had a relaxing effect on Rylan. "I should fill her in on what's going on. I'll walk down there now." She sat back up straight and looked at Paul. "Want to come?"

She definitely seemed more relaxed now, and the question had a flirtatious edge to it. At least Paul thought it did. Half his brain was still considering the perky breasts he'd tried not to see. Before he could say his, "Yes, I do," though, Rylan's cell phone rang. Her mood seemed to flip as she reached for it, muttering under her breath about having to answer more annoying bullshit questions. When she looked at the screen, however, the mumbling halted, and her eyes filled with dread. "It's the ICU."

Paul tossed her back the stress ball.

CHAPTER 15

Dr. Upslinger

It wasn't supposed to be like this.

Reggie Upslinger was *supposed* to be on a golf course somewhere warm, sipping a gin and tonic in the late afternoon sun. He was supposed to be sitting at a little table for two on a stone portico leading into a clubhouse where bartenders in starched, white shirts handled shakers, speared olives, and bandied about legendary hole-in-ones. And, most importantly, he was supposed to be sharing that table for two with Betsy, his beloved wife of thirty-eight years, his partner-in-crime, and more recently, in retirement. Betsy, a woman still every bit as beautiful and vital as the day they met.

But nothing was the way it was supposed to be.

Reggie ambled down the hall toward the elevators. His new snow boots were too stiff in the ankles. They forced him into a clumsy gait that screamed "weirdo," sure as a pink fluorescent sign taped to his back. Nothing new. In the large medical center that he'd retired from, Reggie had – with his old-timer's doctor's bag and Sherlock Holmes cap – willingly played the role of resident oddball. There, his little idiosyncrasies were familiar and reassuring to the staff. They called him *quirky*, even *cute*. Or maybe that was just Betsy who called him cute.

She was a woman like no other.

Reggie sighed and pressed the button for the elevator. Here in Northern Michigan General Hospital, no one seemed to find him particularly cute. Here, he was just a strange old man shuffling around the halls in thick-soled snow boots. Strange and sad. Tomorrow was Thanksgiving, and it would be the first major holiday he would face without Betsy. He had hoped work would do his mind some good, but his mind seemed to have plans of its own. It was intent on finding Betsy everywhere he looked. Little reminders here, big reminders there. Just seeing that psychiatrist in the hall had been enough to set him reeling.

She was a woman like no other.

Her cancer had been quick, efficient. A few stealthy malignant cells took hold and dispatched merciless emissaries in all directions. By the time the attack was detected, the invasion was complete. Betsy left him five months to the day after the diagnosis.

By then, they had both retired from the medical center – he after decades in the internal medicine department, she after decades in psychiatry. The retirement dreams they shared – the safari on the Serengeti, the hike amongst the ruins of Machu Picchu, the sailing expedition to the Galapagos Islands – died with Betsy. A part of Reggie died with her, too. It wasn't something he would say aloud – it sounded a little too Hallmark-Channel for even his ears – but it was true. His conversation skills suffered, his memory suffered. His appetite. His energy. Sometimes, he couldn't concentrate. Sometimes he lost whole swaths of time. He'd walk into a patient's room, he'd walk out again, but he'd have no memory of what happened in between.

They call that grief. And it's a bitch.

Reggie closed his eyes and nodded his head. He could almost hear Betsy's voice, still propping him up and encouraging him to go on. She was the reason he became a locum, or what essentially amounted to a doctor-temp. Locums were doctors contracted through agencies to work time-limited stints at hospitals short on staffing. It was a perfect situation for a recently widowed old doc with time on his hands and desperate need of a scenery change.

This hospital in remote northern Michigan seemed like a good option to Reggie. The land was beautiful, crisscrossed by lakes and charming old town roads. Of course, his timing had been poor. He could blame that on the grief. If he'd had one-tenth of his wits about him, he'd never have come this far north this time of year. The lovely lakes were frozen over, and the charming roads were impassable. It was the night before Thanksgiving, and there was a raging blizzard outside. Not only would there be no Betsy this Thanksgiving, there would be no Thanksgiving, period. Maybe it was for the best.

Still, next time, he'd go south.

She was a woman like no other.

The phrase rattled around his head like a little metal ball in a pinball machine. He wasn't quite sure where it came from or why it was playing on a closed loop in his mind at this particular moment. There had been so many lovely sentiments offered by friends and colleagues at the funeral. So, so many. Everyone had had kind words for his Betsy – but, for some reason, this was the one scratching at his head and heart tonight.

Reggie rode the elevator up, clutching his doctor's bag so tightly that his fingers seized around the handle. His scalp was itchy under his wool hat, his neck sweaty under his collar. And his mind. His mind was doing that thing he didn't like. He called it flip-flopping. It was like his thoughts were the sands in an hourglass moving with gravity in one predictable direction. But then, the hourglass flipped unexpectedly, and this thought moved in another direction. One moment Reggie was pondering the ailments of his patients, mentally juggling parcels of clinical wisdom related to bone marrow, pituitary glands, lung capacity, or the islets of Langerhans. But then the glass would flip, and he'd be thinking again of Betsy. How being able to recite the Merck Manual from memory hadn't been enough to save her. How he hadn't been able to do really anything for her. Nothing except sit by her bed, listen to the clock tick, watch the condensate collect under an untouched glass of ice-water. Hold her hand and stroke her forehead. Listen to shallow breaths rattling inside her chest, palpate edematous fluid collecting under her skin, feel her once-dewy skin turning clammy and cold.

Reggie knew so much about pathology. He had helped so many people, but he couldn't do a damned thing to help Betsy. It was unfair. Some people got sick, and they recovered. Some people got sick, and they didn't. Good people, bad people, it didn't really matter.

Betsy had been a woman like no other, and now she was gone. And Reggie was still here – lost, alone, grieving, depressed.

And maybe a little mad.

CHAPTER 16

Rylan

The ICU in a hospital is somewhat like the confessional in a church: where life meets death and heaven meets hell. One for reconciliation of the body, one for reconciliation of the soul. They differ significantly, however, in the decibel of background noise. While the church is swathed in respectful silence, the ICU is a bedlam of every imaginable, annoying sound that exists on the planet: bells, buzzing, whirring, swishing, ticking, pumping, whispering, talking, groaning, wailing, and squealing. A symphony of distractions.

Of course, noise is not the only feature that sets the ICU apart. Unlike the simpler smells of antiseptic noted throughout any average hospital (occasionally laced with various body odors and gases), the pungent bouquet of the ICU is on a whole different level. A potpourri of body fluids, gases, medicines, and cleansing chemicals thrown into a blender and vomited into the atmosphere.

Rylan stood at the foot of Brad's bed inside his ICU chamber, acclimatizing and taking stock of the situation, much like she had first done in the trauma bay, what felt like days ago but was really only hours. The metallic frames of his external fixators – pins and rods – protruded at awkward angles from beneath his thin bed sheet, adding to the cyborgian appearance created by the multiple tubes entering and exiting his body – central lines, IVs, endotracheal tube, temperature probes, foley catheter. These, in turn, were all supported by a complex, robotic-looking ventilator machine alive with multicolored flashing lights and digital read-outs that sat squatly at the head of his bed, providing life.

Todd had said the ICU docs suspected ongoing bleeding based on the difficulty maintaining blood pressure and a hemoglobin hovering around six, despite at least ten units of transfused blood. The stress ball in Rylan's lab coat pocket was putting in overtime as she squeezed it relentlessly.

An abstract blot of dark, red blood soaked through the dressing and into the white sheet over Brad's abdomen where Todd had performed the laparotomy to remove his spleen. Two units of O neg blood hung off an IV pole, attempting to replace his dwindling blood supply along with a unit of fresh frozen plasma, or FFP, full of clotting factors to help slow down bleeding.

Rylan knew fully well that a phenomenon called *disseminated intravascular coagulation*, or DIC, could strike down even the healthiest of trauma victims with the repeated loss and replacement of blood. The body's clotting factors would begin to fail, and the damaged areas, where blood had previously clotted, would break down, causing the body, basically, to ooze. Brad wasn't quite there yet, but this would overtake him eventually – unless his bleeding stopped. The urgent question, therefore, was to figure out from where he was bleeding.

Could I have nicked the iliac artery placing one of the ex-fix pins in his pelvis?

Rylan shook her head slowly from side to side wanting to believe – hoping – that this wasn't the cause.

She donned a pair of gloves and began a methodical foot-to-head assessment, removing the sheet only where necessary in an attempt to maintain some sense of decency. It suddenly occurred to her that his family still had no idea what had happened or where he was. Although the ER ward clerk had said she'd left a message, as of yet, no one had returned the call. His wife and two young children were oblivious to the fact their world was about to undergo a dramatic and seismic shift. Even if Brad pulled through, it would be years of rehab and recovery. And if he didn't …

She ran her fingers along both legs feeling for crepitus, swelling, or instability – signs of a missed fracture – pausing at the pin sites in his tibia and at the dressing overlying his open wound where the jagged point of his tibia had visited the outside world. There was seepage but nothing more than expected. Next, she arrived at the pelvis and groin area. His scrotum was already the size of a grapefruit from volume overload, and there was a hematoma building in the groin area, but again, not unusual for this degree of trauma.

She palpated his abdomen around the edges of a large midline dressing. It remained firm and bloated. Difficult to know what was happening there. Could be normal post-op; however, Brad was tanking, and the blood had to be coming from somewhere. His chest?

No bruising of the chest wall yet, although he clearly had multiple fractured ribs, and the bruising would come soon – if he lived long enough.

She worked her way from shoulder girdles to fingertips and found nothing amiss. She walked her fingers from the base of his skull down his cervical spine, feeling for steps or other deformities. Nothing. Ideally, she would recruit some nurses and logroll Brad so that she could visualize his back and feel along his spine, but, given his degree of hemodynamic instability, that maneuver might dislodge a clot and result in quick deterioration. It had already been done once by Mike in the ER when they transferred him from the ambulance stretcher to the trauma bed with nothing obvious found. Rylan decided the benefits weren't worth the risk.

Ultimately, she gained nothing from her examination. Exactly what she expected. Now what?

She looked over the ventilator monitors and opened a computer at the bedside to review his bloodwork. That's when she heard a voice that grated on her nerves, like a pen on paper with the ball point retracted.

"Ahem. Dr. Fraser, the answer you are looking for will not be found on that computer screen. The answer is lying in this bed."

Rylan turned slowly to face the ICU attending staff, the man in charge of Brad at this moment in time.

"Dr. Lombroso," Rylan said, gearing up in anticipation of certain confrontation. "I've reexamined the patient from head to toe. It has to be the belly."

Dr. Lombroso was no taller than Rylan but easily outweighed her by a magnitude of five. He had slick, shiny black hair with a Mediterranean complexion consistent with his Italian roots. His romantic entanglements were legendary throughout the hospital, and he was apparently at work on his fourth wife, a former ICU nurse. He was primarily an anesthesiologist but also split his time in the ICU doing critical care, a lucrative gig that helped pay his many alimony checks. Unfortunately, he was as inept in the ICU as he was in the OR. This was definitely not Brad's lucky night.

He stood at the foot of Brad's bed perched on one-inch heeled leather boots and began to lecture. "*You* are standing on *this* hill." He held his left hand in the air with his palm up and outstretched. "Your equivalent general surgery resident colleague is standing on this other hill." His right hand was held high in a similar pose, a shoulder's distance from the left. "And I'm sitting here in the middle, covered in shit, stuck in a crack between the two of you." He had a snickering grin, as if to say, *Get it? You get my metaphor, right?*

He continued, his voice taking on an even more irritating nasal tone, "I hate, hate, hate being covered in shit. If I'd wanted that, I would have become a colorectal surgeon. Right?"

Rylan shrugged her shoulders. Right now, she really didn't give two shits about what this asshole hated or didn't hate. She needed to figure out why Brad was losing blood and why all her patients on the floor were heading for the wrong side of the grass. She squeezed the stress ball tightly, pretending it was Lombroso's neck.

"So, what are we going to do about digging me out of this shit crack, Dr. Fraser? What's the plan? I know Huang is likely stuck in a ditch somewhere, and you're flying solo. God knows there's no way he would have let you do this on your own if he could have helped it. So, you're all we've got. And your general surgery colleague is pointing the finger your way. Could one of your pelvic pins have nicked an artery?"

Bastard men's club. All sticking together... but it was possible. With the X-ray down and the patient crashing, it had all happened so fast.

She pulled the sheet down again to reveal the pelvic external fixator. There was one pin in each side of the pelvis connected by a long carbon fiber bar. The dressings around them were dry. She jiggled the pins, and they felt solid. She analyzed the angle of each pin, forming a 3D picture in her mind of the trajectory. She then covered Brad once again, looked Dr. Lombroso square in the eye, and sputtered the one universal truth in medicine, "It's possible."

The attending placed both of his hands on the rail at the foot of the bed and leaned in. "So. What. Are. We. Going. To. Do. About it?"

Just then, Todd slithered into the room and interrupted. "Dr. Lombroso, this patient needs to go back to the operating room so we can explore the pelvis, change out the errant pin, and repair the lacerated vessel. He's dead if we don't."

Both men were staring at her – actually, make that one asshole and one dickwad – waiting for a response. They were trying to bully her into making a snap decision. She stepped away from the bed and closed her eyes briefly to clear her sleep-deprived mind.

Forget these two jerks. What is best for Brad? How can we figure out where he's bleeding from?

Her pager went off, and she snapped her finger to it, pushing in ever so slightly with a side hip thrust to silence it before the second note could play. And then she had it.

"He needs a stat CT angiogram before he goes anywhere."

This test would involve injecting a dye into Brad's bloodstream before undergoing a CT scan and would not only show the position of the ex-fix pins but also show the arteries in detail around the pelvis as well as where his spleen used to live. If there was a bleeding vessel, they would see it.

"That's a waste of time and resources," Todd said. "He needs to go back to the OR."

The ICU attending furrowed his brow, scrunched his chubby face, and rubbed his chin. "You know, Fraser. You're not having the best night, are you? I pronounced your 35-year-old man with the septic knee on the medical ward earlier. And I've heard there have been a couple of others. I'm not sure I really should be trusting your judgment at this point."

Rylan shifted uncomfortably from one Birkenstock to the other, feeling the walls of the small room close in on her and the ceiling trying to crush her from above. Everything this jackass was saying was true. But, at the same time, it wasn't.

Lombroso tilted his head to the side as if he'd come to a conclusion about something. "However, the CT angio is actually a solid idea. The patient's holding on for now, and if he goes back to the OR, at least we'll have some idea what to look for."

He nodded his head at Rylan and then rushed out of the room, barking orders in every direction to get it organized. Rylan was shocked that Dr. Lombroso agreed with her. Even more notable than his Casanova lifestyle was his distrust and distaste for residents – unless, of course, they were female and attractive.

Todd scowled at Rylan. "Fine. Fine. He can have a CT angio, but it's a waste of time."

Like you have any real say in the matter, Dickwad.

"We both know where the problem lies."

That comment deflated Rylan for a moment. She gave the stress ball a good squeeze.

Todd marched out of the room, bidding adieu to Rylan with a glance that was so smug and self-assured it pissed her off beyond words. He was an idiot and had nothing to be smug about.

"Todd!" Rylan yelled, catching him at the doorway. He stopped and turned to face her.

"What?"

She held the stress ball in front of her face between thumb and forefinger and squeezed. She grinned maliciously, then threw the ball at him. "I found one of your missing gonads."

He caught the ball in a clumsy two-handed catch, gave her the middle finger, and stormed off.

Rylan felt a comfortable warmth flood her chest. A temporary victory on all fronts, or perhaps just a stay of execution. Either way, it felt good.

Unless one of the pins was malpositioned and Brad was dying because of something she had done.

She wished she'd kept the stress ball.

CHAPTER 17

Paul

The call room was a cube with white walls, a brown linoleum floor, and the lingering sour stench of every sleep-deprived overnighter who'd ever stumbled in hoping to catch a few z's. There was a sink immediately to the left beside a door that led into a small, utilitarian bathroom with a stall shower and toilet. Next to the door was a small, ancient, metallic desk, the kind only found in institutions. An old wooden-framed bed was pushed against the wall on the right adjacent to a small rectangular window covered with ragged, faded-beige curtains. The only adornment was a cheap, acrylic mirror nailed to the wall above the sink.

Paul studied his reflection while he cleaned his hands under the faucet. The room's single fluorescent light cast in perverse detail the purple shadows under his eyes and scrappy stubble on his chin. Not his best look. His eyes were so bloodshot he looked like a stoner who'd forgotten the Visine. They told anyone who looked that he was tired, a little dazed, and maybe even out of his depth here tonight at Northern Michigan General Hospital. Looks never revealed the whole picture, though. While it was true Paul's body was tired, his brain was energized, and he was looking forward to the rest of the night. Against all odds, Paul was almost enjoying himself. And he knew why.

Rylan Fraser.

He turned off the water and tugged one of those horrible sandpaper-brown paper towels from a metal wall dispenser, then rested on the bed after a quick inspection for bedbugs and stray hairs.

Rylan Fraser. He'd never known a "Rylan" before, but he liked the name. It was unique. Pretty. It suited her well.

Paul absentmindedly unclipped the pager from his belt and began flipping it from one hand to the other in little somersaults. His brain was a million miles away, contemplating eyes. Those eyes. Rylan's eyes were a startling bright green. Rare eyes, the jackpot prize in some high-stakes genetic lottery. Eyes never to be forgotten. He'd seen eyes like that on only one other woman before, and he certainly hadn't forgotten.

The pager in his hand went off, and Paul fumbled, dropping it into his lap. He knew it meant that someone somewhere needed a tranquilizer, but when he looked at the number, he frowned. It wasn't the psych unit or ER, two numbers he'd come to know well over the night. He dialed. "You called psych?"

"I did."

Paul smiled, recognizing the voice on the other end of the line.

"I'm not waking you, am I?"

Paul glanced up the length of the bed to the single, sad pillow. "Not at all."

"Good. Come to the breakroom on six. There's a fresh pot of coffee."

"On my way."

Paul stepped to the sink and splashed a little water on his face. He straightened the collar on his shirt, gave his underarms a quick sniff, and reached for the jacket he'd lain across the bed. It was his favorite one, a vintage Armani that managed to look sleek and cool, relaxed and casual, all at the same time. It also had lots of pocket room. Enough for stowing everything he needed without unsightly bulges. Notepads and pens, hospital floor plan, Purell, sterile nitrile gloves, wallet. It all fit, no problem. He locked the door behind him and headed for the stairs.

A barely discernible whiff of smoke clung to the air, and Paul immediately suspected Pockface. He kept an eye out as he climbed to the sixth floor but saw no one. The post-op surgical unit was dark and eerily quiet. He glimpsed Linda's stiff caramel hair hovering before a computer screen, but she was sufficiently engrossed in whatever was on that screen that she didn't look up. Paul beelined for the door marked STAFF.

"Wet floor."

The unexpected words were received as an angry hiss, and Paul turned his head to find a janitor working the graveyard shift. Paul mumbled the obligatory thanks while his feet stopped moving, seemingly of their own accord, to force him to take notice of the strangely aggressive energy the man put into his work, punishing to both floor and mop. The mop was clearly bearing the brunt, though, its slim neck choked between two notably dissimilar hands, one perfectly typical and one angrily gnarled.

"All right there?" Paul asked.

The man said nothing.

Paul shrugged since it was too late to really care and entered the break room. Rylan was slouched on a vinyl couch blowing into a coffee cup and peering at a muted television screen. She raised a hand in greeting when she saw Paul. He followed her gaze to the TV which was showing footage of the blizzard. Images of buried cars and mountain-high snowdrifts filled the screen behind a flashing banner that indicated accumulations upward of twenty inches so far.

"Is it supposed to stop anytime soon?" Paul asked.

"They say it should lighten up in a few hours."

Paul helped himself to a cup of coffee then joined Rylan on the couch. "How's your ICU case?"

"Not good," she sighed. "He's bleeding out, and I don't get it. Headed to CT now…" She shook her head and stared into her coffee cup. "I can't catch a break tonight." She sipped the coffee and turned her exquisite, albeit exhausted, green eyes on Paul. "The hospital administrator keeps calling me like every ten minutes. Wants me to track down what the corpses ate for dinner, who delivered their trays, whether they'd recently traveled outside the country. He's making it an issue for the public health and epidemiology people, but, since those people don't do in-house call, it's all falling on me." She put her cup down on a little table, then sat back and ran both hands through her hair. "Don't listen to me, I'm just tired. People died here tonight, and I'm whining about being inconvenienced. I'm usually not this awful, I swear."

Paul looked at her sideways, suppressing a grin. "You're pretty awful."

Rylan gave him a playful punch on the shoulder. She settled back into a slouch and shook her head slowly back and forth. "If the CT angio shows I screwed up …"

"It won't."

"It could."

Paul considered this. "Then you'll fix it."

Rylan groaned. "I'm in over my head here. Best-case scenario is my attending, Dr. Huang, cites me for insubordination. Worst case, he tries to get me thrown out of the program."

Paul smiled. "I seriously don't think that's going to happen. Dr. Huang couldn't get to the hospital, and you were the one-person orthopedic team on for the night. It sounds like you saved a life. Besides, I heard you're the winner of The Most Amazing Orthopedic Resident in the World Award."

Rylan squeezed her eyes tightly shut. "But if I nicked a vessel…"

"You'll fix it," Paul said. He leaned forward and placed his coffee cup on the table beside Rylan's. "I suggest you do some positive visualization."

Rylan forced a stream of air out through her nose. "What? Now you're *my* shrink?"

"Hear me out," Paul said. "If you did, in fact, nick a vessel or something, you're going to have to face it."

"Gee, I feel better already."

"Visualize yourself going back into the OR, re-opening your patient –"

"Precisely what I don't want to do!"

"… and correcting the problem. Stay with me here. Imagine the sound of the blood pressure cuff inflating and deflating, the smell of Betadine, the feel of the scalpel in your hand, the instructions you give to staff. Picture yourself making the cut, applying the suction, and… whatever else you'll have to do… you know better than me. Imagine it all in vivid detail right down to you finding the offending bleeder and tying it off."

Rylan regarded Paul as though he were a child claiming to have seen the Easter Bunny. "Okay, sure…"

"Visualize the whole process down to the successful ending, and then you will make it happen."

"It's that easy, huh?" She gave Paul a dubious grin and sighed. "Okay, I'll try." She sat up a little straighter on the couch and shut her eyes. After about ten seconds, she raised one eyelid. "Are you going to stare at me the whole time?"

Paul coughed into his hand and rose quickly from the couch. "I need some more coffee. Take all the time you need." He poured himself a top-off and leaned back against the counter, watching images flit across the television screen. Whited-out highways devoid of cars. Stranded people sleeping on airport floors. A few minutes later, Rylan beckoned him back.

"Alright, doc, I'm cured now," she said, smiling an unconvincing, good-sport type of smile.

Paul gave an equally unconvincing double thumbs-up on his way back to the couch. "You make a great patient."

"I make a great psych patient! Terrific!" Rylan flopped against the couch's back cushion and stared at the ceiling. "Hey," she said, looking back at Paul, "do people ask you psych questions all the time?"

Paul rubbed the stubble on his chin. "Sometimes. Why, do they ask you ortho questions all the time?"

"Absolutely," Rylan said. She continued in a high falsetto, "I have a pain running through my ass, my knee clicks when I bend, my shoulder grinds, my ankle hurts, …"

Paul chuckled. "Well, I guess it's handy to have a surgeon friend."

"Or family member." Rylan glazed over for a moment and seemed to be revisiting an old memory. Then, a decisive sparkle lit her eyes. "I probably shouldn't tell you this, but what the hell." She smiled mischievously. "Once my father flew clear across the country to perform damage control after my batty Aunt Marla…"

"Yes?"

"… drove her car …"

"Uh-huh?"

"… into… well, into her boyfriend."

Paul raised his eyebrows. "Um, wow." He scratched his head. "There's a lot to unpack there. Not sure where to start."

Rylan laughed. "It's a long story, but my aunt is a bit of a socialite. Her first husband died young and left her loaded. Being both rich and attractive, she has never wanted for male company. At one point, she was dating a – much younger – boy-toy who turned out to be a cheating douchebag. When she found out, well, let's just say she didn't take it well. Dad flew out to mend the douchebag's broken bones along with Aunt Marla's broken heart – and to keep the whole thing out of the papers."

"Was the guy okay?"

"Sure, he received free treatment from one of the best orthopedic surgeons in the country along with a generous sum for his silence. He did fine."

"And Aunt Marla?"

"Aunt Marla managed to keep her name out of the papers and her butt out of jail. So, it worked out well for everyone." She yawned. "You know, I really am feeling a bit more relaxed now. Thanks."

Paul saluted with his coffee cup and returned his eyes to the television. They watched the storm coverage for a few minutes in silence. A warm, gentle pressure built on Paul's right shoulder. He shifted slightly to better support Rylan's head and breathed in the smell of her hair as a few strays tickled his chin.

Rylan's cell phone rang, and she bolted upright, flustered. She yanked the phone from her lab coat pocket and held it at arm's length, squinting to read the screen. "Ugh, it's admin again."

Paul listened to one side of a conversation that seemed very one-sided. The only words Rylan got in were "Now?" and "Can it wait until…" and then, "Okay, I'm going."

"I'm almost afraid to ask," Paul said after she hung up.

"He wants me to go down to the morgue and speak with the pathologist."

"Now?"

Rylan rolled her eyes. "That's what I said. Apparently, the pathologist is snowed in like the rest of us, so he decided to work through the night. He's autopsying the three bodies."

Paul was surprised to hear that the autopsies were happening so quickly. He was also surprised, though less so, by the dictatorial audacity of the administrator in sending a member of the house staff to the hospital morgue – arguably the creepiest place on earth – alone at three in the morning. He offered to accompany Rylan, and she gratefully accepted. Before they walked out the door, however, Paul's pager went off, and he was called away. It turned out someone somewhere needed a tranquilizer.

CHAPTER 18

Jane Doe

The girl they called Jane Doe chewed bread and drank apple juice in her "nest" on the sixth floor. Really, it was just a patient bathroom off a suite in an unused part of the hospital. Mantis had called it the D wing.

That's where you make your home base.

It left a lot to be desired as far as home bases went. It was colorless, smelled of disinfectant, and lit by a fluorescent bulb that made a whiny buzz like a mosquito in a zapper.

Outside the nest, the D wing was dark as hell and probably haunted. She imagined legions of souls that had checked in but never checked out, clawing at the corridors with jagged, yellow fingernails. The only living person she'd seen was some creepy-ass janitor waxing floors at the other end of the hall, silhouetted in an unnatural glow oozing from a nearby room. He'd been sufficiently occupied not to notice when she'd ducked into a room, felt her way Helen Keller-style to the bathroom, and shoved a blanket into the crack between door and floor before turning on the light.

A second blanket held the loot. She'd swiped anything she found, unsure what she might need later on. Artfully, she now arranged specimen tubes, square pads of gauze, a rubber tourniquet, latex gloves, and a dry-erase marker around the basin of the sink. She picked up a specimen tube and turned it in her hand. It would do nicely.

Turning off the bathroom light, she shuffled out of the bathroom and felt her way to the door of the suite. She peeked into the hall. The creepy-ass guy was gone now, and everything was silent and still. Perfect. She found the room's visitor chair beside the bed and placed the tube under its heavy, wooden leg. She took a deep breath, hopped into the air, and landed butt-down on the arm. This resulted in a satisfying crush. She carried a decent-sized shard of glass back into the bathroom and laid it upon the sink with a delicate tinkle.

She snapped the light back on and balanced herself on the toilet seat, where she drew her hospital gown up above her knees. She gazed at the tender white flesh of her inner thighs, tracing a finger along the fine crosshatch of old scars. She retrieved the shard from the sink and gripped it reverently between her thumb and forefinger, like a gemologist handling a precious diamond.

•　　•　　•　　•　　•

"Girl, I see one more cut on those legs, and you're out. Gone. Done. Finito."

Otis, the night manager at the Pink Kitty Lounge, used his hand to make a slicing gesture across his throat. The cocktail waitress uniforms at the Kitty were getting shorter and shorter– so short that what she used to be able to hide under her skirt could no longer be hidden.

"You listen to me, girl. Gentlemen come into the Pink Kitty looking for ladies smooth like silk, not ones carved up like their mama's Sunday roast."

You listen to me, Otis. "Gentlemen" don't come into the Pink Kitty at all.

That's what she said in her head, not with her mouth. Her mouth said nothing while her head kept going, informing Otis that the patrons of the Pink Kitty were nothing but dogs and pigs, worms and vipers.

And, of course, one praying mantis, expertly camouflaged amongst the rest.

She never knew which one was the mantis because he never spoke to her face-to-face. She only knew his voice. The voice instructed her to do things, strange things, and she complied. It was a lucrative arrangement as long as she followed the rules.

No questions asked. Rule number one on the checklist.

You have to be daring.

She could be daring. Check.

You have to be brave …

Check.

… and a little crazy …

Check. Check. Check.

•   •   •   •   •

"You're more than a little crazy," her roommate, Trina, said when she told her about the "interview," unsure what else to call it. All she knew was that the mantis ("Call me Mantis") said he'd watched her at the Kitty and thought she was just right. He needed someone small, light on her feet, and gutsy. He needed someone who could be lots of things to lots of people and blend into the background. He needed someone who could keep her mouth shut and go with the flow.

"You know what this is, don't you?" Trina said. "He's going to wave you like candy in front of gross old men with fat bank accounts and shriveled dicks. This is Jeffrey Epstein-type shit."

Jane Doe just shrugged, adding a few broad strokes to her dollar-store canvas. She was working at a junky easel, the kind kids use where one side is a chalkboard, that she had bought for eight bucks when Toys-R-Us went out of business. "I don't think so." She tapped an index finger on her lip and examined her work. It showed people in an orderly line walking one-by-one off a cliff. Their otherwise ordinary, expressionless faces were distorted by grotesquely bulging eyes. Only one person in the bizarre tableau showed any emotion at all – a child, crying and trying to break free, pulled along dispassionately by the wrist.

"You'll see," Trina said. "Just wait."

．　　　．　　　．　　　．　　　．

Trina had been wrong. Jane Doe's first instruction was for a simple drop. It went off without a hitch. The second was a break-and-enter, a job Mantis said was best suited for someone slight and agile, someone like her. In through the basement window. Out again. Easy as pie.

After that, Mantis started using her a lot. *You're my go-to girl, my it-girl.* He let her know when he needed her. There was no reciprocity to this arrangement. She could not let him know when she needed him. *If you get caught, you're on your own.*

The terms didn't really bother her. She had nothing, so nothing to lose. And Mantis always paid. The envelopes of cash would appear, sometimes in her handbag, the pocket of her raincoat, between the pages of a book she was reading. She never saw how he did it. She never saw him at all.

．　　　．　　　．　　　．　　　．

"He's a voice inside your head." Trina was sitting in their ramshackle living room, painting black polish on her toenails.

"A voice in my head wouldn't pay this well."

Trina sighed, unwrapping a CBD lollipop. "I think you must be a very skilled pickpocket."

"Try secret agent."

"Whatever. As long as you pay your rent." Trina popped the lolli into her mouth and fanned her toes.

．　　　．　　　．　　　．　　　．

The girl they call Jane Doe traced the shard of glass along her thigh, so gently it barely touched. The sensation was enough to raise hairs on the back of her neck. So good. She licked her lips, and with a practiced hand, inserted the sharp glass tip into her smooth skin. A streak of blood, thick and red, erupted from the skin, slowly at first, like early spring grass pushing through sun-warmed soil. Then faster, riding the curve of her thigh to drip onto the stark white floor.

This was her favorite part, that moment when everything felt real. The moment when she *felt*. She ran a finger through the blood and stared at her fingertip, touched it gently to her tongue. A minute passed. She removed a gauze pad from its packaging and applied pressure to the wound. The gauze absorbed the blood, turning from white to red. She used it to dab the inside of the bathroom door. Once, twice, three times. And then she found herself in a sponge art frenzy, dabbing and dabbing until the red smudges coalesced into a tree, lush and full and dripping with sap the color of blood.

She admired her work for a long time. The cut on her leg stopped bleeding. Tomorrow it would be a scab, tight and itchy. It would annoy her, and she'd wonder why she'd done it. She always wondered why afterward. But in this moment, she just knew it felt right. She just knew she felt.

And she was ready to carry on with her instructions.

CHAPTER 19

Rylan

Rylan cautiously negotiated the final steps and pushed open a little-used, creaky metal fire door. She was seriously dragging her ass and would have taken the elevator, but she was still smarting from her earlier altercation with the poltergeist in elevator number two and was determined to use the stairs until they fixed it.

She stopped to get her bearings. She'd only been down here once before. Why were morgues always in the deepest, dankest parts of every hospital? Was it really just a transportation thing, to be near a loading dock for the funeral home? Or was it a psychological thing, bringing the bodies closer to interment? And wasn't that more like going in the direction of hell? Wouldn't it make more sense to have the morgue on the top floor, closer to heaven, if you believed in such things? Rylan shook her head to clear her thoughts. Fatigue seemed to be slowly cutting off circulation to all of the smart parts of her brain, leaving her imagination to run wild.

It was dark at both ends of the hallway with the lights activated by motion sensors, an admin money-saving move – she'd love to see those assholes down here at 3AM looking for the creepy morgue in the dark. Where she was standing was lit with glaring, buzzing fluorescence, and she couldn't remember if the morgue was left or right. There were no signs on the walls since no one ever went looking for the morgue. She knew it was close, though. That unmistakable miasma was creeping up her nostrils. She turned left, inhaled deeply, then repeated the maneuver to the right.

"Yup, definitely to the right," she said aloud, reassured by the sound of her own voice.

She paced languidly down the hallway, each series of activated lights showing the way as she advanced. She was in no particular hurry to arrive at her destination. It was the morgue, where all her mistakes went to be dissected. It was the last place she wanted to go.

She paused and turned to look back. Already, the lights in front of the elevators and stairwell had extinguished themselves. She bit her lip and fingered the cell phone in the pocket of her lab coat, knowing that Helen was one speed dial away.

Before long, she stood in front of a wide, windowless door, the entrance to the morgue. She expected it to be locked. This was, after all, where coroner's cases ended up, murder victims, Jane and John Does. Cases where homicide detectives were potentially involved. The human body was the ultimate piece of evidence and, like all good evidence, was usually locked up tight.

The door wasn't locked, though. It was held partially open, about a foot, by a triangular block of wood on the floor. She assumed the chief of staff had called ahead, and the pathologist had left it open for her. At least, she hoped that was the case.

She tugged on the door and squeezed through, thinking twice about whether or not she should let it close completely behind her. It didn't look like the type of door that would lock you in, so she kicked away the wooden block and let it close. The locking sound made her flinch.

She was in the anteroom. The rank and foul stench of the place hit her like a finger down the throat, immediately making her gag. It was almost impossible to describe, a yin yang of opposites. Sickly sweet, but sour. Fecal with fruity undertones. Throw in a few musty mothballs, and you had the rotting meat of decomposing bodies. She pulled the neck of her scrub shirt over her nose and immediately began breathing only through her mouth.

On the right was a cheap desk with a computer terminal and a series of plastic folders screwed to the wall above with paperwork in them. To the left, much like you'd find in any butcher's shop, was the large silver door of the meat locker, where the dead were kept on ice.

She looked through the door's small rectangular window and saw body bags stacked four high on vertical metal shelves. Far in the back of the refrigerator was a section enclosed by steel bars and a jail-type door behind which, she presumed, human evidence was protected for criminal investigations. She wondered if Mr. Kettering, Mrs. Potter, and Mr. Robinson were in there right now.

Rylan turned away and looked beyond the anteroom to the main laboratory of the morgue where the autopsies were performed. She could see a body laid out on the gleaming, metallic, L-shaped table with the soles of the feet pointing towards her. Interestingly, as she stepped into the room, it didn't smell as bad. She could hear the steady hum of the ventilation system at work punctuated by the clinking sounds of instruments dropping into trays.

The pathologist's back was towards her. He appeared to be wearing scrubs under a lab coat and was sporting a large set of bulky headphones that projected a bug-like shadow onto the wall. As she watched, every now and then, he would bob his bug-head from side to side, following the rhythm of some private beat. He turned to place an organ on a scale and then leaned into a microphone hanging from the ceiling and muttered something.

She didn't want to startle him, so she walked around the perimeter until she was facing him on the other side of the table. As she approached, Rylan glanced at the body on the table and realized it was Mr. Kettering. Her legs suddenly wouldn't move, as if they were both paralyzed. She could feel the thumping of her heart, and a breath was lodged firmly in her chest, refusing to come out. Was she having a panic attack? She clenched her eyes shut, and the feeling slowly passed.

Probably more of a guilt attack, she thought. When she opened her eyes again, the pathologist was staring at her with an unnerving smile.

He was tall, with a thin, pale face and black, curly hair that sprouted from all around his headphones. He had a quirky, lazy left eye that never seemed to leave the body he was working on, even though his attention appeared to be focused on her. He wasn't particularly attractive, but he certainly wasn't unattractive, either. She thought "unconventional looks" would be the best way to describe him. Using his forearms, he pushed the headphones back to partially expose his ears. She could now hear muffled, tinny music playing.

"You must be Rylan Fraser," he said. "The chief of staff called ahead to let me know you were coming." There was a musical, lyrical note to the cadence of his words. Rylan imagined he had been belting out tunes before she arrived, singing to the dead. "I left the door blocked open for you." He pointed his bloodied, gloved forefinger in the direction of the door.

"Thanks for that. I buzzed to let you know I was coming, but –"

"Yeah, I know, I had my music blaring pretty loud. The hum of the ventilation system gives me a weird tinnitus sometimes. The noise cancellation headphones and music seem to help."

He glanced up at the clock on the wall and sighed. "Jesus, I've been down here more than eighteen hours. I thought *I* was having a rough day, but you …. Damn. One for the record books. Three deaths in one night."

Rylan sighed inwardly. Those were not the kind of records she wanted anything to do with. "Yeah. Definitely not having my best night. My junior res took the weekend off, and my staff is stuck somewhere in the storm and unreachable. Plus, I have this really sick patient in the ICU."

She had no idea why she was telling him all of this. Maybe she felt sorry for him? All alone down here since yesterday morning with only her dead patients to keep him company.

"So" – Rylan tilted her head towards Mr. Kettering – "find anything, Doctor…?"

Mr. Kettering's chest and abdomen were split open, and each of his organs was sitting in a small pool of blood on metal trays lined up in an orderly fashion on the "L" portion of the table separating Rylan from the pathologist. The pathologist removed both of his gloves and slingshot them into a nearby garbage can. Rylan approved of his technique. He then reached over the table of orderly carnage and offered a hand.

"Apologies. I'm Dr. Greyson. Just started a few months ago. Does this kind of snowstorm thing happen a lot around here?"

Rylan shook his hand. "I've been in and out of this hospital on rotation for almost five years, and this is a first for me."

"Good. Otherwise, I might have to go looking for a sunnier work environment."

Rylan thought he could really use some sunshine. He was so pale.

"Anyway, I've autopsied Mrs. Potter, and I'm just finishing up Mr. Kettering here. So far, nothing out of the ordinary. They both died of cardiac arrests, and they both had all the usual comorbidities."

"So, nothing unusual about their deaths?"

"Not so far. I still have to do Mr. Robinson. He just arrived a little while ago. Also, I still have to go over all of the bloodwork and imaging before I complete my report. The chief of staff and the higher ups are all over my ass to get this done quickly. If you come back in an hour, I might have more info for you."

Rylan sighed. She'd been hoping for some answers and was no further ahead. "Call me right away if you find something unexpected. Otherwise, I'll circle back later. Thanks for your help."

"My pleasure. Say… not sure when you're finishing up your shift, but maybe we could grab some breakfast in a few hours, and I can fill you in on my findings."

Holy shit! It's 3AM and he's hitting on me. Her mind veered directly to Paul Bennett. "Appreciate the offer, but I already have a breakfast date." She didn't at this point, but she might.

His shoulders sagged, and she felt sorry for him again. He began putting on new gloves.

"Maybe another day?"

He perked up. "Absolutely. Some other day. You okay to find your way out?"

"Pretty sure it's the same way I came in."

He smiled coyly at her and then dove both gloved hands back into his work, picking up something that looked like a spleen. She was reminded of Brad and wondered if the CT was done.

She walked towards the anteroom and called back, "See you in an hour."

No answer. She turned her head. Dr. Greyson already had his headphones back in place and was once again bobbing his head from side to side.

Rylan opened the door to the morgue and stepped into the hallway, letting the door close and lock behind her. The overhead lights buzzed to life with her movement. She inhaled a deep breath of fresh (*fresh?*) basement air – a marked improvement over the green miasma of the morgue – then walked towards the darkness of the stairwell.

She was only a few steps in when she heard a squeak. At first, she thought it was a mouse, which would not be unexpected in this part of the hospital. Then it came again but now sounded more like a small wheel in need of oil. She scanned the area outside the morgue door and noted a trolley as tall as she was, partially backed into a cubby hole, filled with metal trays, the kind she saw inside the morgue on which organs or instruments were placed. Each tray was in a slot about four inches apart. She imagined the morgue went through a lot of these trays. She looked to the floor and saw that the trolley had four swivel wheels.

She stared at it and heard the squeak again. Did it move? It was difficult to say for sure in the poor lighting. She hesitated and then stepped in front of the trolley to examine it more closely.

Was there someone hiding behind it?

Her hand went to her phone in her lab coat pocket. The first thing that came to mind was the woman who had escaped from Paul's custody. If she was a danger to herself, it was Rylan's duty to help her, and it would help Paul in the process. Then she remembered Pockface was also roaming the hospital, and he was unpredictable. But he was also her patient, and she had a duty towards him as well. She inhaled deeply, looking for the smell of Pockface's cigarettes – or whatever else he smoked – but she still had the morgue stink firmly lodged in her nostrils.

"Hello? Is anyone there?" Her voice quavered, just a little.

She withdrew her phone from her pocket, and just as she activated the flashlight, a hand suddenly reached for her between the metal trays. It swiped at her phone, missed, latched onto the lapel of her lab coat, and drew her in. She panicked and pulled back. A tug of war ensued. Rylan may not have been very tall or heavy, but she did have the muscular wiriness of playing competitive hockey most of her life, often in the men's league, and the trays provided a buffer layer between her and the aggressor. Reflexively, she grabbed for the hand and tried to force it away but lost her footing and fell backward, dragging the towering trolley of trays as well as whoever was behind it with her. The trays were ejected from their slots and clanged to the floor in a discordant ruckus that could have awoken all the occupants of the morgue.

The back of her head hit the floor first, and then the rest of her body. The trolley followed. Somewhere in there, the hand let go.

And then everything went dark.

•   •   •   •   •

"Rylan, sweetie. Are you alright?"

That was Helen's voice. Rylan opened her eyes slowly. Someone was shining a flashlight on her, and she had to shield her eyes. She could just make out the deep, concerned wrinkles of Helen's sixty-year-old face hovering above her. She looked every bit the role of a mother.

"Oops, sorry." The beam of the flashlight veered away. That sounded like Dr. Greyson.

Rylan tried to speak, but her throat was too dry, and nothing came out. She sat up with the support of Helen's arm behind her back and tried again. This time a coarse whisper emerged. "Yeah. I think I'm okay. The back of my head hurts."

She scanned the area. It looked like all the trays that had been on top of her had been pushed to the side along with the trolley. Helen was there with two other security guards and Dr. Greyson. There was no sign of the person behind the trolley.

"How did all of you end up here?" she asked, now sitting with her legs outstretched on the concrete floor.

"You can thank Dr. Greyson for that," Helen said. "He heard the noise out here and, when he saw you trapped under the trolley, immediately called a *code white*."

Rylan remembered that a code white was for a potentially violent or out-of-control person. She looked at Dr. Greyson. "Did you see anybody else?"

"No. I'm sorry. They ran off. I heard rustling down the hall then the stairwell door open and close, but never saw anyone."

She looked at the trays scattered all over the floor. "Must have been one hell of a crash for you to hear it with your headphones on."

"You're lucky. I had my headphones off to listen to where my dictation on Mr. Kettering had finished up when you came in. Even then, I barely heard it."

She smiled and thanked him. He may have saved her life.

She was lucky, and she was feeling better. The post-impact brain fog seemed to be lifting. She rubbed the back of her head and tried to stand. Dr. Greyson and Helen both offered her support, but she waved it off. She was fine.

"Are you sure you're okay, Rylan?" Helen asked. "You look a little wobbly. Maybe we should get you in a wheelchair until you've been checked?"

"I think I'm –" Her knees both buckled at once. Fortunately, one of the security guards had the presence of mind to find a wheelchair nearby and already had it positioned behind Rylan. With the help of both Helen and Dr. Greyson, she fell gently back into the chair.

Rylan looked at Helen. "Okay, maybe I'm not quite fine."

"We're bringing you up to the ER to have Dr. Mike give you a once over."

There was no use arguing with Helen, so Rylan sat back for the ride.

CHAPTER 20

Pockface

Jiggle, jiggle. Turn, turn. Nothing.

IIe stepped through the near-dark hallway to the next door and placed his hand on the doorknob. Jiggle, jiggle. Turn, turn. Nothing.

"Dammit."

At the next door, however, someone else's quickened holiday departure became Pockface's small degree of fortune.

"Open sesame, you little whore."

The knob turned, the door swung open, and Pockface absorbed the layout of a standard hospital administrative office: one desk, one chair, and a series of filing cabinets. His hand wavered for a fleeting moment over the light switch before he closed the door behind him and shuffled to the office chair, guiding himself by the faint yellowish glow pushing through the opaque window glass of the door from the hallway light. He threw the pillow he was carrying under his armpit onto the desk, dropped heavily into the plush leather chair, leaned back, and kicked his size-sixteen feet up onto the corner. He grimaced a little as his infected forearm struck the armrest of the chair. He closed his eyes for a moment to steady himself and then reached into the pocket of his hoodie and produced a handful of small pink pills which he swallowed dry. He smiled, thinking how easy it was to score narcotics in a hospital.

They were basically everywhere. Plenty of pills and plenty of neatly-packaged hypodermic needles made the place a bonafide candy store for a guy like him. Maybe he would never leave. As he inhaled a deep breath through his nostrils, he enjoyed the anticipation of the high he knew was coming.

He looked around the office, trying to get a sense of who worked there, but it was too dark to make anything out. He wished he had his phone. Not to mention the rest of his clothes. And his sneakers.

He reached for a small side drawer in the desk, pulled it open, and rummaged blindly through with one hand.

"Yes!" he muttered to himself, pulling out what felt like a small penlight that had probably been sitting there, unused, for years. Would the batteries still work? He toggled a button with his thumb, and the room lit up. He was amazed that such a small penlight could put out so much energy. He moved the circle of illumination around the room, initially very slowly and then faster, as if he were holding a lightsaber, cutting the dark night into fragments with rapid thrusts, slashes, strikes, and stabs.

Finally, he tired and rested his arm on his knee with the beam of light reflecting off a glass-enclosed painting hanging on the wall. Was it a painting? Something caught his eye. He played with the focus on the end of the penlight and then leaned forward in the chair until he could make out the frame of a medical diploma with an emblem at the top that he recognized as his own alma mater. He couldn't read the name of the graduate, though.

He leaned back in his chair once more and scanned the contents of the open drawer with his penlight until he found an old prescription pad with the name Dr. Alan Whitaker, Orthopedic Surgeon, written in italics across the top, along with the address of Northern Michigan General Hospital. Wasn't he the asshole in charge of that bitch, Fraser? He hadn't seen him once since being admitted. Had no idea what he even looked like.

He then pointed the penlight back at the medical diploma on the wall, specifically at the emblem, and stared at it a long moment until pulling his gaze away to look at his bandaged arm. He placed the penlight in his mouth and held it pointing at his elbow and forearm area. He worked the sleeve of his hoodie up his arm, revealing the markings of an emblem, similar to the one on the medical diploma, except different. Instead of the snakes and post the medical crest displayed, his showed the staples, greyhound, and alligator of Yale Law School.

He smiled as a series of neglected memories flooded his mind. Good memories at first – meeting new friends, particularly new *girl*friends; new professors presenting stimulating ideas; classmates that were much more interesting than those of his undergrad years; fencing club where, for once in his life, he actually demonstrated prowess at a sport. For the first time, he had felt like he was part of a group of people that really could change the world. In fact, the whole first year of law school was unquestionably the best time of his life.

He released a long sigh. His life could have turned out completely different. *He* could have been completely different. If only his new roommate in second year hadn't –

What the hell was his name again? He was having more and more difficulty remembering things like people's names. No doubt a side effect of years of daily drug cocktails.

But was it his fault? Everything that happened?

No, definitely not just his fault. He hadn't made the program so ridiculously, exponentially difficult. And extreme circumstances called for extreme measures. At first, there was the pill his roommate suggested to keep him awake for late-night cramming, and then another to make him sleep, and then another to help him relax. There was a pill for everything.

At the time, his roommate seemed like a godsend, the only way to get through the tunnel of academia that lay before him. It was too late when it became apparent his body couldn't endure the escalating synthetic chemistry required to face the towering workload and unrelenting stress. And the downward spiral began.

Everyone he ever knew abandoned him like he had wet leprosy. Eventually, he abandoned them, along with his name that belonged to another life, his old life. He went through several monikers but none of them stuck until he met a woman, Susan, who saw him for what he had become. He was deeply into meth at that time, and she coined the name *Pockface*. For her, it was a term of endearment. And, for him, it became one as well. He was abandoned once again when she OD'd. But he kept the name and the not-all-bad memories that went along with it.

Those memories were practically all he had left, and it pissed him off, really infuriated the fuck out of him, that *she*, that goddamn lady surgeon …

He released another long sigh and tore off a piece of clear plastic tape. He slowly unwound the bandage on his arm, beginning at the lower end. Not his first time at this rodeo. He'd removed the bandage before, shortly after the surgery, wanting to make sure it was still intact. And that's when he had seen. Of course, the psycho nurses had just shouted at him like a toddler caught with a fistful of freshly baked cake and rewrapped the arm without even listening to him. Not one of those bitches actually cared about what mattered to *him*.

Pockface watched thick, milky fluid drip down his arm and onto the alligator. He continued unwrapping, wiping pus away in the process until he found what he didn't want to see. He quickly unraveled the remainder of the bandage, letting it fall on the desk. The skin was beet red with pus oozing from the edges of the large incision that traveled from his elbow down his forearm, stopping just above his Yale law crest. But that's not what bothered him. Not what made his skin hot and his breathing fast. Not what drove him over the edge. Just above the crest, the face of his beloved Susan had been transected in two halves, right between the eyes.

He shook his head violently from side to side, spittle dripping from both sides of his mouth. He picked a paperweight off the desk and launched it across the room at the wall. The glass protecting Dr. Whitaker's Yale medical school diploma shattered and sprayed shards everywhere. Pockface stared at the glint reflecting off the pieces of glass that had landed on the desk and couldn't help but make the connection to his life. A shattered life reduced to shards and scattered everywhere. Unfixable.

He propped the penlight on the desk and rewrapped his wound with the dirty bandage. He stood and tucked the pillow back under his armpit.

That bitch had robbed him and deserved to pay.

CHAPTER 21

Paul

Paul was just leaving the psychiatric ER when he saw Rylan coming. Her luminescent green eyes telegraphed her approach like low beams in a fog. She was in a wheelchair being pushed by Helen, the security chief he'd met earlier. While Rylan did not appear to be in major distress, she looked far from happy. The skeptical resignation on her face told Paul that she was not pleased by the prospect of being a patient in her own hospital, and further, that maybe the wheelchair treatment was overkill.

"What happened?" Paul asked, intercepting the women at the electronic doors to the medical ER.

Rylan waved a dismissive hand. "I'm okay," she said. "Somebody grabbed me and knocked me down."

"What?" Paul looked to Helen for an explanation, but she was busy snapping her fingers in the air, trying to get someone else's attention. An instant later, that someone appeared in the form of Dr. Mike Curran. He swooped in on Rylan and repeated Paul's question.

"What happened?"

Helen spoke over Rylan, quickly explaining the assault outside the morgue and how she had found her on the ground under an instrument trolley, unconscious.

"Jeez," Mike said. He was shining a pocket light in Rylan's eyes, speaking to Helen. "What the hell is going on here tonight? Did you at least catch the guy?"

"No one said it was a guy," Helen said.

Mike looked up from running his hands over Rylan's head. "It was a woman?"

Helen shrugged. "Not sure. We never found that young girl who ran away earlier this evening."

"True." Mike gave a disapproving grunt and returned to separating the hair on the back of Rylan's head, examining the scalp. "You have a nice little bump on the back of your head here, Rylan, but no bleeding."

"Good. Now stop touching it because it hurts."

Mike asked a nurse to grab an ice pack. He proceeded to examine Rylan right there in the middle of the ER, all while firing off a series of questions about things like nausea, ringing in the ears, and double vision. When he was satisfied that she was neurologically intact, he asked about the rest of her.

"Maybe just a few bruises," Rylan answered. "Nothing broken."

"That's fortunate," Mike said, "because we wouldn't have an orthopod to fix you." The two conferred briefly about the value of getting a head CT and decided to hold off for the moment since, given her minimal symptoms, she didn't meet the threshold criteria.

Paul stood by this whole time, idly watching the exam. He was unsure whether he should disappear or stay put. On the one hand, it felt somehow voyeuristic to be there, but on the other, it felt important that Rylan see his concern and his interest in finding the person who'd hurt her. "Helen," he asked, "are there any closed-circuit cameras in the basement? Perhaps we can see who did this to Rylan."

Helen frowned. "No, though we are on the verge of an upgrade. It'll be nice to move into the twenty-first century like the rest of the world. In fact, a guy from the camera company just called last week, and we went over all the locations we need new cameras. I told him about the basement, the stairwells, the medical wards –"

"Helen, where *do* we have cameras?" Paul asked.

"Come on. I'll show you." Helen led Paul, Mike, and Rylan from the ER to the security kiosk at the main entrance. Rylan ditched the wheelchair and walked on her own two feet. Paul noted her gait was steady, although she still held the icepack to the back of her head. Helen directed them to a series of screens behind the kiosk. "Basically, we have views of the entrances, the elevator banks, the emergency rooms, and the psychiatric unit."

The doctors gazed at the grainy black-and-white images on the screens. "So, there's no way we can see who has been on the surgical or medical floors?" Rylan asked.

"Not with this limited system."

"And you say this camera guy just called last week?" Mike asked.

Helen nodded, and Paul observed a look pass between Rylan and Mike.

"What about this camera here." Mike pointed to the one on the far left. "Why is it blank?"

Helen huffed. "Hasn't worked for months. It overlooks the docs parking lot on the south side. I did tell the camera guy about it, and he said they'd fix it when they did the upgrade."

Mike and Rylan exchanged dour glances once more. Paul realized they weren't very happy with the idea of their daily parking spaces not being at least a little bit protected.

"Helen, can you play back some of the footage from earlier in the evening?" Rylan asked.

Helen said she would, although she didn't think they would see anything useful. Over the next several minutes, the group perused the recordings. First, they looked at the entrances where there was very little activity given the storm outside. Then, they examined footage from the emergency rooms. Mike was seen in many of the frames, walking the length of the ER hall, often popping behind curtains to examine patients, then stopping at a computer to check labs or write orders.

"That's one handsome son of a gun there," he said, pointing a finger at the screen.

Rylan groaned and asked Helen to switch the view to the psychiatric ER where Paul became visible, though his presence was more sporadic than Mike's had been in the medical ER. Paul watched Rylan follow his comings and goings on the screen with her eyes and wondered what she was thinking. She glanced up and caught him watching her watch him. Her cheeks pinked up, and she smiled sheepishly. Next, they looked at the elevator banks where they picked up only that which was expected – housekeeping and transport staff, the occasional overnight resident in scrubs. Finally, Mike agreed there was nothing of particular use to be gleaned from the footage. He said he had to get back to the ER and was about to go when Rylan jabbed a finger at the screen.

"That guy!" The footage showed a man exiting the fifth-floor elevator. He was older, slightly hunched, shuffling along in snow boots, a black instrument bag in his hand.

Mike squinted at the screen. "That's Reggie Upslinger. He's a locum hospitalist. The admin had to practically beg the agency to send someone because we're so short-staffed."

"And this guy was the best they could do?" Rylan asked.

"Be nice," Mike scolded, looking from the screen to Rylan and back again. "Reggie seems to be a good enough guy." He scratched his chin and watched the man amble across the frame and out of view. "He retired after thirty years or so at a big academic center, then lost his wife unexpectedly. I think he's doing locum work now just to have something to do. Seems a bit depressed if you ask me. But he appears to know his stuff."

Rylan's face softened a bit. "I tried introducing myself, and he just seemed so … unfriendly."

"And you wondered how anyone could resist the charms of the enchanting Rylan Fraser."

"Shut up."

"Both of you shut up and look here," Helen said, pointing to a different monitor. "Isn't that Pockface?"

It was amazing to Paul that everyone in the hospital seemed to know Pockface. He looked at the screen where Helen was pointing to a large man in sweatpants, a dark hoodie, and hospital socks. He had traded his hospital pajamas for street clothes, albeit without shoes. Even without shoes, though, he moved across the screen at a good clip. Something large was jammed under his left arm.

"That sure is Pockface," Rylan said, "and that fucker is carrying a pillow. Do you see it?"

"He's probably hospital-squatting because of the blizzard," Mike said.

"No," Rylan said, her voice rising, "he's probably smothering innocent patients in their beds!"

"Now, Rylan, don't be cra –"

"Mike, listen to me. Three of my patients – stable patients – have died here tonight. This is our explanation." She thrust her finger forcefully at the screen and turned imploring eyes to Helen. "Helen, you have to find him! He's supposed to be on MRSA precautions, he left his room AMA, and I think he's super *dangerous*. We need to get the police here."

Helen raised both hands, palms outward, in a placating gesture. Paul was unsure, however, if she was trying to placate Rylan or herself. Her face was undeniably troubled. She took a deep breath, perhaps buying time to consider her words before she spoke them. "Rylan, we have no evidence that he is doing anything more than sleeping in some quiet corner of the hospital."

"But –"

Helen held her hands firm. With an exaggerated nod of her head, she said, "But even that is against the rules, particularly since he left his room AMA. Listen, we are already searching for him, but we'll try and escalate things. Okay?" She pulled her walkie-talkie from her belt, pressed a button, and it crackled to life. Before she even said word one, however, an excited voice on the other end began speaking. "Helen, that you? I need you on the fifth floor, D wing. STAT."

"What's going on?"

"You … um, you need to see this for yourself. Just come. And be careful."

Helen replaced the talkie at her hip and shook her head back and forth in consternation. "What's that saying?" she muttered, lifting her hands to massage the back of her neck. "Everything that can go wrong will go wrong?"

And that's when the power went out.

CHAPTER 22

Rylan

The overhead lights crackled and sputtered everywhere, and Rylan swore she felt the whole hospital vibrate. She tried to picture what kind of monolithic generator would be required to power a hospital of this size but really had no concept. Big? Really, really big?

The darkness was total during the five-minute switchover, and the sounds changed abruptly from mechanical hospital buzzing, beeping, and humming, to a crescendo of human whispers eventually erupting into yelling that only subsided once the power was restored.

And then it all happened again. Complete blackout with now only the emergency battery-powered lights, the ones typically unnoticed in the upper corners of every hallway, offering some vestige of illumination.

The fucking generators are on the fritz! What does that mean for my ICU patient? A man completely dependent on electricity to stay alive. And what about his CT and the OR?

Rylan's phone vibrated in answer.

"Rylan, it's Todd. The power's out. We need help in the ICU. There's no one left to bag your patient. His surgery's obviously on hold."

No shit, Einstein.

"Coming," she said, already dashing off. Her Birkenstocks squealed as she looked back at Mike, Helen, and Paul, still standing in front of the now blank security screens at the darkened security kiosk desk.

"Gotta run to the ICU. Helen, you have to catch Pockface!"

Within moments, setting a new personal two-flight stairwell speed record, she burst through the double doors of the ICU and landed directly at the foot of her patient's bed where someone she didn't recognize in the darkness was bagging Brad-the-unfortunate. Only the pathetic glow from the face of her smartphone provided any visibility. When Rylan moved closer, she could see a sheen of forehead sweat and eyes as wide as those of a woman before the gallows.

Rylan suddenly recognized her. She was the temp ward clerk who covered the ICU occasionally. Undeniably out of her element.

"I've got it, Marsha," Rylan said, moving to the head of the bed.

"Thank you, thank you, thank you. This is so … gross!" she said, changing places with Rylan and then throwing her gloves to a dark corner of the room.

"Any idea what's going on?" Rylan asked.

"No. Just the obvious. The generators aren't working. I've gotta go somewhere else and do some … work."

Rylan wondered what kind of work she could possibly do with all the computers offline.

Marsha exited Brad's room, but not before grabbing her phone, leaving Rylan with only a sliver of light stealing its way in from the hallway.

Rylan yelled, "Hey. Out there. Can anyone bring a flashlight?"

There was no response. Rylan was not surprised since the ICU was short-staffed and everyone was already on task. She felt her lab coat for her phone with her free hand and found it. She could bring some light to the situation, like Marsha, but she was 22 hours into her shift from hell with no end in sight. She may not find time to recharge it. And really, what did she need to see anyway?

Her right hand squeezed the bag rhythmically, pushing air into Brad's lungs through the endotracheal tube. From there, the oxygen would go into his bloodstream to be delivered to every part of his body, most importantly his brain. She could feel his chest rise and fall in time with her squeezes. And then she had a disconcerting thought.

How do I know if he's even still alive?

He was already living on the precipice of death. The brief time it took to switch over to manual ventilation could have been the kick that put him over the edge. She looked towards the blank monitor and cursed the luck of this night.

Back to basics, she thought, as she walked her fingers to Brad's neck and palpated for his carotid pulse. She felt something but realized it was her own pulse, fueled by adrenaline and the work of bagging. She shook her hand, closed her eyes, and felt again. And there it was: faint and thready but definitely there. He was still alive, but he wouldn't be for long if they didn't get him to the OR.

Time dragged on, like watching paint dry or blood coagulate, and exhaustion began to ripple through her body, settling in her eyelids, weighing them down. She lost herself briefly in a daydream where her new friend, Paul the handsome psychiatrist, invited her back to his place one evening after a dinner date. His apartment was sparse but well decorated. There was a couch and a bed. He poured her a nightcap and sat close to her on the couch, his knee touching hers, his arm resting on the back of the couch with his fingers lightly grazing her hair, occasionally brushing an errant strand away from her face as a riveting conversation that began over dinner was carried on. Until, finally, he leaned in …

The little interosseous muscles in her hand squeezing the bag suddenly cramped, jolting her back to the moment. "Damn it!" she whisper-yelled as she switched hands.

"You okay?" a voice asked from just outside the door.

"Todd?"

"Yeah, it's me. Got spelled off by Marsha, although it took some convincing. How you holding up?"

He actually sounds sincere, like he cares.

"I'm fine. A little tired."

"That CT was done, by the way. Unfortunately, it hasn't been read yet. They were about to bring him to the OR from CT when the power failed."

"So, no one's seen it?"

"Nope. And we can expect the whole IT system to be scrambled for quite a while when the power does come back on. Assuming it comes back on."

"What exactly are you saying?" Rylan asked.

"If the power comes on, and we can go to the OR, we may not have a choice but to go blind. We reopen his belly and follow the bleeding to the source. Either the iliac artery on the inner table of the pelvis where your external fixation pin is likely protruding, or some other source."

"Such as the area around the spleen?"

"Possible. Unlikely, but possible."

"And if the power doesn't come on?"

"We both know Brad's as good as dead."

There was an instant of fatal premonition, as if the same current that was suddenly passing through the wires in the walls was also passing through Rylan. Blinding light suddenly burst on the scene, like a solar flare, and the rumble of the hospital HVAC system accompanied a thousand other sounds as all the electronics of the ICU came back to life. When the glaring white before her eyes finally settled, she noticed Todd was gone. She also noticed some rudimentary vital signs appearing on the monitor. And they weren't good.

She removed the Ambu bag and placed Brad back on the mechanical ventilator by reattaching the flexible circuit to the endotracheal tube. She watched his chest rise and fall for a moment to ensure it was working properly after rebooting and then ran out of the room.

She found Todd, who was cornered by Dr. Lombroso and seemed to be involved in an intense conversation. She stepped up and interrupted. "Brad's crashing. He needs to go to the OR now."

"CT?" Dr. Lombroso asked as he swiveled his eyes to meet Rylan's.

"Done. But not read or available," Todd said.

Rylan squirmed a little under Lombroso's intense gaze. "Hopefully, we can look at it in the OR after the PACS system reboots."

Dr. Lombroso sighed heavily, his rotund chest diminishing at least three sizes. "Alright, I'll call the OR to let them know you're coming. They should already be expecting you. We've got nobody to spare here at the moment. The two of you can wheel him over. Go. Now!"

Rylan looked at Todd, who gave her a condescending mock bow and pointed the way with an open hand, as if to say, "Your problem, but I'll graciously help you out." Rylan flared her nostrils at him and took the lead.

They quickly transferred Brad's vital sign lifelines – ECG, oxygen saturation, blood pressure – to a portable unit, disconnected the ventilator, and reattached the Ambu bag. They wheeled Brad out of his room, accompanied by a fanfare of ventilator alarms they didn't know how to shut off. Rylan was squeezing the Ambu bag with one hand and pushing the bed with the other. Todd was at the foot, pulling the bed and wheeling a heavy IV pole stacked from top to bottom with monitors and medication delivery devices.

Todd hit the large push-plate button on the wall with his knee to automatically open the double ICU doors. They picked up speed as they maneuvered the bed down the hall to the OR, converting to a light jog.

Everything was happening so fast. Rylan needed to at least try and call her staff again. It was one thing to slap on external fixators and clean out a wound; it was another entirely to deal with the potential complications in a dying man. As she reviewed in her head exactly what she was going to do, she heard Todd yell something and felt the bed swerve. She looked up and saw the scary, decrepit old janitor with the fucked-up hand wearing a headlamp and mopping a section of the hallway just outside the main doors to the OR.

Seriously, Rylan thought, *he was working during the power failure?*

Rylan followed Todd's lead and swerved the bed around the area of wet floor and a yellow sign that said, "Caution." As they approached the door, she saw the janitor punch the push-plate on the wall with his deformed hand and grimace. The doors slid apart allowing them through. She glanced at him as she passed, wanting to offer thanks, but he pointed his gnarled fist at her and gave a look of pent-up rage that stifled her vocal cords.

CHAPTER 23

Paul

Paul followed the beam of Helen's flashlight along the dim hall. Little electrical bursts of energy pulsed through his spine, and his brain tingled in anticipation. The night had already veered off in all sorts of unexpected directions, from blizzard to blackout. What would be next?

Helen had been convinced that the summons she'd received at the kiosk was connected to the escaped patient from the psychiatric ER, so she'd asked Paul along to assist in soothing the girl and de-escalating any tension that might arise during the confrontation. Her pace was brisk, and she was all business now. She swept the flashlight in a continuous arc from side to side, determined, it seemed to Paul, to prevent anyone lurking in the shadows from getting the upper hand.

They rounded a corner and found two security guards at the end of the hall, turned so their backs faced Helen and Paul. One was slowly shaking his head back and forth. The other was scratching the back of his neck. They were staring at something on the wall in the way museum visitors do when engrossed in an exhibit.

Helen's walkie-talkie belched static into the relative quiet of the hall. The security guards tensed and swung their heads around. Their startled faces met the beam of Helen's flashlight.

"What is it?" Helen asked impatiently, coming up behind them.

The two men stepped aside, and the light hit the wall, revealing a crudely drawn, monochromatic mural that covered an area Paul estimated to be about six by ten. The work appeared to have been rendered in haste, though by an artist with a fair amount of skill – and perhaps psychosis.

"What the hell is this?" Helen jerked her flashlight up and down the display. Scrawled across the top of the diagram was a short verse. She read it aloud:

The tally in the valley
Grows like toes
And where are my clothes?

"What is this garbage? It's complete nonsense."

Beside Helen, Paul nodded his head. It was complete nonsense. Under the lackluster poem was a drawing of a squat two-legged creature, naked and barefoot with long, fingerlike toes extending from each foot. The figure was short-necked and round-backed – like a Neanderthal – and had distinctively female touches, like breasts and long, flowing hair. Its head had a canine appearance with nose and mouth forming an elongated snout. The jaw held a set of angry, gnashing teeth, and gore and blood leaked down the creature's chin and pooled at its long toes. Large, human-shaped eyes peered from the top of its head, bulging and frenzied so that a full ring of white conjunctiva was visible around the solid, red cornea. Little pear-shaped droplets poured from the eyes, dripping onto the floor. The image was grotesque and unsettling. It reminded Paul of a Japanese manga cartoon, and, although he didn't know much about the art form, he thought it showed a fair amount of technical skill. The artist's state of mind was a separate matter entirely.

"Trash," Helen snapped. "Did your patient do this?" She gave Paul a stern look.

"*My* patient? You mean the one who ran away while *your* guys were transporting her to the unit?"

Helen pressed a thumb and index finger into the corners of her eyes and rubbed the bridge of her nose. "That came out wrong," she said. "First of all, I'm not in charge of transport, and second of all, I just meant –"

Paul waved her off. "I know what you meant, it's okay. But I have no idea who drew this picture."

"Of course not." Helen nodded her head and tried on a weak smile that didn't quite work. Paul thought she looked very tired.

"Look, Chief," one of the security guards said. "This isn't really such a big deal." He moved almost flush to the wall and swiped at it with the lapel of his uniform jacket. The ink disappeared. "It's dry-erase marker. It comes right off. No lasting harm."

"For goodness' sake," Helen said. "Why would anyone do a thing like this?"

"A bit of fun …" the security guard said.

"Drawing graffiti on a hospital wall is fun? People have no respect for anything anymore." She pulled a cell phone from her pocket and took a few pictures of the strange mural while addressing the security guards. "Listen, Jones, get someone from housekeeping up here ASAP to clean this mess. A few damp rags and a bottle of Fantastik should do the trick."

She slipped the phone back into her pocket and scrunched up her face. "What's that noise?"

There was a howling whoosh coming from somewhere down a connecting hallway. Paul hadn't noticed it at first with his attention on the bizarre mural, but he heard it now. He turned toward its source. "It sounds like –"

"– like wind," Helen finished for him. "And it's freezing here. A window must be open."

She was right. Paul's fingertips were practically numb. An open window in a blizzard did not make a lot of sense, but then he thought of Pockface. "Maybe someone opened it to smoke?"

"Maybe," Helen said. She started walking, and Paul followed along with one of the security guards while the other stayed behind to call housekeeping. Once they'd gotten about halfway down the hall, there was no doubt a window was open. The howling winds amplified as they got closer, and it was easy to figure out which room was the offender. Its closed door shook and jiggled frantically against the jambs.

"This can't be good." Helen shined her flashlight on a little plaque identifying the room in question as a "multipurpose room." With a deep breath, she pulled open the door and immediately stumbled backward. The force of the blizzard winds whipping through the open window tipped her against the accompanying security guard. As they righted themselves, Paul squinted into the dark room. It looked more or less like a small classroom, with a smattering of schoolroom desks scattered about, their silhouettes just visible by the weak hallway emergency bulbs. A window directly across from the door was most definitely open, and the frigid air made Paul's eyes water. As far as he could see, no one was inside – which made sense since it was *way* too cold for anyone to be hiding there. Paul stepped into the room and made a beeline for the window. The sooner it was closed, –

"Oof!" Before his brain grasped what was happening, his feet flew out from under him, and he was down.

"Dr. Bennett!" Helen pointed her flashlight at Paul and hurried into the room. "What happened?"

Paul sat up slowly and suppressed a swear word under his breath. He bent his right knee at a forty-five-degree angle and massaged his thigh. "Snow and ice on the linoleum. I didn't realize. Pretty stupid."

This little mishap, Paul knew, was going to screw him up for the rest of the night. He'd gone down on his right hip, and the impact had reverberated down his thigh to the knee, waking up pain receptors and setting them ablaze. He'd had a serious leg injury years before, and the surgeon who'd fixed him up had a bad attitude and colossal chip on his shoulder. Paul remembered his smug, smarmy face, his steely eyes, and his deaf ears as Paul begged for stronger painkillers. "You're going to be just fine," was all he said, as if his just saying it was enough to be grateful for. What Paul would learn later was that "just fine" meant his leg would ache intermittently for the rest of his life, throb when barometric pressure dipped, and burn after bouts of exertion. *Asshole.*

"Come on, let's get you up," Helen said. She offered a hand and Paul took it, grunting as he rose to his feet.

"Well, that was fun," he said, straightening his blazer and smoothing his sleeves.

Helen gave Paul a quick once-over with her eyes. Once she seemed convinced he was intact, she moved to the window. She shone her flashlight into the night where it was instantly swallowed by the storm, then poked her head through the aperture and looked downward. It was a fruitless effort. Her neat, grey bob instantly transformed into a wild mane that flew across her eyes and blocked her vision while sheets of relentless snow rammed her face and skull.

Helen pulled back inside and slammed the window shut. "I don't like it," she said, shaking snow from her hair and combing her fingers roughly through the damp, tangled strands. "This window is big enough for someone to fit through. I need security to get out there and check the grounds below the window."

"You think we had a jumper?" the security guard asked, craning his neck to peer through the glass.

"I sure as hell hope not, but we did have a psych admission go AWOL earlier tonight." She glanced at Paul and their eyes connected for a silent moment. "For all we know, there could be someone down there buried under the snow. It's impossible to see."

"Right. I'm on it," the security guard said, turning to leave the room."

Paul's fingers found the newspaper clipping in his pocket and rubbed the frayed edges. He chewed his lower lip and harnessed whatever mental energy he could to quash the agitation blooming in his chest. This was not how things were supposed to go tonight.

A mechanical whir cut the air, and the lights in the hall came back on full strength. "Thank God," Helen said, turning off her flashlight and tucking it into her belt. The room they were standing in was still dark since none of them had hit the switch when they entered. Paul crossed the room, his throbbing leg a reminder to tread carefully over the slick, wet floor, and flipped it on. The shadowy shapes surrounding them instantly transformed into identifiable objects. There were the desks that Paul had picked out earlier and also a squat bookshelf crammed with anything but books. Two CPR practice-dolls lay in an undignified heap in a corner. Paul was wondering about the contents of a large, bright orange toolbox-on-wheels when he realized Helen's gaze was fixed on a spot on the floor. There, about three feet from the window, lay a red dry-erase marker.

"For heaven's sake," Helen said. She lifted her walkie-talkie to her mouth and began urgently firing off orders. Paul heard her revoke the earlier instruction about washing the diagram on the wall. "Tell housekeeping to wait," she said. Then, she holstered her walkie-talkie and pulled out her cell phone. Paul didn't know who she was speaking with, but he assumed it was some higher-up in administration. He heard the phrases "AWOL psych admission" and "sick, red graffiti on the wall" and "open window." All the while, Helen kept her tone calm and professional, and Paul admired her for that.

While Helen spoke on the phone, Paul considered the optics of the situation. How did this look? Or, more to the point, how did it look for *him*? New psychiatrist, escaped patient, writing on the wall (literally!), possible suicide. He feared someone might want to talk to him, take a closer look at the new hire, perhaps explore his past. His fingers again caressed the newspaper clipping in his pocket. *Troubled teen, 17, latest suicide on Y-Bridge.* No, he could not handle that level of scrutiny right now. He made for the door. His bad leg complained with each step, and Paul tasted blood where his teeth worked his lip.

"Hey, doc, where're you going?" Helen asked, placing her palm over the phone at her ear.

"Paged," Paul muttered, holding up his beeper for evidence.

He thought he saw a flicker of doubt on Helen's face, but she nodded. "Come back when you can, okay?"

Paul was already walking when he grunted in the affirmative. He retraced his steps to exit the floor. The bizarre mural looked even weirder under the harsh fluorescent lights. He re-read the silly poem. *The tally in the valley grows like toes … and where are my clothes?*

He walked on, turning the little verse in his head. *And where are my clothes?* Paul thought of his young admit from the psychiatric ER. She'd been in hospital pajamas when he'd seen her. Her clothes had been taken away. Was the poem her way of saying she wanted them back? Did she think she was going to put on her street clothes and walk out the hospital door? If so, she must've missed a memo.

And the window … had she opened the window? She had no business fooling around at the window. *No one* should have been at a window tonight. The thought of things unraveling made Paul angry, and he had an impulse to kick the wall, but his leg hurt too much.

Paul was so entwined in thought that he barely registered the janitor with the mangled hand walking straight for the mural armed with a squeeze bottle. Perhaps he'd missed a memo, too.

It was only when Paul was several steps beyond the janitor that it dawned on him. This time, the guy's face actually hadn't been wrapped in a scowl. In fact, this time he'd been chuckling.

CHAPTER 24

Rylan

"If it isn't the two lovebirds and their little broken baby."

Rylan scowled at Dr. English, realizing that any retort was useless. She and Todd wheeled the bed adjacent to the OR table and prepared to transfer. She glanced across theater one to the PACS computer screen mounted on the wall. Even from where she was standing, she could see a mostly blank screen with the reboot symbol rotating at the center: the waiting game.

I don't have time to wait! Brad doesn't have time.

"What a lovely gift. Gracing me with the same patient once again, now even more on the verge of death, and expecting me to overcome all your screwups and keep him alive. Is there any chance that either of your staff men has made it into hospital?" Dr. English was prepping his anesthesia equipment on his gas machine and readying his medications.

"You know, birdies, I have half a mind to call this off. With no staff here, I'm not in any way obliged to continue this farce. In fact, I'm sure what I'm doing here, allowing two residents to operate on their own with no staff presence, is completely against hospital policy. I could lose my license." He stood at the head, one hand holding a syringe and the other an IV bag, waiting for a response.

Rylan met his gaze straight on. "We can't just let him die."

"He's as good as dead already. Why should I potentially let him take my career down with him?"

Rylan gathered what was left of her inner strength and inner anger, sucked in a quick, ragged breath and planted both Birkenstocks on the floor. She thrust her chin forward and yelled, "Because, it's the fucking right thing to do. Okay? It's the right thing."

Todd, standing dumbfounded at the foot of the bed, took a step back and looked like he was about to break into a run. No one talked to Dr. English that way. No one.

For a second, it appeared Dr. English's head was going to erupt like a volcano, spewing shocked and angry brain matter all over the shiny clean walls of the OR. And then, the muscles of his neck relaxed, and his shoulders sagged just a little. He pulled his mask down under his wrinkled chin, revealing weary eyes and a mischievous grin. In a complete about-face, he said, "Finally, someone with a bloody spine. So, what are you waiting for, Dr. Fraser? Fix him."

Rylan was so surprised, one of her knees buckled, and her bladder almost spontaneously burst.

Dr. English held Brad's head with one hand on either side. "Ready for transfer!"

Rylan assumed a position on Brad's left while Todd ran around to the other side with a roller device in hand.

"Donna, assume the urology position, if you please," Dr English said. Donna, the circulating nurse, ran to the foot of the bed and grabbed both feet.

"Rotate!"

Rylan rolled Brad's torso towards her with both hands, being careful to avoid the external fixation rods and pins.

"Insert!"

Todd inserted the roller device under Brad's back and pelvis.

"Push-pull!

With Rylan pushing and Todd pulling, Brad gently glided over the roller from his ICU bed to the OR table.

"Rotate!"

Todd rotated Brad towards him as Rylan extracted the rolling device.

"Well done, my little birdies. Now I suggest you come up with a plan while I take a few minutes to stabilize the patient and deepen his anesthesia. A final phone call to your staff would be in order. Yes?" He looked pointedly at both Rylan and Todd, who both nodded while backing away from the OR table.

They pulled phones from their side pockets like they were drawing pistols and tapped away. Seconds later, they both realized their cell phones were nothing more than little minicomputers with no connection to the outside world.

Todd looked up. "Anything?"

"Big zero."

"We're on our own." Todd put his phone back in his side pocket.

"Yes, we are."

"Nervous?" Todd asked.

Rylan paused to think her response through. Todd was asking how she felt. Was he setting her up? Or was he actually concerned? The worst of times sometimes brought out the best of people.

"Yeah. A little. You?"

"Mmm, a little. I just hope –"

"Little birdies!" A booming voice echoed through theater one. "It's time to fly."

Fuck, Rylan thought as she glanced at the blank PACS computer screen once again.

They rushed out to the scrub sink and squirted sterilization fluid on their hands and forearms. They methodically rubbed their hands together as they re-entered the OR with arms outstretched. Rylan saw that Larry, the scrub nurse, had an armamentarium of tools available on his nursing table. She continued to hope that she wouldn't need any of them. He was already prepping the abdomen and pelvis, including the pin sites of the external fixator, with Proviodine, an antiseptic.

"We obviously can't just pull the ex-fix pins out without having exposure of the potential bleed site in the pelvis first," Todd was saying. "So, we need to re-open the abdomen and go into the pelvis. We also don't know whether it's the left or right-sided pin that's the culprit. We'll have to just pick a side and start there – unless there's one side you felt less sure about than the other?"

Rylan shook her head from side to side. "No. Honestly, they both felt perfect."

As they were getting gloved and gowned, Rylan had a flashback. When she was seven or eight years old, her dad had to rush to the OR for an emergency spine case, and there was no one to look after her. He had left her with the nurse at the front desk. On the wall behind the main OR desk was a series of small television screens used to monitor progress in each of the rooms. She remembered her eyes being glued to the screen as she watched her dad enter the room. He was a tall and intimidating man, and all heads turned to look at him. She couldn't hear what was being said, but she could tell that he commanded a great deal of respect and authority. His mere presence seemed to bring a whole other level of confidence to the room.

I am not my dad, not yet. I have to win over everyone's respect, one person at a time.

She had made a good start with Dr. English, and she knew Larry, the scrub nurse, was in her corner.

They stood on either side of the patient and squared off the surgical site with a variety of sticky drapes. And then they just stood there, a foreboding stillness enveloping the room. It was one thing to talk through a procedure. It was another to dig in with the knife.

This isn't the aura of confidence my father projected.

A disembodied voice yelled from behind the curtain at the head. "Cut!"

They both reached for the knife on the mayo stand simultaneously. Rylan looked up. A bead of sweat was trickling down Todd's temple, and his glasses were starting to fog. He said, "Okay. I'll start the approach while you prep for removal of the ex-fix."

Rylan nodded her head in the affirmative and let Todd take the knife. "If it's not one of the pins, and I release the ex-fix, his pelvis will open up, and he'll bleed to death. So, I'm not touching anything until we see what's what." Rylan was going to hold her ground until the last minute. Her ex-fix pins were perfect. At least that's what she was telling herself.

"It's definitely an errant pin, but suit yourself." Todd used the knife to cut the previous sutures holding the long midline abdominal incision together. "Make yourself useful, then. Grab a hemostat and help remove the sutures."

Rylan did exactly that, all the while her eyes darting repeatedly between the PACS viewer and the wrench Larry had placed on the mayo stand for her.

As the incision opened up, a well of bright red blood oozed to the surface.

"That's not good," Todd whispered loudly.

"Suction and lots of sponges," he commanded, as he blindly plunged his hands up to his elbows through bowel, deep into the pelvis. "It looks like it's coming from the left side. I'm going to feel around the inner table of the pelvis and see if there's anything sharp and metallic."

Todd's eyes widened. "I think I feel something. Get ready to remove the pin."

Rylan glanced at the blank PACS viewer one more time, a bead of sweat now running off her brow. She still couldn't believe this was her doing. She sucked in a quick breath and grabbed the wrench from Larry's waiting hand. She engaged the wrench on the clamp mechanism holding the pin and was ready to release it, when a voice she didn't recognize yelled, "Got something."

She paused and looked up to the PACS screen. Lines of code were racing up the screen, like in a Matrix movie, as the computer came online. She noted the X-ray technician working the keyboard. Within moments the image of a pelvis materialized. Brad's pelvis.

"What are you doing?" Todd asked. "Get ready to remove the pin. I think I feel the tip."

"Think?" Rylan asked. "Wait. They've got the CT up."

Todd swiveled his head ninety degrees as if he didn't believe her. "We don't have time!"

"We have time to avoid a lousy decision, Todd." She spoke urgently to the tech. "Scroll down the axial views until I tell you to stop."

Images of Brad's pelvis flipped across the screen. "Stop!" Rylan could now see the position of the pin within the body of the ilium, the flare of the pelvis. She ripped off a blood-soaked outer glove, leaving a clean inner glove, and then marched over to the keyboard. She waved the tech away and placed her hand over the mouse.

"Look," she said, "the position of the pin is perfect."

"Well, then, what's this sharp thing I'm feeling?" Todd asked.

Rylan quickly scrolled the images once more and went back to the table. She tore off her remaining glove, contaminated by using the mouse, and Larry helped her don two new ones. She went to Todd's side, wanting to get the right angle of approach, and gently hip-checked him out of the way. She plunged her hand into the wound and carefully felt along the inner table of the pelvis. At first there was nothing but normal anatomy. And then, she felt something sharp. She smiled and looked at Todd as she grabbed his hand, pushed through bowel, and guided his fingers towards the problem area. "Is this what you're talking about?"

"Yeah, that's the tip of the pin. Isn't it?

"Moron," Rylan said. "That's a shard of bone from his pelvic fracture. You can see it on the CT."

"Oh." Todd removed his hand and deflated visibly. "Well, how the hell would I know that? I'm not a bone surgeon."

You got that right, Dickwad.

"Wait, could that spike of bone have lacerated the vessel?"

Rylan felt around some more. "It's nowhere near the external iliac vessels and, even if it was, the spike of bone is tiny. Look, Todd, my ex-fix is fine and not the source of the bleeding. It must be somewhere else. The splenic bed? A residual bleeder you may have missed? A tie that came loose?"

"It can't be."

Together, they explored the area where the spleen had been removed and discovered a large clot. Rylan had only seconds to bask in the glory of being right before all hell broke loose when Todd removed the clot and a fountain of blood gushed from the wound.

A flurry of activity broke out from behind the drape at the head of the table accompanied by a "What the bloody, fucking hell!" as multiple pints of blood were flung onto the IV poles, one after another, wrapped with blood pressure cuffs to squeeze the blood in even faster.

They quickly found exactly what Rylan had predicted, a small branch of the splenic artery where a suture tie had come off.

"Incompetent third-year resident," Todd said. While Rylan could tell Todd was trying to divert the blame to the third-year general surgery resident who had helped with the original procedure, she was sure Todd would never have allowed that resident an opportunity to tie off such a crucial vessel. No, this was all Todd's doing, and she would never let him live it down. She would hold it over his head like the sword of Damocles until his dying days. Such was the surgical culture. No one ever forgot a screwup. Ever.

"Speak of the devil," Rylan said as the "incompetent third-year resident" entered the room.

"Where the hell have you been?" Todd yelled like a wounded animal. "Get your ass scrubbed and get in here. This is your fault …"

Shit rolled downhill, and Todd went on a tirade that mingled expletives, insults, and derogatory comments as to the resident's upbringing, all in equal portions. A classic tactic of "the best defense being a strong offense." No one in the room was fooled, though. Fortunately, the poor resident heard little of it as he was outside at the scrub sink, and by the time he reentered, Todd had run out of breath.

Rylan looked over the drape separating the surgical field from the head of the bed. The squall had died down, and the patient appeared to have stabilized. She noticed Dr. English was watching her. When they made eye contact, he simply nodded his head, as one colleague did to another.

Rylan felt for the first time in her life the smallest ounce of what her father must have experienced on a daily basis. Respect with a capital "R." And it felt amazing.

Rylan said to Todd, "Looks like you've got a handle on this."

"Yes, yes, I've got a handle on this," he said in a pissy voice. "You may go."

I may go? Once a Dickwad, always a Dickwad.

She turned to Larry, who was gowning and gloving the third-year resident, and gave him a wink and a crinkly-eyed under-the-mask smile. "Thanks, Larry. Can you put the same dressings on the ex-fix pin sites when everything is done?"

"With pleasure."

"And, no offense, Larry, but I hope I don't see you again tonight."

"Ha. Same here, Rylan. Hope you get some sleep."

Her pager twinkled, and she suddenly remembered everything else that was going on in the hospital.

Sleep seemed very unlikely.

CHAPTER 25

The Janitor

Sid dumped his spray bottles and rags in a corner of the janitorial closet and stretched his arms wide. He'd seen some red hot crazy working the halls of this hospital, but those doodles on the wall took the cake. Whoever had done that was not a happy customer, not happy at all, and Sid felt a sense of comradery with the writer. Yes, Northern Michigan General sucked. He had the hand to prove it. He arched his back and looked up at the old grimy white ceiling panels in the janitorial closet. The filth was disgusting. Why wasn't he surprised? This hospital was dirtier than a stinking pigsty. He had half a mind to make an anonymous call to the state. *That would show 'em.* At any rate, he wouldn't be tackling that ceiling tonight. Or ever.

Holding the stretch, Sid glanced at the watch on his good wrist out of the corner of his eye and mumbled to himself, "Four-fucking-thirty." He sighed heavily and used his good hand to rub the base of his neck and then his lower back. Twelve-hour shifts always wrecked him, and he had many hours to go. The power failure hadn't helped. He worked through it, though, trusty headlamp and all. By God, his work would get done, and nothing would stop him.

Sure, he resented being a janitor, but he was a good worker. And he needed the job. That's why he wouldn't actually call the state – he'd just be shooting himself in the foot if something were to happen to this job. Besides, Sid knew the hospital was already doing a good job bringing itself down. A janitor hears and sees plenty of things without being noticed, and Sid had caught the death talk creeping through the halls. Everyone was wondering about the "unexplained deaths." *Unexplained,* yeah. Sid could explain them. He could give those curious administrators an earful if any of them would give him the time of day. He could tell them that with "doctors" like that Rylan Fraser running the show, they were lucky anyone escaped the place alive and unmaimed. Every time Sid even thought her name, he felt the pain amplify in his bad hand. How he hoped she'd get nailed for malpractice or worse. It was time for her to pay her debt.

He pulled his old iPod from the front pocket of his overalls and scrolled. He needed something that would calm his nerves and get him through the rest of this miserable shift. He made his choice and adjusted his earbuds. The sounds of ocean waves gently pushing onto the beach filled his brain. He loved the tranquility of the beach. Meditation was something he'd learned at the chronic pain center in the years after his accident, something that actually helped, at least sometimes. A soothing male voice began reciting a mantra as Sid placed a bucket under the sink faucet and prepped for a final cleanup.

"Take a deep breath," the voice said, "a long deep breath in through your nose and out through your –"

Disorienting darkness suddenly enveloped his little room, and he felt something cinch tightly around his neck. Someone grabbed his good arm and jammed it up high behind his back and then forced his body into the wall and held him there.

He cursed loudly, but his voice seemed to echo directly into his ears. He brought his bad hand to his face and felt plastic. His heart accelerated and he sucked a deep breath, coming up short, like when your diaphragm cramps after a run. The plastic stuck to his dry lips, sealing his mouth. Panic gripped him, and he flailed with his bad hand at the plastic bag over his head. He grabbed at the tie around his neck, trying to pry his fingers under, but he couldn't push hard enough to make a space. He tried to spin but was pinned heavily against the wall. He tried hitting the assailant with his bad hand, but that only ignited lightning bolts in his fingers.

Sid became lightheaded and felt his knees buckle. The sounds of his struggle became distant to him, and he slowly slid down the wall. Strong arms dragged him, lifted his body, and dumped him into his large sink, like a sack of filthy rags. The light in the room flicked on, and through the fog of his own residual breath, he saw a blurred figure hovering over him.

"Nothing personal. You were just in the wrong place at the wrong time."

Black spots flickered through his vision and a tunnel formed. He knew he wasn't just fainting. He was dying. One earbud was still in place, and the last sounds he heard were the ocean and a voice calmly directing him to *relax and take a deep breath.*

CHAPTER 26

Paul

Paul stepped into the hall and pulled the call room door shut behind him. He'd had just enough time to wash his face and swish a bit of toothpaste around his mouth before his next curtain call. This time, a page to the fifth-floor medical unit for a patient with acute mental status changes.

He took the stairs. Probably not the brightest move, he realized all too late. His bad leg whined in protest with each step. How appropriate that on this night of all nights, it was acting up again. How fucking perfect.

Navigating the hospital's sleepy corridors, it dawned on Paul that Helen hadn't paged. He supposed that meant Jane Doe's body wasn't buried under the snow after all. Thank God for that.

Paul heard rubber soles squeaking along the linoleum. The elderly doctor – the one with the deerstalker cap and leather bag – approached from about fifteen yards down the hall. Paul was surprised to see the old guy still awake. But, then again, he probably hadn't been able to snag a call room. They had disappeared faster than chum in a shark tank when it became clear that no one in house was leaving tonight thanks to Mother Nature and her sick sense of humor. A raging blizzard on the eve of Thanksgiving. How fucking perfect.

Paul gave the old man – *what was his name again?* – a sympathetic smile. In return, the man gave Paul a look of squinty-eyed suspicion. His gaze flitted between Paul's face and ID badge, and he passed by without a word. Paul shook his head. Something was definitely not right about the guy.

Up ahead, an elevator door opened, and Rylan emerged in a little puff of manic energy, like a racehorse out of the gate at the Belmont Stakes. She took off toward unit five. Paul shouted her name.

She stopped and turned. "Hey, you," she said, almost smiling – but not quite. She waited for Paul to catch up, and he could actually see pleasure and dread sparring on the battleground of her pretty face. "What brings you here?" she asked.

"Paged," he said.

"Me, too." She sucked a big breath into her lungs and squared her shoulders, then pushed open the heavy double door that led to unit five.

By now, the scene that greeted them was all-too-familiar. A forsaken crash cart in the hallway. A few staff debriefing in hushed tones by the nursing station.

The little clique at the nurse's station looked up when Rylan and Paul approached. There were stifled coughs and a bit of uncomfortable shifting.

"Dr. Fraser. Hi," said one of the nurses. Her tone was artificially bright, and her expression was unmistakably guilty.

"What happened here?" Rylan gestured towards the crash cart. Paul thought it was pretty obvious what had happened.

"Mr. Briggs in room 532 coded. He didn't make it. We were just about to page you."

"I was already paged, like five minutes ago. The caller said he had a fever, not that he was coding."

A few dubious looks passed around. "No one paged."

Paul stepped forward, holding up his beeper. "I was also paged. Same patient." His announcement was met with blank faces.

"And you are …?" one of the nurses asked.

"Dr. Bennett. Psychiatry."

Someone snorted. The idea that anyone would page psychiatry during a code was absurd.

"Can someone please tell me what happened?" Rylan's imploring eyes landed on one particular young woman. "Millie?"

A nurse in sky-blue scrubs separated from the group. Her fingers closed gently around Rylan's elbow, and she tugged her aside. Paul searched the faces of the small group left behind. Perhaps they could get to the bottom of this. But they only gazed back at him with quizzical expressions, like they were wondering why he was still there. So, Paul turned and followed Rylan. Like a puppy.

"What is going on?" Rylan asked. Her voice was loud. Too loud, Paul thought. Another quarter turn of the dial and she'd be shouting. She was losing control. "I was up here a few hours ago. No one said Mr. Briggs was having any complications."

"He wasn't," Millie said. "All vitals were stable, everything was fine, and then he just flatlined."

"People don't just flatline. There has to be *some* reason."

"I know." Millie fidgeted uncomfortably, then dropped her voice. "Listen, Dr. Fraser, I have to tell you that there has been a lot of strange talk around here tonight. People are saying that you've lost several patients and maybe …"

"Maybe what?"

"Maybe it's your fault."

"Oh, good God!" This time it was most definitely a shout. She buried both hands in her hair and tugged angrily.

Millie continued. "I know it's not true, Dr. Fraser, but just so you know, we are not allowed to let you see patients one-on-one until things are sorted out."

Rylan's face turned white, then red – as red as if someone had slapped her. Paul understood that someone had, in fact, just sort of slapped her. "On whose orders?"

"Dr. Whittaker."

"Dr. Whittaker, that fu –" She stopped herself and took a deep breath. When she spoke again, it was with forced calm. "Dr. Whittaker thinks I'm killing his patients?"

Millie blustered. "I don't think –"

Rylan raised a hand. "It's fine," she said. Her voice was suddenly smooth as cream. "Fine. I won't see any more patients tonight. I'll go sack out in a call room for the rest of the shift, and Dr. Whittaker can do whatever he wants."

Millie shook her head. "He still wants you to see patients since you're … you know … on call." She closed her eyes and scrunched her face, saying the next part very fast. "You just have to be chaperoned in patient rooms."

"Chaperoned," Rylan repeated. She pressed her palms together and touched them to her mouth. "Great. That's just great." She dropped her hands back to her sides and balled them into tense fists. "I may be a suspected murderer, but under no circumstances should I be relieved of even ten minutes of call." She gawped at Paul with a *can-you-believe-this-shit* expression.

Paul, actually, could believe this shit. After all, it was, what, Rylan's fourth patient to die that night? He was certain, absolutely certain, that Rylan was guilty of no wrongdoing, but there were definitely some bad optics. He tried to bolster Rylan with a look of appropriately supportive outrage then asked, "What about me? Do I require a chaperone, too?"

Millie studied Paul for a moment like she was just noticing him for the first time. "Who are you again?"

This did nothing to stoke Paul's ego, but it was fine. "I'm Dr. Bennett, the psychiatrist. I have also been paged to all the rooms with the dead patients."

Millie stared at him like he was a buzzing fly begging for a swat. "None of us know who you are."

Paul's lips formed a tight smile, and he took a step back. *Okay then.*

Rylan, kindly, tried to soften the sting of Paul's indignation. "He's our new psychiatrist. He just started …" But she quickly gave up, having her own fish to fry. "Oh, never mind, it doesn't matter." She shook her head impatiently and took a deep breath. "More importantly, have you seen Pockface up here?"

"*Pockface?*"

"You know who he is, right? He's this big –"

"Yeah, I know who he is. We've had him on the unit plenty of times, but I haven't seen him tonight."

Rylan frowned and looked up and down the hall like she doubted the veracity of this statement.

"What about a strange, old doctor?" Paul asked. "He carries a black bag."

"Dr. Upslinger?" Millie looked at Paul like he had finally uttered something not ridiculous. "Sure, he's been in and out all night. He assisted with the code on Mr. Briggs."

I'll bet he did, Paul thought. He tried to telegraph his suspicion to Rylan, but she didn't seem to pick up. She just said, "Let's get out of here."

Paul could not deny the wisdom of this plan. "Gladly."

Together, they headed back toward the double doors. They clicked shut behind them, and Paul waited for what he sensed was coming. Three, two, one …

Rylan exploded. "What the fuck?!"

Paul sighed. "Look, Rylan, don't take it personally."

"Don't take it personally?" She gave him an incredulous look. "Rumors are flying around the hospital. I am being accused of incompetence, or" – she cackled hysterically – "murder. How do I not take it personally?"

Paul considered the question before responding. She had a point. "Listen, you're being scapegoated. It happens all the time in systems like this. Something has gone wrong, so there has to be some finger-pointing. You just happen to be at the wrong end of the finger."

"I have a finger right here I'd like to show a few people."

Paul laughed. "I get it." They walked on a bit, and Paul said, "You know, this will all blow over soon, and your good name will be restored to all its resident-of-the-century glory."

"Are you sure?" Rylan asked. "How do you know I'm *not* the killer?"

Paul gave Rylan an appraising look. "Please. I've seen plenty of killers, and you're no killer."

"Plenty of killers?" Rylan gasped, fighting a smile. "Your experience is vast and impressive, Dr. Bennett."

"Plenty."

"And what, pray tell, does a killer look like?"

Paul stopped walking. Rylan stopped a few steps later when she realized he had fallen behind. She about-faced until the two stood gazing at each other in the middle of the hallway. The mood shifted, and their playful smiles faded. Paul tilted his head to the side and studied Rylan's features. Gently, he tucked an errant piece of hair behind her ear. "Not like you," he breathed quietly.

Rylan's green eyes connected with Paul's. She did not say a word, but those eyes said many things, and, spellbound, Paul listened. At least until a pair of orderlies – Paul couldn't help but name them *Tweedle Dee* and *Tweedle Dum* – stepped out of the elevator, and the noise from their graceless movements split the air like thunder on a summer night.

Paul and Rylan resumed their walk.

"So," Paul asked, reluctantly ejected from the spell, "is that our working hypothesis? The patients are being murdered?"

"That's *my* working hypothesis," Rylan said. "That Pockface is going around smothering patients with his big, raw hands and his stolen, hospital-issue pillow."

"But why would he?"

"Because he's a psychopathic asshole!"

Paul considered this argument. Though persuasive, there were flaws. "But how does he know exactly which patients are yours? And why would *I* be involved? Pockface doesn't know me."

Rylan threw up her hands in exasperation. "I don't know."

Paul tapped his fingertips along his thigh. Rylan was pretty fixated on Pockface, but the strange, little doctor kept flitting in and out of Paul's thoughts. The way he scrutinized Paul's face … his nametag …

"Hey, maybe we can get some answers from the autopsies. I'm going back down to the pathology lab. Do you want to come along?"

"Well, I believe you need a chaperone."

Rylan swatted his shoulder. "Considering I was assaulted last time I was down there, I really do need a strong chaperone." She made a show of reaching for her cell phone. "Maybe I should see if Helen is available."

Paul cleared his throat. "Very nice."

•   •   •   •   •

Five minutes later, Paul found himself under bright fluorescent lights deep in the bowels of the hospital. The autopsy suite was manned by a tall, lanky pathologist shaped like a human Q-tip. Dr. Greyson had a bushy mop of curls on top of his head, and he was covered in skin so pale it glowed. While Rylan made introductions, Paul regarded the soiled gloves that shielded Dr. Greyson's hands, anxious that one might soon be extended his way. Thankfully, it was not, and the two men just mumbled the socially appropriate *nice-to-meet-ya's*.

Greyson had an open, earnest face, and Paul couldn't help but notice the unmasked delight that appeared on it when he addressed Rylan. "How's your head?" he asked.

"Just a little bump. Thanks again for calling security."

"You bet." Greyson peeled off his gloves and dropped them into a biohazard bin. "I'm just glad you're alright. You were unconscious for a few minutes there." He scanned Rylan's face as if checking for evidence of lingering damage. "Anyway, it's good you came back. There's something I want to show you." He crossed the room to a computer terminal. "The preliminary labs are back on the first two autopsies – I had them rushed – and there's something."

They moved over to the computer as he fiddled adeptly with the keyboard, and the images on two of the three screens were quickly replaced with lab values. Rylan scanned the screens, noting Mr. Kettering and Mrs. Potter's names at the top.

Dr. Greyson stepped back and pointed. "Potassium," he said.

"Potassium," Rylan repeated, studying the values. "I don't understand. The potassium looks a little high, but nothing crazy. Isn't that totally normal after death?"

Greyson nodded. "That's right. The blood level is nothing crazy, but the concentration in the heart is high. Unusually high. Plus, there are lanceolate crystals in the heart tissue, which are indicative of potassium accumulation. We'll need to study the tissue under electron microscopy, but –"

Paul put up a hand. "Hold up. Psychiatrist in the room," he said, tapping his forefinger on his chest. "Remind me of what high potassium does?"

Greyson nodded and turned to face Paul. "A bolus of potassium given quickly will stop a heart. That's why potassium chloride is the juice of choice for lethal injections on death row."

Paul nodded. He understood. And he was surprised that Greyson had figured out so much in so little time. "So, what you are saying ..."

"What I am saying" – Greyson glanced back at the screen and then at Rylan – "is that Dr. Fraser's patients are being executed."

CHAPTER 27

Pockface

The man in sweats and hospital socks stood tucked into a small recess – really, nothing more than an armpit – where the surgical ward met the D wing. The hood of his black sweatshirt was pulled tight around his face in a half-hearted attempt to conceal his identity, though he knew the effort was futile. Size always gave him away. He placed the palm of one gigantic hand on the door latch while taking one last peek toward the surgical unit to make sure none of those night-shift skanks were looking his way – he especially hated the helmet-headed Linda who was always pissing and moaning about something (and reminded him way too much of his mother) – and found the coast clear. "Okay," he muttered, "time to see what's behind door number three." Pockface pushed the door open and walked through.

It was dark on this side of the doors save for a gentle glow coming from the nursing station halfway down the hall. The doors behind him clicked shut, and a smell of fresh wax overwhelmed his olfactory senses, triggering an epic wave of nausea. Pockface pressed against a wall and waited for it to pass, squeezing his eyes shut and taking sharp, uneven breaths through his mouth. His stomach was a mess, and his heart was thumping an angry rhythm that had nothing to do with nerves. He needed more candy pills, and he needed them fast. The thought of that condescending bitch, Fraser, refusing to discharge him with a pain script distracted him with rage, and he only crested the wave of nausea by fantasizing how satisfying it would be to pummel the holier-than-thou look off her face with a jagged two-by-four. Recovered, he wiped sweat from his prickly, bald head and stood stock-still, listening for sound or movement. There was none. Time to find the medication room.

Pockface ambled quietly down the hall on his ginormous, socked feet and followed the light to the nursing station, skirting a dumpster filled with construction debris. The nursing station was deserted, as expected. A smell of drywall and fresh paint competed here with the floor wax smell, and his queasiness returned posthaste. He shook it off as best he could and swept the newly renovated station with his eyes until they landed on a door to the left. He peered through the door's thick glass pane. "Bingo!"

Although the light was off on the other side of the door, enough streamed through from the nursing station that he could see neatly stacked shelves of meds. He tried the handle and found it locked. Of course, it was locked. "Goddammit, shit!" He squinted through the window, trying to make out labels in the dark. He knew it was unlikely to contain any of the heavy stuff, but he bet there would at least be some percs. With his hammering heart and shaking hands, there was suddenly nothing more important to him in the whole world than getting inside that room. Only a wired glass panel separated him from what he wanted, and wired glass panels could be dealt with. He just needed the right tool.

Pockface swung around and headed straight for the dumpster to see what he might find amidst the construction waste. Just as he turned, however, he caught sight of a young girl, a child, really, in a hospital gown running down the adjoining hall. He blinked and she was gone. Pockface paused for a second and thought of going after her. But just for a second. It made no sense that a child would be on a deserted unit in the middle of the night. His mind was playing tricks. It certainly wouldn't be the first time he'd seen things that weren't there when he needed a fix. Besides, even if there was a loose kid on the unit, so what? Not his problem.

He scanned the dumpster for something that could smash glass. There was nothing obvious on top, so he began rooting around, searching for a metal pipe or even a broken chunk of the old laminate countertop. With a sense of growing desperation, Pockface convinced himself he could make almost anything work. Finally, his hand closed around a hard and smooth object. He leaned forward over the dumpster, tossing obstacles aside in a frenzy to free the instrument of his salvation. *Come to papa, baby.* A beautiful, 18-inch galvanized steel pipe snaked a path upward from the dark depths of the dumpster and broke through to the surface. Pockface gripped it with his right hand and lifted it over his head in triumph. *Yes, yes, yes!* The mental high-fiving ceased instantly, though, when a needle pricked his skin, and white-hot fire flamed through his neck.

CHAPTER 28

Rylan

"Let's have some fun?" Mike asked wearily, his mask off and dangling from one ear. His furrowed brows hovered over bloodshot eyes, and his head was cocked to the side, threatening to fall from his neck.

"That's what the voice said. Right after congratulating me on my award," Rylan said. "It happened earlier this evening before my patients started dying. With everything that's been going on, I'd completely forgotten about it until we got the results back from the patholo … pathologel – Fuck! I'm so tired I can't even say pa-tho-lo-gist." She enunciated slowly and carefully, her tongue fat and uncoordinated. She covered her face with both hands and rubbed her eyes.

Rylan and Mike were leaning against the main desk in the ER, a crutch to prevent them from toppling to the floor with exhaustion. Rylan had convinced Paul that the safety of the ER was the best place to figure things out, a sort of headquarters. That, and she wanted to alert Mike. It was just past 6AM, and the world remained pitch black outside, with snow plastered two-thirds up the windows. A weary, wide-eyed Carla, the ER clerk, looked up at them from behind the desk. "Wait," she said in her deep voice, "are you saying there's someone in the hospital killing our patients?"

Both Mike and Rylan turned to "Shhh" her. "Carla," Mike said, "let's keep this on the down low, okay? No need to create a panic."

Rylan, looking at Carla's worried face, immediately thought, *There's no way she's keeping this quiet. This whole hospital will know in the next ten minutes.*

"Seriously, Carla," Mike said, "you can't tell anyone. If this nutjob catches wind, who knows what could happen?"

Carla stood abruptly. "Seriously, Mike? We are completely snowed in. Completely isolated. No one can get to us, including the police. The phone lines are down, and cell phone connection is touch-and-go. The power always seems to be on the brink of going out. You're telling me there's a serial killer on the loose in our hospital. And you want to keep it quiet?"

As if to emphasize this last statement, silence descended upon the ER. Staff and patients froze in position, and tired, inquisitive faces swiveled toward Rylan, Mike, and Carla. The only sound now was the low, groaning howl at the windows, as if the wind also was trying to find a way through to listen in on the conversation.

Mike sighed, gave Carla an evil stare, and then put both his hands in the air with his palms facing the crowd. He cleared his throat and began:

"Look, everyone. It has come to our attention that there have been several unexplained deaths in our hospital over the past twelve hours. We are investigating as best we can, given the circumstances. As everyone already knows, all roads are blocked from the storm, so we are currently without police assistance. I want everybody to keep calm and hunker down. Use the buddy system. No one goes anywhere alone, okay? On the plus side, we have no patients coming in, so we only have to deal with those already here."

A barrage of questions filled the air.

"Have any staff been killed?"

"Where are the deaths happening?"

"What kind of investigations?"

"Do we know anything about the killer?"

"Who is being targeted?"

Mike did his best to calm staff and patients alike, fielding each question in turn. Rylan took the opportunity to back away, and as she was doing so, her pager twinkled its deadly tune once again. She glanced at the four-digit number and didn't recognize it. She stepped over to an in-house landline and dialed. A male voice answered immediately.

"Dr. Fraser, you have an off-service patient in room E603. A 28-year-old male status post-tibial nailing from yesterday morning."

"With whom am I speaking?" Rylan searched her beleaguered memory, trying to recall any such surgeries yesterday morning but came up blank. It was possible, of course, that she was not involved in the case. Typically, though, it would have been signed out to her for the holiday weekend.

"Who is this?" she asked again. "And I don't know of any tibial nailing done yesterday."

"It looks like compartment syndrome. Come quickly."

"Compartment syndrome?" This ominous pronouncement caught her attention, tugging it away from her determination to learn the caller's identity. "What makes you think that? Does he have any of the "P" signs and symptoms?"

Rylan paused to catch her breath. By "P" signs, she was referring to the five signs – pain out of proportion, pallor, pulselessness, paresthesia, and paralysis – that every medical student knew by heart about a serious orthopedic condition called "compartment syndrome." In this syndrome, swelling (usually due to a traumatic event) caused the pressures in the compartments of a leg or arm to become so great that muscles, nerves, and vessels were compressed to the point of non-viability, creating a dead limb and a surgical emergency.

"Well, does he? And who's speaking? Is this a nurse?"

The line was silent. A repeat performance of every other phone call where someone ended up in the morgue.

"Hello? Dammit!"

This reeked of another killing, but there was always that possibility it could be legit. The last thing she wanted to do was ignore a potentially limb-threatening situation. She looked to Mike for help, but he was up to his eardrums in staff and patient questions.

There was no way she was going without backup. She walked over to Helen's security desk. She needed to tell her that she had just received another suspicious call in a series of suspicious calls, each of which ended with an otherwise-stable patient being found dead. Were other on-call docs having this experience, or was it just her? It seemed a real-life murderer was on the loose in their hospital. No, not just a murderer – a fucking serial killer. A serial killer targeting Rylan's patients. A shiver crawled up her spine, sending little bursts of unwanted adrenaline into her hands and feet.

She rounded a corner, exiting the ER just as the blare of a fire alarm reverberated through the halls. A code red was announced overhead. It gave her an instant, splitting headache. When she arrived at the desk, Helen was already on her radio. She looked up at Rylan and said, "Gotta run, hon. Someone pulled an alarm in the admin wing. What a night. Catch up later, okay?"

Before Rylan could utter a word, Helen's heavy-set frame was accelerating away from the desk and down the corridor. Rylan sighed and pivoted 180 degrees, still holding the pager in her hand, trying to figure out what to do next.

She wandered back to the main ER desk with the klaxon still howling, and she felt like it was following her. She put one finger in her ear and was still staring at the pager when a newly familiar voice yelled, "You have that look. Did you get another page?"

Rylan looked up at Paul, smiled wearily, and nodded her head in affirmation.

Paul was shaking his head slowly from side to side with a grim look on his face, also holding his pager. "Me too, but I haven't answered it yet."

It was a special thing to have someone she could talk to. She impulsively grabbed his hand and pulled him into a nearby empty examination room. She closed the door, muffling the fire alarm.

"Sorry," she said, her hand still gripping the sleeve of his Armani jacket as she turned to look at him. "That was giving me a killer headache."

Paul paused for a long moment, then stepped closer. He gently placed his hand over the back of Rylan's neck and began massaging the base of her skull. "Well," he replied, "I can sympathize. It's been a crazy long night. I've had a wicked sleep-deprivation headache for hours, and that fire alarm isn't helping."

Rylan, for the first time tonight, let down her guard, closed her eyes, and melted. She wanted so much to collapse into his arms and make all the terrible events of the night go away. A chance to dream a better reality where no one had died, her trauma victim had survived, and her shift finished in the cafeteria with she and Paul discussing future dinner plans over shitty coffee and stale muffins.

The fire alarm stopped as suddenly as it had started, leaving an uncomfortable silence between them that was quickly filled with the awareness of a serial killer on the loose and a 28-year-old patient about to lose his leg.

Her eyes sprang open, and she saw that he was staring at her. She dug deep and did the exact opposite of what she wanted to do. She pulled back and said, "There was another phone call."

She filled him in on the details, biting her lower lip ferociously while she flipped the pager that was still in one hand over and over like a domino.

When she was done, Paul placed his hand around hers and gently squeezed, holding the revolving pager in check. "Even if this is another fake out, I don't see that we have any choice. We can't let a 28-year-old man lose his leg."

We. Rylan thought. A *We* was a powerful thing.

Comforted, she looked into his tired hazel eyes. He smiled back at her, released her hand, and, for the second time tonight, reached out with a finger to tuck an errant strand of auburn hair behind her ear. His hand lingered there as he said, "Your hair seems to have a mind of its own."

She self-consciously brought her hand to her ear, her index finger grazing his, their eyes connected. "It does sometimes have a mind of its own."

Their fingers remained touching for a fleeting moment, sending a different kind of adrenaline coursing through her hand, the kind that shot straight down to the lower half of her body.

We can't let a 28-year-old man lose his leg.

She stepped away abruptly. "We have to go."

•　　•　　•　　•　　•

Rylan and Paul stood in front of the large steel doors that led from the surgical wing through the D wing, past the area where she had met the janitor, through another set of steel doors, and finally to the E wing and room E603 where Rylan's patient supposedly was. She had checked with Carla, the ER ward clerk who had been working at the hospital forever, and a glance at her computer screen confirmed there were patients on that floor, overflow from the regular medical ward. The standard way to get there was accessing elevators from the ground floor in the E wing, however, Carla had pointed out that passing through the 6th-floor surgical ward was much faster. Despite Rylan's hesitations, and with some prompting from Paul, they agreed that if they were going to do this, speed was of the essence.

Rylan felt a few drops of perspiration trinkle down between her shoulder blades. She had begun the charge from the ER at breakneck speed up the stairwell until she noticed Paul limping behind, struggling with one leg. She suggested they take the elevator, but he said he was fine. She slowed down, and he explained to her the findings on the fifth floor, the crazy mural, the marker, the open window, and the slip and fall that injured his knee. He said it was an old football injury and would get better on its own. She remarked coyly that he didn't look like a football player. He half-smiled and picked up the pace.

When she thought about the mural, the marker, and the open window, she couldn't see how it was connected to her four deceased patients. Certainly, it wasn't something she could see Pockface doing. Her mind raced with questions that had no answers.

She reached for the door handle, and memories from her last encounter with the janitor and his gnarled hand surfaced, cavorting around abruptly in her mind until the pieces fell into place and a clear picture formed.

Damn! That's who he is.

She now remembered his was one of the first operative cases she'd scrubbed in on during her plastics rotation at the beginning of residency. She recalled the janitor was none too happy with the results and, for some reason, seemed to blame her. Although she and the plastic surgeon had done the best they could, the outcome was dismal with poor motion of the fingers and considerable residual swelling. More importantly, though, was the ongoing severity of the pain. Her staff man had remarked that that's just the way it was sometimes; you win some and you lose some. She knew now that he was probably in the early stages of complex regional pain syndrome, a terrible complication of traumatic injuries to the upper extremities that produced severe pain, swelling, and stiffness that often never went away.

Rylan stopped in her tracks partway down the hall. How was it, she wondered, that the janitor with the gnarled hand was working at Northern Michigan General Hospital? He obviously had an axe to grind with Rylan. Could he have orchestrated this whole thing? She scanned ahead and noted that, other than the fluorescent light overhead, only one other light was visible, the one creeping under the door of the janitor's closet down the hall. The nursing station which sat at the junction of two intersecting hallways was eerily quiet. Well past the nursing station, she could see the set of windowless steel doors that led to the E wing. She couldn't get there fast enough.

"What's wrong?" Paul asked. "Why are we stopping? Did you see –?" The overhead lights suddenly went out.

Other than the sliver of light from the janitor's room, it was complete blackness.

"Shit!" Rylan yelled. "Generator's out again." She backed into the wall as she fumbled for her phone. It was partway out of her lab coat pocket when it slipped out of her hands and fell to the floor.

"Fuck!" Rylan cried out. "Paul? Are you okay? Do you have your phone?"

No reply.

She felt a whoosh of air pass her, and the tiny hairs on her forearms stood at attention. She crouched to the floor and frantically swept her hand in circles until her fingers met the rectangular shape of her phone. When she touched the screen, a blueish glow emanated from her screensaver. She activated the flashlight and stood. Holding the phone at arm's length, she spun around in a circle.

Paul was nowhere to be seen.

CHAPTER 29

Dr. Upslinger

Reggie Upslinger was the type of man who just naturally blended into the shadows. Sure, on first meet he sometimes earned a raised eyebrow – what with his ever-present deerstalker cap and signature old geezer medical bag – but once that initial curiosity wore off, he became something familiar and harmless, like the rolling blood pressure machines and phlebotomy carts scattered around the hospital floors, lurking at the periphery of awareness until needed.

That's why he was not surprised when the two doctors brushed right by him in a flurry of manic energy without casting so much as a glance his way, that tall psychiatrist in his expensive-looking jacket and his bouncy friend in her surgical scrubs. Reggie wondered where they were racing to at this hour, though his brain was too fatigued to wonder too hard. He had found a quiet, dark waiting area in a delightfully un-trafficked part of the sixth floor, really just two rows of four chairs bolted to the ground beside a neglected water cooler. It wasn't much, but to an exhausted 67-year-old man up way past his bedtime with aching ankles and no call room in which to rest his wearies, it was a gorgeous desert oasis.

Reggie sipped tepid water from a paper cup and rotated one sore ankle, then the other, trying to coax a bit of circulation back into existence. His awful new snow boots were tucked neatly under a chair beside him, the worst $140 he ever spent. Maybe if he shut his eyes and mumbled the right incantations, they would transform into the soft, shearling mules he padded around in at home.

He gave it a try. No luck – the only type that ever spared him a visit these days.

Reggie sat back and rested his eyes. He contemplated his luckier days. Those days when he knew whom he'd be eating Thanksgiving dinner with. Those days when he knew whom he'd be eating every dinner with. Those days that were gone, leaving Reggie neglected and alone in the shadows.

He rubbed a hand across his brow and cupped his forehead in his hand. The weight of his loss was just too much to bear at this hour. And, if the grief tornado didn't succeed in driving him to distraction, there was that little something extra swirling around in the miasma. For hours now, a single, vague, slippery thought had repeatedly nipped the line, then swam off before the reel-in. Insanely frustrating. Reggie shook his head to see if he could knock the wily thought into focus but only managed to instigate a headache. He rolled his eyes, settled back, and gazed left, following the direction in which the two doctors had rushed off. He had seen them open the double doors to the area marked "D-wing" and disappear inside, which he found strange since he'd had the distinct impression the unit was closed. Or, on second thought, maybe not so strange. Two attractive young people, a snowed-in hospital, a deserted unit …

He knew how it went. He had been young once. In the early years, it seemed he and Betsy couldn't go fifteen minutes without putting their hands on each other. Just a certain look or meeting of the eyes would tug them both back to bed like a couple of yo-yos on delightfully tense strings. In those early years, they had been so careful, taking the necessary precautions – by mutual agreement – to delay children until they completed their medical trainings and established careers. Then, there were the later years when they abandoned the precautions and eagerly awaited the children. But the children never came.

Reggie looked down at his toes, slightly gnarled and bony under his wool socks, and thought they looked about as forlorn as he felt. His vision blurred as he – not for the first time – pondered the what-ifs. What if he and Betsy had had children? What if they had known days filled with skinned knees and math homework and violin recitals? What if there was a daughter to wear Betsy's soft smile and hallmark dimples after she was gone?

Thoughts like these did no good. Reggie could catalog his regrets from here to Sunday, and it wouldn't change anything. He slouched back in his chair and steepled his hands over his belly. He needed to pull himself back to the here and now. He began to rhythmically tap his fingers together and run through items on a mental checklist. *Let's see …*

That patient in heart failure had been successfully transferred to the ICU – he'd check on her status before he went home.

He was still waiting on the CBC for the fever on five …

He opened his eyes and glanced at his watch. He'd check the computer to see if results were back in another – he yawned into his right hand – twenty minutes or so. Then he could check those potassiums he was waiting on, too.

Twenty minutes or so.

Reggie started to drift into that space between sleep and wakefulness where the conscious mind surrenders control. Reggie was pretty sure his unconscious mind was ruled by some cruel and vindictive second-rate miscreant, some fat guy in sweats grinning maniacally and gripping one end of a tug-of-war rope, forever yanking Reggie's thoughts back to the same familiar, grief-soaked place.

Betsy.

Okay, he'd play. He had no choice. Whether asleep or awake, he had to tug his end of the rope to find the bearable equilibrium between grief for what was lost and gratitude for what he had. So, he grieved the fact that there were no offspring to carry Betsy's intelligence, wit, and grace into the future. But he was grateful Betsy had left a legacy all the same. She left a beautiful and humble one that would carry into the future and affect the lives of many – although the many would probably never know her name. Reggie knew that every young doctor Betsy mentored was a better doctor because of it. Every student, every resident, every research fellow. Betsy had taught them how to recognize and treat illness, sure, but, even more importantly, she taught them to recognize and treat people. Never forget, she would tell her supervisees, every person you meet with a mental health issue is someone's son, someone's daughter, someone who entered this world bathed in an aura of dreams and potential like every other person ever born.

A woman like no other.

Reggie sank further into the hard, plastic chair. His head lolled to one side. His lips parted a little bit. And, like that, he was dreaming. A good dream, this one. Snippets of Sunday mornings. Those first Sundays of the month when Betsy would have her research fellows to the house for bagels and coffee while they reviewed data and planned for the upcoming weeks. Typically, there would be some intense formal discussion for, oh, about twenty to thirty minutes, then there would be the inevitable devolvement into affable chatter and laughter. Voices would comingle and escape into the kitchen where Reggie would be biding his time, reading spectacles on, newspaper spread across the table. But he'd be listening, always listening, for the moment when the business portion of the meeting was complete, and the camaraderie portion would begin. Because then he would be invited in. And there would be scones. The most delightful blueberry scones. Together, they would eat and talk and laugh, a makeshift family of sorts. Every two years, the group would shift. Some fellows would leave the nest and launch into their careers. New fellows would come. The Sunday morning tradition, legendary, would continue.

Betsy's last cohort of fellows had been a particularly enjoyable group. There was Sophia, a dark-haired Italian beauty with a throaty laugh who always had one button too many undone on her blouse (although Reggie, of course, never looked.) She'd talk about what restaurant she'd eaten at the night before while regaling the group with mishaps from her dating escapades. There was Jervais, a lean Haitian man with broad shoulders and funky braided hair who had a membership to the Rock and Roll Hall of Fame and always seemed to have an inside line on where to catch the best live music. Then there was the thoughtful young man Reggie thought of as The Bringer of the Scones. That one was a true child of the heartland, raised on chicken and dumplings, cold winters, and church potluck suppers. He was soft-spoken and polite to a fault, with pure, blue eyes behind wire-rimmed glasses and a slightly receding hairline. He lived with a steady boyfriend, and both were self-proclaimed "foodies" – which is why he knew the best café in the city to pick up the very best blueberry scones (and also may have accounted for the little extra padding around his middle). He always struck Reggie as being older than his years, more mature somehow. It was he who spoke those lovely words to Reggie at Betsy's graveside.

She was the best teacher I ever had …
… an all-around great person. Truly, a woman like no other.

Reggie awoke with a start. For a moment, he was confused about where he was, but then things fell into focus. Crystal clear focus. Finally, he understood what had been bothering him, niggling at his brain. Betsy's young psychiatry fellow, the one with the blueberry scones and kind words of condolence … was Paul Bennett.

CHAPTER 30

Paul

Paul caught sight of her while the lights were still on. Just a glimpse of pale skin and tangled, brown hair. The Jane Doe from the psych ER poked her head from one of the rooms along the south hall, then ducked quickly back inside. Paul glanced at Rylan, but she had stopped moving and was looking in another direction altogether. "Why are we stopping?" he asked, pivoting his head between Rylan and the apparition down the hall. The question bounced off Rylan's back, and she neither turned around nor responded. Whatever had caught her attention was holding on tight. Paul began, "Did you see –"

But the lights went out while he was mid-sentence. He heard Rylan swear and fumble. It sounded like something dropped to the floor. Paul took the opportunity to move off down the south hall, a little discombobulated in the dark and praying his homing signals were up to snuff. He had a general sense of where the room was. He also had a penlight in his pocket, but he didn't want to use it. Not yet.

Paul heard Rylan call his name, but to respond would have been to give up the advantage of stealth, so he remained silent and walked quickly, arms outstretched before him like a mummy. This was something he needed to handle alone.

Feeling his way to a woman in the dark, Paul couldn't help but recall a game he used to play with a former lover. A game that involved dark rooms, blindfolds, and a great deal of tactile exploration. He had been very good at it. And, if memory served, so had she. Lord, that game had been fun. An improbable tingle stirred around his groin but was fast stifled by the incessant throbbing in his bad leg. That part had *not* been fun. Paul frowned in self-admonishment. He needed to remain on task. A stroll down memory lane could wait for later. Right now, there were much more pressing concerns.

He reached the doorway into which the girl had disappeared. At least he thought it was the right door. He squinted inside but didn't see anyone. He paused with a hand on the doorjamb and turned back to where he'd left Rylan who had just managed to get the flashlight on her cell phone working. Paul quickly passed from the hall into the room without being seen. If the girl from the psych ER was here, and he was pretty sure she was, then he was dealing with a delicate situation that required careful damage control.

Glass crunched underfoot and Paul froze, straining his gaze this way and that to detect movement, but everything remained still. *Why was there glass?* He carefully extracted the penlight from his pocket and swept the room. The floor was littered with small shards of glass and dark red dots that looked suspiciously like blood spatter. The bathroom door, which was open into the room so that he could see its inside surface, was covered in what one might generously describe as smudge art. Reddish-brown smudges. Paul thought of the mural on the fifth floor and the discarded dry-erase marker, but he knew immediately that this rendering was not the product of any marker. It was blood, absolutely. He could see it and smell it, and it was making him a bit queasy. It was all wrong, and he wanted to shout *What the fuck!?* But then Jane Doe rose from where she was crouching behind the bed. Startled, the beam of Paul's penlight collided directly with her face.

"Put that fucking light away!" she hissed. Her skin glowed white, and her eyes were bloodshot. She looked like someone tired, angry, and one thousand percent out of patience.

Paul dropped the light into his pocket. The vaguest hint of daybreak was on the horizon, lightening the sky outside the room's single snow-pelted window just enough to cast everything inside in eerie silhouette. "What have you been doing?" he hissed back, sweeping an arm from the floor to the bathroom door and back again. "What's all this?"

"Don't you worry about *this*," she half-shouted, half-whispered in response. "I've done everything I was supposed to do. And then some." She laughed as if someone had just told a funny joke. "It's time for me to be going. Get it? I need to be *going*." She put exaggerated emphasis on the last word. "Going, going, gone!" Paul thought she looked positively deranged. "Understand?"

"Why the blood?" he asked.

"Don't ask me about the fucking blood! It's none of your goddamn business!"

She was still whisper-shouting. Paul worried that Rylan might hear. He really hoped Rylan would not hear. He took extra care to keep his own voice low and steady. "You shouldn't have –"

A moment too late, Paul realized the young woman before him was in no mood for any sentence that started with, "You shouldn't have …" She clenched her teeth and snarled, "I am done here. Done. Do you understand? I am going!"

Going, going, gone, Paul finished for her in his head, quick to suppress a smile. There was something almost comical about this tiny little thing trying to call the shots but, he knew better than most, that people could be full of surprises. He considered her teeth, small and crooked and glinting in the dark like the teeth of a wild animal, and he wondered if she was a biter. Biters were the worst. He felt a distinct sense of displeasure when she took a bold step from behind the bed and encroached on his space. "Where are my clothes?" she demanded, a little too close for comfort.

"Your clothes?" he repeated, tapping his chin thoughtfully. "Hmm." Paul took a nonchalant step back, never taking his eyes from Jane Doe. He saw that she was dragging something in her right hand. It looked like a bedsheet.

"My clothes, mutherfucker!"

A bit of spittle hit his chin, and Paul wiped it against his shoulder, unnerved and nauseated. She was literally spitting mad, and he needed to proceed with caution. No room for mistakes here. He raised his hands in a placating manner. "Yes, your clothes. Sure, just give me a minute." While stalling for time, he performed a rapid visual appraisal. Jane Doe was still in her hospital gown. A piece of ripped bedsheet was wrapped around one skinny thigh, bandage-style. Dark stains bled through the fabric. Blood. Of course, blood. Paul sighed. He hadn't known she was a cutter. Another unforeseen complication. What he did know is that he *really* didn't want any of her blood to touch any part of him. He dropped a hand casually into his jacket pocket, relieved to find the small bottle of Purell still there. He stroked it like a kitten while his eyes made a dramatic show of roaming the room in search of a pile of clothes that had thus far escaped notice.

Jane Doe's agitation swelled alongside Paul's hesitation. Finally, it burst into a series of rants that she hissed into the dead space between them. She rambled about how she'd done everything she came to do that night, how she'd done it all perfectly, how it was time to end it, how she wanted to go, and how no one was helping her. How *he* wasn't helping her. Paul listened patiently, feigning wide-eyed interest, nodding his best psychiatrist's nod at appropriate intervals. He wanted her to feel calm because he knew only too well how a cornered human – or a caged animal – could pounce in desperation. And, though she was far from stable, she was also not desperate. At least not yet. She still knew enough to keep her voice down, to keep her presence concealed. She still thought she was getting out of here, and to ensure that end, may have still had a trick or two up her sleeve.

Or perhaps behind her back. It was with increasing alarm that Paul noticed only one of her hands was visible, the one holding the torn bedsheet flecked with blood that she was presumably using to make bandages. (*Resourceful.* Paul had to give her that.) But the other hand, he couldn't help but note, she held behind her back. This whole time, it had been behind her back, and, this whole time, Paul was trying to get a handle on what she was concealing back there. One wrong move and things would go sideways real fast.

The distraction came in the form of a woman's scream. It exploded into the room like a thunderclap, then receded into oblivion, leaving the room in silence. Paul looked at Jane Doe. Jane Doe looked at Paul. Everything was the same except for one thing. A new silhouette in the pre-dawn light. A plunger on one end, a needle on the other. Going, going, gone.

CHAPTER 31

Rylan

"Dammit! PAUL!! Where the hell are you?"

Rylan was frozen in place mid-way down the corridor, both feet stuck to the newly waxed floor, as if she'd stepped on one of those cruel glue-type mousetraps.

Her father's words pushed to the front of her mind: *In our line of work, indecision kills, Rylan. Remember that. It kills.*

Rylan crouched over and pushed the palm of her free hand to her forehead. *I have to do something.*

She looked down the hallway from where they'd come into complete darkness. Was there someone there? Someone who would step out of a shadow and do ... what? Kill her? Was there really a killer on the loose? It all seemed so surreal, so impossible. These kinds of things happened in the movies and on TV, shows like Dexter or True Detective. Not in real life at every day, bland Northern Michigan General Hospital.

She looked in the other direction, and her eyes were immediately drawn to the light sneaking from under the door to the janitor's closet. It was like a beacon, drawing her in. She needed to go to the safety of the light. And she needed to push forward to the E wing to get to her patient. She squeaked one foot forward and then another, holding the phone in front of her like a talisman. Eventually, she found herself planted in front of the door, standing stone still. She listened.

She heard nothing but the kick-drum beat of her heart.

The little hairs on her neck prickled with fear, and her guts snaked into a tight knot. She closed her eyes for a moment to steady herself and drew a deep breath. She reached for the handle, turned, and pulled slowly, her other hand still holding the iPhone flashlight directly in front.

The flood of light blinded her, sending a spectrum of crackling colors racing through her optic nerves. There was the outline of a figure near the large janitorial sink. *In* the sink? Everything was so blurry and hard to make out. She blocked the florescent light overhead with her open hand, and her vision cleared.

She wanted to scream, but her throat's immediate response was to squeeze shut in terror. Her whole sleep-deprived body started to shake uncontrollably. She sucked hard to get breath through her convulsing windpipe, but it was like breathing through a paper straw.

There was someone lodged butt-first in the sink with their legs hanging over one edge and arms and head hanging over the other. A plastic bag was secured with a zip tie around the neck, and the bag was fogged with the victim's final breaths, so Rylan couldn't see the face. But she didn't have to. One look at the man's right arm revealed the gnarled fingers of the janitor, Sid Kosinski.

This time she had no problem getting the scream out.

She covered her mouth with a hand to stop the noise and backed out of the janitorial closet into the dark hall. She turned a slow and quiet one-eighty. A faint glow was coming from the vicinity of the nursing station, suggesting a light in one of the back offices. She realized this was not another generator failure. This was someone messing with the light switches.

Desperately, her hands raked the walls looking for a switch to reverse the darkness, but they were shaking too badly to be of any use. She understood now with perfect clarity that she was the mouse in a sick game of cat-and-mouse. And she needed to get the hell out of there. To run. She just couldn't figure out which way to run in the dark.

Choosing the wrong direction might run her straight into the arms of the attacker.

"Paul?" she called again, but slapped her palm back over her mouth, afraid of giving away her position. No response.

She flattened her back against a wall, willed her legs to stay put, and called 911.

Dead air.

She checked her signal.

No bars.

She crushed her useless cell phone into her chest and squeezed her eyes shut. *Think!*

There would be a landline behind the desk in the nursing station. Internal lines were still working. She could call Helen.

Decision made (*Indecision kills, Rylan*), she took off running towards the nursing station but slammed face first into a large garbage bin, the kind used for renovation-type work. She fell to the floor, her eyes tearing up from the pain in her nose, and her mind spinning with cobwebs. She reached for the side of the bin to pull herself upright, and her hand closed on something cold and fleshy. She drew back and stared at the thing, wiping away the tears with the sleeve of her lab coat. It was a large hand attached to a large forearm.

She leaned into the wall unsteadily, a sharp pain piercing between her eyes, as if a shard of bone from her nose had lodged straight into her frontal lobe. Blinking through tears, she focused on the arm that dangled lifelessly over the edge of the garbage bin.

Part of her brain, the self-preservation part, cried out to get up and run, but she couldn't, or wouldn't. Despite the fear and sleep deprivation, she still had her training etched into each cell of her body, like a soldier after military boot camp. It was the one thing she could fundamentally rely upon when everything else turned to shit.

She shifted her gaze onto the fingers, looking for any movement. There was none. She reached slowly and placed her index and long finger around the wrist, checking for a pulse. There was none.

Her crooked gaze walked up the hand to the forearm where she noted a tattoo of a school crest made up of an alligator, some kind of dog, and staples. She'd seen this before. Then she saw the bandage and had to clench her eyes tight to steady herself. She pulled herself upright, still holding on to the wall for support, and peered over the edge of the bin directly into the open bloodshot eyes of Pockface. A syringe and needle were lodged in the side of his neck. Her mind completely rejected what she was seeing. This couldn't be happening. She stared into Pockface's eyes waiting for him to lunge forward and shout some insulting and demeaning words to her face.

But Pockface was done shouting. He was dead. Another one of her patients dead.

The room began to spin, and her eyes teared again. She was spiraling into tunnel-vision darkness. She had to warn someone before she passed out.

Helen!

She had to call Helen.

She stumbled past the bin, entered the nursing station, and found a landline. She dialed Helen's four-digit extension. The line connected.

"Helen? Helen? Are you there?"

Please be there.

"Rylan?" Helen answered after a moment. "Is that you? You sound strange. Where are –"

"Helen! You need to come. Pockface and the Janitor are dead. Paul is missing."

"What are you talking about, Rylan? Are you alright? Where are you?"

"I'm in the –"

Rylan was so numb from the last 24 hours that she barely felt it. A poke on her shoulder, like a needlestick.

And then she collapsed forward onto the desk.

CHAPTER 32

Helen

Helen stared with baggy, tired eyes at the phone receiver in her hand. Rylan's voice had been on the other end one moment, and then it was gone.

"Rylan!?" she shouted into the phone, but there was no response.

Helen swore and placed a hand to her chest, calming a sudden burst of palpitations. She patted the pocket of her pants, making sure her blood pressure tablets were there. Could this night be for real?

She checked the display for the origin of the call, but it was blank, indicating the receiver at the other end had been hung up. Helen kicked herself for not paying closer attention when the call came through. The four digits on the display would have told her exactly where Rylan was. Now, she could be anywhere in the hospital … with a killer on the loose.

Pockface and the janitor are dead.

What janitor was she talking about? Who would have been working overnight in the middle of the year's biggest snowstorm? And was Paul that new psychiatrist? They must have buddied up, Helen decided, as per Dr. Curran's instructions. But where were they?

Helen rubbed her temples, trying to squeeze an idea out.

Alright. Whatever was happening would certainly create a commotion. If it was on one of the wards, someone would have called the security desk by now. So, it must be somewhere more isolated. She pulled a floor-by-floor map of the hospital from a desk drawer and began flipping through the pages, making mental notes of places in the hospital that she thought were isolated enough.

The basement for sure. Rylan had already been attacked there once.

The first-floor admin area was empty. But she had just been there with her whole team for the false fire alarm and saw nothing out of the ordinary. Although, she supposed the false alarm was out of the ordinary.

The whole rehab area on the fourth floor would be empty and suspect. And then there were the call rooms on the second floor ….

She leafed through the map pages until she arrived at the sixth floor. Something was scratching at her brain, something to do with the janitor. She scanned it in detail and paused when she saw the D-wing.

"That's it." She pulled a clipboard from a hook and flipped through the pages until she found what she was looking for: A notice about the renos and preparations underway to ready the D-wing for the upcoming flu season.

"Of course, there would be janitorial staff working there to prepare it," she said aloud. "And a perfect place for Pockface to hide out."

She drew her walkie-talkie to her mouth and barked a series of orders sending one security guard to check the rehab floor and call rooms, two to the basement, and one more to join her on the sixth-floor surgical ward.

She unconsciously fingered the taser she kept in a holster at her hip and was about to dash for the elevator when that strange locum internist, Upslinger, approached her.

"Excuse me," he said abruptly, slamming both hands on the desk. "I have some very important information I need to share."

Helen looked at him, his wild hair curling out from under his ridiculous hat, his long trench coat flowing open like a cape, and his absurdly oversized snow boots. She didn't have time for his eccentricities.

"I'm sorry, Doctor. I have to run. We have an emergency to attend. I'll speak with you when I get back."

Helen nodded her head at Dr. Upslinger, as if dismissing him, and then ran to the stairwell. The elevator probably would have been faster, but she didn't want to get stuck in conversation waiting for it.

"Wait!" Dr. Upslinger yelled. "This is important. It's about the man you call …"

But Helen was already through the steel door to the stairs at this point, and the remainder of the sentence was drowned out.

CHAPTER 33

Rylan

Flickers and spasmodic arcs played out like an electrical storm on the backside of her eyelids. An angry buzzing sound filled her head, and her right leg felt as if it was filled with sand. There was a bitter, chemical taste on her tongue. Worst of all, the room seemed to be spinning like that house in The Wizard of Oz.

Rylan heard a gurgling sound, as if someone was choking on their own spit, and this stirred her consciousness and pulled her from a deep slumber. She attempted to open her right eye, but it seemed to be welded shut with crusted tears. She mobilized one hand, opening and closing her fingers, and then peeled the eyelid open, breaking the crusty seal. Harsh, white light assaulted her retina. She did the same for her other eye with the same effect. All she saw now was the proverbial ghost in the snowstorm. She closed and opened her eyes repeatedly to get some lubrication flowing and ease the dryness. As she did this, she shifted her weight from one buttock to another, immediately feeling a rush of blood to her right leg. She knew what was coming next, the intense pain of revascularization. But this would take a few minutes.

She felt around and realized she was propped up with her back in a corner and her legs sprawled in front. She leaned her head back, rubbed her face with her hands, and sucked a deep breath. Her vision was clearing to the sight of blood on her hands. Her nose began to ache, and she remembered face-slamming the garbage bin, and she remembered Pockface.

Now her long vision was coming into play. She looked past her blood-soaked hands to something swinging overhead in the center of the room, like a pendulum. This was accompanied by a squeaking noise, barely audible over the buzzing of the fluorescent lights. It reminded her of an eerie playground swing she avoided as a child.

The brutal, sudden recognition of what the "thing" was reflexively caused Rylan's eyes to snap shut, and her body to squeeze further into the corner. Her mind was still dulled and swimming with sleep-inducing chemicals. It was all a horrid nightmare. It had to be.

And then she heard another sound, beyond the buzzing and the squeaking. A groan, someone trying to say something.

"Help. Please help me, Rylan."

Hearing her name was the magic "Open Sesame" that lifted a veil. Her eyes sprung open, and she looked past the swinging body to see a man bound to a chair.

"Paul?" Rylan croaked in a dry, raspy voice. "Are you okay?"

They made eye contact. "I think so," Paul managed.

Rylan pushed forward from the corner and scanned Paul from head to toe. She noticed his hands and legs were bound to the arms and legs of the chair with plastic zip ties. From his thigh, a syringe dangled.

Rylan held the wall for support and tried to get her legs and feet under her. The back of her head ached fiercely, like the worst sleep deprivation headache she'd ever had. The blood had returned to her right leg with a vengeance, burning like it was on fire. Still, she managed to shuffle one leg in front of the other towards Paul. She tried to arc her way around the swinging body, averting her eyes, but her curiosity was too strong, and she looked.

A petite woman in a hospital gown hung by her neck from a bed sheet tied overhead to a pipe. Her bowels and urine had released, and a puddle was forming under her feet. Rylan couldn't smell anything but assumed that was because of the damage to her nose. She stared at the woman, at the wide, bulging eyes, trying to make sense of what she was seeing. But there was no sense to any of it.

As she stared, her eyes fixed on the woman's feet and began automatically following the rhythmical, pendular motion, like the watch of a hypnotist. And then it hit her hard all at once: the fatigue, the pain in her face, the insanity of everything she'd witnessed in the past hours. She'd had enough. More than any one person could endure. Her face turned ashen white as the vessels in her neck opened and gravity drained the blood from her head. Her eyes rolled back into their sockets, away from the carnage in front of her. Her legs turned to jelly, and she dropped to the floor.

Her hearing was the last of her senses to shut down, and Paul's pleas of, "Rylan, stay with me. Help me," bounced around her brain for only a few seconds before the bliss of emptiness engulfed her.

CHAPTER 34

Paul

"Rylan!"

Paul watched Rylan crumble to the floor with a thud. And then he watched her stay there. *No,* he thought. "No! Rylan, wake up! Please!"

But it was no use. She was out. *Dammit.* Paul strained against the plastic ties at his ankles, cutting into the skin beneath his wool socks. He managed to get the legs on his chair to produce an angry *tat-tat* on the tile floor, but when he stopped moving, the sound died away, and no one came to his rescue. He rotated his neck left and right – anything to avoid looking straight ahead – but all he found was silence and shadows. Then, he tucked his chin to his chest and stared at his lap where the hypodermic needle that had pierced his right thigh stood at attention.

"Rylan," he tried again. "I need you to wake up."

Beyond the windows, the sun struggled to ascend on the new day, but the clouds remained thick. Punishing winds still rattled the glass, though the snow was finally letting up. Hazy, unsure light filtered into the room, just a hesitant toe-dip at this point. Paul grit his teeth and raised his eyes, just enough to see the dangling feet of the late Jane Doe swing languidly from side to side. She was close to him, so close that he could have touched her with the tip of his shoe if not for the ties. Not that he would, of course. This girl before him was somebody's somebody. He had to remember that, no matter what else had happened here. He thought of the tattered newspaper clipping in his pocket, the one that reported on the death of Kayla Jennings, survived by her grief-stricken parents, Mr. and Mrs. Jennings. He wondered who would grieve for Jane Doe.

Rylan still wasn't moving. Paul contemplated the unsavory reality that he was, at that moment, both literally and figuratively stuck. The smell of feces and piss in the room was overwhelming, so he did some aggressive shimmying and succeeded in relocating his chair back a foot or two. Not that it helped. All he really accomplished was to splash his jeans with little drops of dead-girl pee when the tips of his Oxfords slapped the expanding puddle by his feet.

He'd burn his clothes when he got out of here.

"Rylan!" A woman's voice shouted somewhere down the hall.

Paul whipped his head around. Maybe he was about to be unstuck. The woman's voice called, "Rylan, are you here?"

Out in the hall, doors banged, voices called. The lights went on.

"Why the hell were the lights off?"

Paul recognized the voice as Helen's. "Here!" he shouted. "In here!" He shook and shimmied again, nearly tipping his chair backward with the effort.

Helen bounded through the door, Taser in hand, another security guard on her heels. She muttered, "Dear God," and covered her nose and mouth with her free hand. She assessed the situation in a single instant and beelined to Rylan's side. Folding her legs into a heavy crouch, Helen ordered her partner to call for backup. "The snow is stopping, so no more bullshit – we need the police this instant! Tell them to follow a goddamn plow." Her eyes darted between Rylan, the bloated face of the dead girl hanging from a bedsheet, and Paul tied to his chair with the needle in his thigh. "Tell them we've had a hanging, we've had foul play, and we need their asses here *now*."

"I'm on it, Chief," the guard muttered, bolting from the room.

"And get the rest of our team up here in the meantime. And Dr. Mike, too – tell him Rylan is unconscious!"

Helen put two hands on Rylan's head and brushed her hair back gently. "Rylan," she murmured, running two fingertips over her neck, "talk to me, honey."

Helen looked up at Paul. "She has a pulse. She's breathing. What should I do?"

"Untie me," Paul said.

Helen nodded. "Of course." She stroked Rylan's cheek tenderly before rising from the ground and pulling a Swiss army knife from the pocket of her uniform. She moved to attend to Paul's left wrist, but just before blade met zip tie, she paused and looked at Jane Doe. "What happened?"

"Just untie me," Paul said again, "and I'll tell you everything. Come on, I'm losing feeling in my hands and feet."

"But who did all this?" Helen asked, waving a hand about the room.

"*She* did!" Paul said. He jutted his chin in the direction of Jane Doe.

"*She* hurt Rylan?'

"No, Rylan fainted. Rylan's fine. Just cut me loose –"

"But she's such a tiny thing …" Helen said, gazing at the suspended corpse. "How –?"

How did she knock out a big, healthy man and zip tie him to a chair? Is that what you're wondering, Helen? Paul's angry thoughts raced full speed ahead astride his exasperation. He tensed and strained further against the ties. "Helen, please!"

Helen looked from Paul to the knife in her hand, and Paul caught a whiff of uncertainty, but it disappeared quickly. "I've got it," she said and made quick work of cutting him loose. "What about this?" she asked pointing to the needle in his leg. "Is it safe to just pull out?"

Rylan chose that particular moment to gain consciousness, and Helen pounced like a kitten on a red laser dot, leaving Paul to unceremoniously yank the needle from his own thigh.

"Rylan, are you okay?" Helen asked.

Rylan looked slightly dazed. She sat up straight and rubbed the back of her head. "I think so," she said. Then something seemed to click into place, and the expression on her face transformed through several phases of horror before, finally, relief. "Oh, Helen, thank God you're here! Did you see?"

"Yes, honey." Helen's voice was calm and soothing, the kind a mother uses to tell a child her puppy got loose and ran into traffic. "She hung herself. She was very troubled. There was nothing you could do."

"No, not her!" Rylan yelled with such force that Helen startled. "Did you see Pockface and Mr. Kosinski?"

Helen looked to the hall, frowning. "Mr. Kosinski?"

"The janitor! He's dead, and so is Pockface!"

Helen swung around and looked at Paul, the appointed translator for the hysterical and the deranged. "What is she talking about?"

"Paul!" Rylan gasped, as though just remembering he was there. She twisted her neck to see around Helen, and Paul stepped forward into her line of sight. "Oh, my God. Paul, are you all right?"

"I'm okay," he said, offering a hand to help her up.

"But you were tied to the chair and there was a needle …"

"I'm okay." He hoisted Rylan up to standing and ran his hands along her neck and down her shoulders, reassuring himself she was still intact. "It was the patient I saw at the beginning of the shift – Jane Doe – in the ER. When we came onto the ward here, I saw her and wanted to convince her to return to the psychiatric unit, to get help …" His voice broke, and he hesitated before continuing. "She was psychotic. Not making sense at all. She said she was … following instructions." He ran his hands through his hair and tugged until his dark waves stood upright. "Auditory hallucinations. It all happened so fast …"

Rylan stared into Paul's face, her jade green eyes glistening with sympathy and sadness. Beside her, Helen listened in quiet, rapt attention.

"She had a needle," Paul continued. "She injected me with something and maneuvered me into the chair. I must've lost consciousness at some point. When I woke up, I was tied to the chair. I screamed for help, but no one could hear me. You were out cold. There was no one to help me … or her." He tilted his head ever so slightly at Jane Doe.

Paul's voice drifted off. The sympathy in Rylan's eyes was too much to bear, so he broke contact and focused on a spot somewhere across the room.

"Why? Why would she do that?" Helen asked.

When Paul said nothing, Rylan shouted, "Because she was crazy!" She reached out and took Paul's larger hands into her smaller ones and kneaded them with protective tenderness.

"She made me watch," Paul said, still staring at the faraway place.

A distressed groan came from Rylan. She shut her eyes, and Helen placed a steady hand on her shoulder. Neither seemed sure what to say.

Paul continued, mumbling now to himself more than anyone else, "A front-row seat for a suicide, and I couldn't stop it." A moment passed, and his eyes ventured to meet Rylan's again. A tear spilled over his lower lashes and rolled down his cheek.

"Oh, Paul!" Rylan wrapped her arms around him and hugged him tightly. "I'm so sorry."

They stood that way for a while, both crying. Helen looked about the room. The blood on the walls, the glass on the floor. "There's more to it," she said, almost too quietly to be heard.

But Rylan heard. She pulled her head off Paul's chest. "What do you mean?"

Helen just shook her head. "It's a matter for the police now." She stepped toward the hall where the other security guard, the one she'd told to call for backup, assured her that the police were close.

"Thank God. Now, Rylan, what on earth were you saying about Pockface and the janitor?"

Rylan swallowed hard. "Pockface is in a dumpster around the corner …"

Helen looked at the accompanying security guard. A silent communication passed between them. He nodded and trotted off to have a look.

Rylan continued, "… and the janitor is in the sink."

"What sink?" Helen asked, but before Rylan could answer, they heard the door to the unit swing open and bang against the opposing wall. Thundering footfall was punctuated by walkie-talkie static as Helen's security team burst onto the unit. A second later, Dr. Mike Curran came tearing around the corner and stopped short before Helen and Rylan and Paul. "What's going on?" he asked, leaning forward with a hand on each knee, gulping air.

Rylan stepped aside and extended an arm in the direction of the hanging girl. Mike's eyes widened, and he instantly recoiled, then corrected course and stepped forward for a closer look. "This is the girl from the ER," he said, covering his mouth and nose with his arm and glancing at Paul.

"Boss!" A flurry of activity erupted down the hall, and a security guard called for Helen. "Come have a look, there are two bodies here!"

A whimper escaped from Rylan, and Paul gave her hand a gentle squeeze. Mike, conditioned to leap into action at the merest sign of human distress, started toward the activity, but Rylan wrapped her free hand around his upper arm, anchoring him in place. "Don't go. It's too awful."

"Nobody. Touch. Anything!" Helen shouted, storming off in the direction of the commotion.

Mike watched her go, then turned his attention to the hand on his arm. "Who?" he asked, staring at Rylan's fingers.

"Pockface and Sid Kosinsky, a janitor."

Mike nodded slowly, still studying the fingers around his arm as though they might sign him the answers to the many questions in his head. He inhaled, then released a breathy whistle. "Dead? You're sure?"

Rylan nodded. She knew dead.

"But who would do such a thing?"

"Her," Rylan said, pointing to the girl swinging from the noose.

"*Her*?" Instead of looking at the girl, Mike looked at Paul. His eyes searched his face, inquisitive. They asked, *does this make any sense to you?*

"And she's responsible for all of Rylan's patients in the morgue?" Mike continued.

Paul covered his own eyes with a hand and shrugged. "She ... she was psychotic ..."

"But still –"

Paul was losing control. To his horror, he started to retch. It was just too much. The swinging body with the bulging eyes, the filth on the floor, the smell. He needed to get out of there. The unit door banged again down the hall, and Paul wanted to get on the other side of it more than anything. He took a deep breath, trying to regain some semblance of composure. "I really don't know what to tell you."

"Well, figure out what to tell *them*," Helen said, materializing behind them, leading three men and one woman in dark, burly jackets with matching polyester pants. "The police are finally here."

CHAPTER 35

Rylan

Rylan felt like she was meandering through fog as she worked her way down the final corridor to the call rooms with Paul at her side. The same sentence looped through her hazy, adrenaline-fueled mind:

What the hell just happened?

The police had been thoughtful and considerate of what they'd been through, including the sleep deprivation. They took preliminary statements and told them they would be in contact after the forensics team had done their work.

A hand landed on her shoulder.

"You okay?" Paul asked gently. "It's a lot to take in."

It was so much to take in, Rylan thought, *that nothing was getting in*. A funnel that was clogged at the spout. She found herself incapable of following any thought pattern to an endpoint. It all just swirled around her head, like a cartoon character sucker punched in the jaw. They arrived in front of the ortho call room. It had been years since she'd slept overnight in the hospital. This room was for the lowly third-year resident who did in-house call. She paused mid-step. Paul had asked her a question.

Am I okay?

For everything he had gone through in the past, and for everything he had just been through, the question, really, was, "how could *he* possibly be okay?" She turned and looked at him. Her cheeks reddened as she brushed the tip of one finger across his face – with no idea why she'd done that – and landed her hand comfortably on his shoulder.

"You're right," Rylan whispered, her voice cracking just a little, as a tear forced its way into the corner of one eye. "It's a lot to take in. For both of us. And, to be honest, I'm not okay. My brain is fried, and I'm completely fucking confused as to what just happened. I can't make sense of a goddamn thing. And I really need some sleep." She reluctantly removed her hand from his shoulder, wiped her eye, and turned away. She grabbed the call room doorknob and pushed.

Nothing.

She turned and pushed again. They had lost the key long ago, and it was understood that no other medical service would use the room. Ever.

It didn't budge.

Expletives of every sort lined up single file in her mind, prepping for a verbal explosion that was about to tear whoever was in there a new sphincter. *Rectum? Damn near killed 'em.*

She curled her hand into a mallet and was in mid swing, about to simultaneously launch the physical part of her assault, when smooth fingers curled tenderly around her wrist.

"At this point, will you really be able to sleep?"

Rylan's head of steam lost pressure as she turned and met his eyes. She was immediately transfixed. Hypnotized. For not the first time tonight, it struck her just how handsome Dr. Paul Bennett really was.

"Look," he said, pointing, "it just so happens my room is right next door. Join me."

Who was she kidding? As tired as she was, she would never fall asleep. In fact, after every psychological cut she'd suffered tonight, she might never sleep again. Why even try?

Paul drew the key from his disheveled black Armani blazer pocket, opened the door, and pulled her in behind him. The door closed with a thud. Bright morning sunlight poured through the one small window, reflecting off the snow-swept landscape outside. "Argh!" Rylan cried, shielding her face with a hand. She leapt across the room and tugged the flimsy curtain into place with savage determination. "Better," she said.

"Better," Paul agreed.

Rylan turned so she and Paul stood facing one another from either side of the room, neither sure what to do. Rylan glanced at the single bed to her left, felt her cheeks warm, and looked back at Paul. She took a few tentative steps toward him and paused, staring directly into his eyes.

Paul reached down and tucked a loose strand of hair behind her ear. "Those bangs are always dangling over your left eye."

Rylan shrugged. "I guess I need a haircut."

"No. I like it." He ran a gentle finger along her brow, tracing the path of the errant lock. He reached his other hand around her back and pulled her close. When she smiled, he plunged his face in her neck and ran his lips along her collarbone.

The touch of his lips was so soft, it made Rylan quiver. She tossed her head back, and a thick, throaty moan filled the room, allowing the weight of a night's treachery to escape into the ether. Her arms found their way around Paul, and she pulled him in tight, flattening her body against his, delighting in the hardness she found pressing against her belly. Her mind went blank, and everything that happened next was without thought, driven only by sheer, carnal want. A frenzied whirlwind, hands and lips everywhere at once. Within seconds, Rylan was down to bra and panties. She held Paul's shirt in one hand and his pants in the other. His blazer lay in a heap on the floor next to her lab coat.

Prowling fingers pushed her panties to the floor, and two hands hooked her armpits and lifted her off the linoleum, seating her on the desk. The cold was shocking at first, but rapidly dissipated as Paul ran his hands through her hair, cupping her head in his hands and covering her lips with his. Rylan wrapped her legs around his waist and pulled him into her with a desperation that made her woozy.

So woozy that her doctor brain almost turned off, but she knew better. Reluctantly, she pulled her lips from Paul's, placed a hand on each of his shoulders, and gazed into his face. "What about –"

Understanding immediately, Paul nodded and pulled back. "I have something …," he mumbled, extracting a wallet from the clothing heap on the floor. Rylan held her breath, barely daring to move, hoping they could resume course exactly where they left off after this necessary little detour. She heard a crinkle and saw a foil wrapper fall to the floor. Barely an instant later Paul was back in front of her. He hunched forward and placed his hands on the desk, one beside each of her thighs. "Ready now?"

"Ready," Rylan moaned, circling his waist with her legs.

When Paul entered her, Rylan felt a waterfall of electricity rumble through her body. It rolled into her toes, her fingers, her hair, her ears, her lips, and even erased the dull ache in her nose. Renewed energy lifted the veil of darkness that had been suffocating her over the past few hours. Invigorated, she pushed Paul backward with a strength that surprised her, gently but firmly toppling him onto the single bed with a loud squeak of decade's old springs. She heard him laugh.

"Does this mean we're done?" he asked.

"Not a chance, doc. Just time for a change-up," Rylan responded in a low and sexy voice. She crawled on top of Paul and straddled him.

Paul sank his head into the bed as his eyes rolled back in unconcealed pleasure. A series of rhythmic squeaks followed, gradually getting faster and faster, punctuated only by loud gasps and urgent moans.

A final wave of delight rippled through Rylan's sweat-soaked body just as Paul tensed and grunted a final time. For a moment Rylan kept very still, sitting astride Paul, eyes shut, waiting for her breath to normalize. Finally, she opened her eyes and looked down at Paul, who was watching her, unblinking. He had a look of blissful satisfaction on his face, like he'd conquered the highest mountain. He reached out to grab her torso and maneuvered her to a side-lying position. He paused, pushed a strand of hair behind her ear once again, and politely excused himself.

Bemused, Rylan watched Paul roll off the bed, listened to his feet thump across the floor, and watched him bound toward the bathroom while the sheen on his perfect bottom reflected the incoming sunlight. *Guess he really had to go.*

Rylan turned onto her back and lay there grinning, thinking about how perfect an ending this was to the worst night of her life. She sat up in the bed and rested her back against the headboard. Paul had been right. No way would she have fallen asleep alone in her call room, not after all the horrors of this night. But now, well, things felt different now. After that one hundred percent satisfying major class A tension release, her eyelids were feeling heavy. In anticipation, she smoothed the patch of bed next to her, ready to rest her head on Paul's chest when he emerged from the bathroom. Then, she would finally sleep.

She cocked an ear and heard the shower running.

Strange, she thought, trying to hold her disappointment at bay. She took a quick sniff of her armpits and scrunched her nose. Then again, maybe not so strange. After a brutal 24-hour call shift, she reeked. She'd have to jump into the shower when he was done … or maybe before he was done. A latent ripple of pleasure coursed through her pelvis, and she released a happy sigh.

Still, she didn't feel quite so sexy anymore. She leaned over the bed and found her scrub shirt and slipped it over her head, then covered the rest of herself with the bed's scratchy, worn blanket. She picked her cell phone off the night table and was pleasantly surprised to find a four-bar signal and some power left in the tank. She worked her fingers over the screen. At first, she was tempted to call someone – her dad? She had so much to tell him – but then she realized Paul would likely be back momentarily, and that would be awkward.

Just gimme a minute, Paul, I'm talking to my dad, telling him how great the sex was. It's all good.

She sighed again and rubbed her face, attempting to wipe the silly grin off.

She waited as her phone loaded up emails and missed messages. She scrolled over the local news updates which were mostly about the snowstorm and all the damage it had done. One story was about a snowplow that had crashed into a cell tower near the hospital.

Well, that explains that. She tapped her phone in emphasis.

There was another story about how her hospital had been snowed in and ambulances had been rerouted to a hospital further south.

She was about to check her social media feeds when a final headline caught her eye:

NEW PSYCHIATRIST AT NORTHERN MICHIGAN GENERAL HOSPITAL FOUND DEAD IN HIS APARTMENT.

WTF?

She quickly read through the article, her pulse accelerating, until her eyes focused on a name: Dr. Paul Bennett.

WTF!

Troubling thoughts that had been circling the outer reaches of her mind suddenly coalesced. It never made sense. No way could Jane Doe have lifted Pockface's body into the dumpster. Maybe not even the janitor into the sink. No way. Even if she was psychotic and incredibly strong for her size. No way.

Her heart split in two as stomach acid awaiting breakfast streaked to her mouth. She retched and tasted bile. It was like someone had given her the antidote for post-coital bliss.

She glanced at the bathroom door. The shower had stopped.

Her skin turned clammy, her breathing became raspy, and the sound of her heartbeat flooded her ears. She didn't have much time. The bathroom door was only a few feet from the main door, her only way out. She heard rustling behind the door and shuffling footsteps.

"Fuck. Fuck. Fuck. What do I do?" She mumbled to herself, sitting straight up on the side of the bed with her feet touching the cold floor.

She grabbed for her phone but fumbled. It fell to the floor and bounced under the bed.

No!

Next best thing and probably faster, she yanked the receiver from the landline sitting on the night table and dialed those four digits.

Helen answered after the first ring.

More shuffling behind the bathroom door.

"Help!" Rylan whispered.

The doorknob to the bathroom began to jiggle, and she completely lost control, her primitive instincts taking over. She dropped the receiver to the floor and bolted like a startled deer for the door.

CHAPTER 36

Jake

Jake worked the little sliver of antibacterial soap over his skin with strategic precision. Up and down and round and round until every disgusting body fluid he'd touched that night circled the drain in a swirl of no-frills foam and disappeared – along with the suffocating persona of the late Paul Bennett.

Paul Bennett.

Now, that had been a sweet morsel of serendipity. Meeting that guy was like Charlie finding the golden ticket to the Chocolate Factory. Gentle and trusting Paul Bennett, new to town and a verifiable emotional basketcase. The man was everything Jake could have hoped for in a target, and so much more. Reeling from a recent breakup *and* a professional crisis, Paul was only too happy to allow someone like sexy Jake Alister to buy him a drink at the bar. And then a second, and a third. A roll or two in the hay later, and there were no secrets between the starstruck lovers.

Not true. There had, in fact, been a lot of secrets between them – but Paul didn't know that. Without reservation, he bared his soul to Jake when he showed him the newspaper clipping reporting on his young patient's suicide. He didn't think twice about entering the passcode to his Mac with Jake at his elbow. He sought no privacy while he filled out his onboarding paperwork for his new job at Northern Michigan General – to be presented to HR that week for issuing of a photo ID – while Jake stroked his hair and watched him input personal data over his shoulder. He even went so far as to tell Jake the PIN for his bank card. Granted, Jake had him in a chokehold with the tip of a syringe of potassium chloride poised at his jugular at that point, but Paul told him all the same. And he got the needle, all the same.

Sorry, Paul Bennett.

But people were disposable. Life was nothing more than a glorified videogame with room for just one victor. The rest was collateral damage. A person needed to be smart about how they played the game. That's why Jake spent a good portion of his formative years practicing. Out behind the garage, he sliced throats with clinical detachment (helping to control the neighborhood population of stray cats in the process.) He learned that blood, thick and hot and teeming with biological cells, made him sick. He snapped necks for a cleaner alternative, but soon discovered that the exertion was a bit too hands-on for his tastes. He toured the dark web and found snuff porn, props, and paraphernalia, all readily available if a person had a little cash to spare. He invested a little time and money in exploring the merits of various poisons – arsenic, cyanide, strychnine – but these substances were a little finicky to work with. In the end, Jake realized there was no need to reinvent the wheel. A tried-and-true option already existed, and it was called potassium chloride. The executioner's drug. Easy to come by, easy to use. The first cat he gave it to succumbed within a minute. It was a bad minute, though. The thing yowled and screamed, bared its teeth, and went wild before it collapsed belly up in the weeds and was unceremoniously shoveled into a patch of upturned earth.

Same thing happened to the first girl he tried it on. A warm spring night in the park around dusk. A tenth-grader with wavy brown hair and denim cut-offs. Jake smooth-talked her behind a tree where they passed a bottle of Fireball and smoked a joint. When the girl dropped her heavy eyelids and rested drowsily against the tree trunk, Jake gave her the needle. Fast, easy, efficient, clean. The only problem was the screaming. He should have expected it after the cat, but it still caught him by surprise. He had to hold her down with a jacket pressed over her face until it was over. That was irksome. Lesson learned: Potassium chloride hurt like a bitch. Next time, he added a bit of Propofol to keep things civil.

Even now, years later, the memory of that first girl was still wildly arousing. Jake slid his hand up his thigh and wrapped his fingers around his burgeoning hardness. A few strokes, and he was entirely ready to go again. He closed his eyes and imagined Rylan straddling him, just as she did about ten minutes ago. He imagined Aunt Marla straddling him, too, just as she did about eight years ago. Then, he got a little creative and imagined the two together …

Almost there. He grunted and worked his hand a little faster.

Marla. Now there was a name that could still make him stiff any day of the week. Rich, wild, petulant Marla. She had married well, divorced even better, and spent the rest of her days in a frenzied pursuit of fashion, entertainment, wine, and sex. That's where Jake (aka "Ethan Coolidge" in those days) came in, spending the better part of a year as Marla's sexy little sugar-baby. Lord, she had been phenomenal in bed. They had good times, he and Marla. At least until she found him in a downtown hotel bar with a curvy blonde and rammed him with her car in the parking lot.

Jake leaned forward and placed a palm flat against the tile wall for support as his body convulsed in sweet agony. He stood in the hot steam, panting, then took a deep breath and re-centered. He rotated the shower head so the stream pounded his sore leg. It hurt like a motherfucker and chased the endorphins right out of his system. Goodbye Marla Fraser, hello Patrick Fraser.

Patrick Fraser was responsible for this pain.

Patrick Fraser, Marla's hotshot orthopedic surgeon brother, flew into Chicago on a red-eye the morning after the hotel parking-lot debacle. He carried 500K in cash and a case of "surgery tools," which, to Jake, looked suspiciously like the ones the workers of Local 662 were using on a construction site down the block. By late morning, this

Patrick Fraser had tortured Jake's bone back into some kind of "reasonable" alignment with a few backroom maneuvers on his leg – quite literally in the *back room* of an orthopedic practice belonging to one of Fraser's old colleagues – and then slapped on a toe-to-groin plaster of paris cast. The deal was this: free orthopedic care and a cool half-mil so long as "Ethan" didn't go to the police. (The family believed it would result in "bad optics" if Aunt Marla was convicted of aggravated assault. Um-hmm.)

Once Dr. Patrick Fraser had fixed him up, "Ethan" would present to a local clinic for follow-up care, giving some rehearsed story about how he'd obtained his injuries abroad. Aunt Marla would handle all the medical bills. Sufficiently mended, "Ethan" would leave town and never contact Marla or the Frasers again. All good. While Jake really didn't give a steaming heap of cow dung about Marla's reputation, he was disinclined to seek legal action for reasons of his own. For one, trying to explain the whole "Ethan Coolidge" thing to the police certainly would have been awkward, particularly since Ethan Coolidge was a dead guy in Spokane.

So, everything could have worked out for everyone involved if only Dr. Patrick Fraser hadn't had a ten-foot stick up his ass.

Jake knew some surgeons told jokes to pass the long hours in the operating room. Others traded notes on Netflix binges or sang along to a streamed-in playlist. Patrick Fraser, Jake learned, had his own way of making time fly. He muttered an incessant barrage of insults under his breath, words that smoldered with white-hot rage causing wispy curlicues of smoke to float from his ears.

I know what you are. Bottom-feeding scum.

The choice phrases diffused lazily through Jake's painkiller haze. He was too numb to worry about them. They meant nothing so long as his broken parts got expediently fixed. A Chinese-food delivery guy's semi-decomposed body had recently turned up in an abandoned lot not far from Marla's apartment, and Jake needed his legs to work so he could walk the fuck out of town.

A grifter, a liar, a cheat …

When Patrick had cut Jake's mangled wool trousers off, the contents of his wallet spilled across the floor, and low and behold, an alternate ID was discovered. It might have said "David Gold" or "Samuel Hutchings," but Jake couldn't remember now. It was so many identities ago.

An imposter, a criminal, a lawless thug …

Patrick never knew the true identity of Marla's lover. One thing he did know, however – that he made clear to the tiny circle of collaborators in this covert mission – was that he was furious with this fake Ethan character for making a mockery of his sister's name. For indulging his carnal desires with her body. For accessing her home and her credit cards without restraint. For humiliating Marla by taking up with other women on the sly. But the thing Patrick was *most* furious with, the thing he couldn't get over, the fat fly that stuck in the ointment, was fake-Ethan's nerve in making one particular, single utterance. More specifically, in uttering one particular, single name. It wasn't Marla's name, no. It was *her* name.

How many times had Jake endured Marla's tiresome family show-and-tell? All those nights when a cocktail hour had stretched well beyond the confines of sixty minutes, and Marla stumbled through her lavish apartment sipping yet another Manhattan, pointing to this and that framed family photo. She had gobs and gobs of family pride and spoke as if she rubbed elbows with the Kennedys and Astors.

Uncle Jack was mayor of such-and-such town for eight years.

Gifted concert pianist, Cousin Julia, sold out Carnegie Hall not once, but three times!

Dear brother, Patrick, was to orthopedic surgery what DiMaggio was to baseball.

Jake tried to listen but usually just pretended to, nodding here, chuckling there, throwing in the occasional "wow." But there was really only one photo in the room that interested him, one to which his eyes were magnetically drawn back to time and time again. The one of Marla's young niece with the mesmerizing green eyes.

You have a very pretty daughter, Dr. Fraser. Her name is Rylan, isn't it?

A few simple words that caused a seismic shift in power. Patrick's shoulders tensed, and his eyes narrowed. A vein bulged in his neck. It seemed Jake had discovered an Achilles heel.

Years later, Jake believed it to be a sign when he found Dr. Rylan Fraser's name in print. *Young Surgeon Makes Hometown Proud.* It wasn't exactly a random coincidence because he had kept tabs on the family for years. At first, it was nothing more than a bit of voyeuristic curiosity. Later, though, when the gnawing pain in his leg failed to recede, Jake concluded that Dr. Patrick Fraser had provided substandard medical care, that he had knowingly and willfully sabotaged his recovery. And then Jake's interest in the family became something more, something fueled by the desire to right a grievous wrong.

Young Surgeon Makes Hometown Proud. The universe was nudging him to action.

Jake turned off the water and reached for a towel. He pulled back the curtain and waited for the steam to clear enough to see the clean scrubs he'd stashed in the corner.

Like everyone else, Jake knew the legal purpose of a malpractice suit was to redress a wrong suffered at the hands of a negligent practitioner. Jake also knew he could not, given the circumstances surrounding his injury, sue Dr. Patrick Fraser in any legitimate court of law. Therefore, an alternative was needed. An alternative in which Jake, and only Jake, served the key roles. Judge and jury.

The verdict: Guilty.

The redress payment: High.

Jake slipped the scrub pants on and reached into the back pocket. Everything was just as he'd left it.

Finding Rylan Fraser on call last night had not been serendipity. It had been strategy. Jake knew that, in teaching hospitals like Northern Michigan General, a serious motor vehicle accident always meant the senior orthopedic resident would be called in to assess and operate. He just had to ensure there would be a serious motor vehicle accident. Easy enough to arrange. And, once Rylan was in the hospital, Jake had just needed to make sure she wouldn't leave. The disappearance of her junior resident and a steady stream of urgent calls on her already-dead patients took care of that. Not to mention, as a bonus (and further indication that the universe was in his corner) the storm of the century provided by Mother Nature.

Everything had gone remarkably well with only the smallest of blips. One was that close call down by the morgue. He hadn't expected a pathologist to be working overnight. Jake had followed Rylan to find out whether they were onto his little potassium chloride cocktails. He hid in the shadows waiting for her to leave to have a "discussion" with the pathologist and only flinched because a rat scurried over his shoe. Filthy germ-carrying vermin. The other blip was the unplanned presence of the two buffoons, Pockface and the janitor, on the D-wing. Talk about wrong place, wrong time.

He unwrapped a syringe and expertly filled it from a small vial. He gave the tip a few quick flicks and smiled. Rising star Rylan Fraser was about to go out with a bang. Another bang. One more for the road. With exquisite timing, Jake would plunge the needle into the soft hollow at the base of Rylan's neck just as they climaxed in synchronized ecstasy, what the French so aptly called *La petite mort*. The little death.

Judge, jury, and executioner.

CHAPTER 37

Rylan

There was one visual focal point: the silver-colored, slightly dented doorknob with the smudged patina acquired from decades of wear and tear. Eight feet, two powerful strides, and she was there. A way out. Escape from this catastrophic nightmare.

And she came close to making it. Her hand was on the doorknob, turning, until the bathroom door opened outwards. Who the fuck designs a bathroom door that opens outwards into the path of the main door? Really! Who could ever think there was any architectural sense to that design?

The bathroom door hit her squarely in the head, face, and already battered nose, knocking her to the floor, her hand limply sliding from the doorknob. She heard a sinister chuckle, and felt two hands lift her into the air like a trophy and toss her onto the bed as if she were a load of dirty laundry – or a corpse being thrown into a mass grave.

Rylan struggled to focus through the tears and blood that flooded her eyes, through the haze and fear that enveloped her mind. Disoriented, she felt her hands and feet being bound to the wooden bed posts, but she was too stunned to react. It was as if her body was paralyzed, and she was looking down upon it from above. She was repelled by the image, a vulnerable, half-naked body spread-eagled on the bed. Rylan tried to scream, but a wad of fabric was stuffed into her mouth.

A cool, wet facecloth slapped down on her face, roughly wiping blood and tears away, and then the most horrid odor assaulted her nasal passages: harsh acrid ammonia. The chemical of choice for awakening a fainted damsel. She turned her head violently away, but the smell followed her until she opened her eyes and gazed upon the face of a traitor.

He wore an ugly, self-satisfied smirk – narrowed eyes, cocky brows. His head was stiffly angled to one side, and his shoulders were hiked, accentuating bony shoulder blades, like the wings of a gothic gargoyle. He looked nothing like the Paul she knew. Gone were the playful, sparkling eyes, the strong jawline sporting sexy morning stubble. Like Superman after a phone booth pitstop, Paul had emerged from the bathroom utterly transformed. The sparkling eyes now glowed only with malice, and the skin wore a pale and doughy sheen, like that of a creature living beyond the reach of natural light. He had changed into scrub pants but was still naked from the waist up. A bead of sweat, or perhaps water from his shower, trickled down his hairless chest, and Rylan observed with great distaste how underdeveloped his chest was, practically pectus excavatum. *What had she seen in this man?*

"Wakey, wakey, sleepy head," he said, sitting on the bed next to her. Rylan had the desperate urge to smack the smarmy expression off his face, but the ties on her wrists made this impossible. Instead, she just stared at him, trying to convey pure hatred with her eyes alone.

"Listen, if you promise to be a good girl and not yell, I'll remove your gag."

Fuck him. There were no rules here. If she wanted to yell, she would yell. There were surely people in the surrounding call rooms that would hear and come running. How could he stop her?

"Save your breath," he said, as if reading her thoughts. "Of course, you'd yell. I would if I were you. But there's no point. I snatched the keys to the call rooms nearby before the storm got serious." He reached over to a drawer in the desk and showed Rylan a handful of keys which he tossed into the garbage can, along with any hopes of rescue. "And if you're thinking about the asshole who stole your call room next door," he continued, glancing at the wall separating the two rooms, "that asshole was me." He smiled smugly, inhaled, and drove a final message home. "Regardless, as soon as you open your mouth, you'll get the jab."

At this, he stood, reaching into the back pocket of his scrubs and withdrew a syringe. He played with it for a moment, passing it back and forth between his long, slender fingers. Whirling and twirling it like a baton. He looked her hard in the eyes, smiled, and then put the syringe back into his pocket.

Terror creeped up Rylan's spine into her brain as she grasped the full meaning. She squeezed her eyes as tight as she could and refocused, drawing on years of training designed to wall off her emotions. She needed the gag out of her mouth. Her only hope was if she could talk to him.

She nodded her head, showing him that she understood the stakes. She understood that he held all the power.

Paul, or whoever this asshole really was, watched her for a moment, and said, "Okay, let's give this a shot. One-sided conversations are never much fun." He pulled the syringe from his pocket with one hand and placed his thumb on the plunger. With the other hand he reached forward and yanked the gag from her mouth. He waved it victoriously before her face, and Rylan recognized her panties dangling from his index finger.

"Fuck you, asshole."

Paul raised an eyebrow and began wadding up the panties again, like he was going to stuff them right back into her mouth. "We had a deal."

"I'm not yelling," Rylan snarled through gritted teeth.

Paul considered this. "I guess not," he said, keeping the syringe in his right hand visible at all times. He pushed a strand of auburn hair from her face behind her ear. She turned her head away violently, dislodging a large lock that landed squarely across her nose.

"Ahh. There's the sexy, come-get-me look I love so much," he said, standing and positioning himself at the end of the bed.

"Who are you? What do you want from me?" Rylan asked, now acutely aware that, although she was at least wearing a scrub shirt, her bottom was bare, and he was standing there, at the end of the bed, leering at her. The sense of exposure, of vulnerability and powerlessness she felt at that moment was so overwhelming, it took every bit of self-restraint she had not to scream. Her eyes welled with angry, frustrated tears.

Paul appeared to bask in her mortification, feeding off her humiliation like a swamp leech sucking blood. He squatted at the end of the bed so that only his eyes were visible above the old wood footboard, and Rylan could see him staring between her legs, subjecting her to a lascivious scrutiny that made her stomach turn. Her face caught fire, and she reflexively attempted to close her legs – which only caused the sharp edges of the zip ties to shred the flesh around her ankles. She winced and spat, "What. Do. You. Want. From. Me. You psychotic asshole?"

He stood to his full height, gazed down upon her, and said nothing, which was far creepier than anything he'd actually said thus far. He twirled her panties round and round his index finger and then slingshot them off the syringe and onto her belly. He smiled at his handiwork, then held the syringe point-upwards in one hand and gave it a few expert flicks with the fingers of the other.

Oh my God, he is really going to kill me. Rylan was going to die like all her patients unless she did something. She writhed from side to side, shaking her head furiously in all directions. She caught a glimpse of the landline sitting on the night table, its cradle empty of its receiver which lay on the floor next to the bed.

Helen! She remembered. Maybe. Just maybe, she got through. She needed to stall. To buy time. She closed her eyes, formulating her sentences.

"I just need to know why. Why all of this? What did I ever do to you?"

He sighed and dropped the hand holding the syringe. "You really didn't do anything, Rylan. It's just bad luck you were born to a smug son-of-a-bitch."

"What?"

"Your father, the mighty Patrick Fraser, is the most arrogant, narcissistic, self-serving piece of shit I've ever met."

"What are you talking about? You met my father?"

"Unfortunately, yes," he said, standing up and staring depravedly at the area between her legs rather than her face. "And you know what that self-righteous scumbag had the nerve to say to me? He said I wasn't fit to lick your boots." Fake Asshole Paul gave a nasty chuckle and pulled his phone from the pocket of his scrubs. He stood at the foot of the bed and snapped a photo of Rylan in her compromised position, bare from the waist down. "I can't wait to tell him I licked that inner thigh."

The thought of her father seeing pictures of her *like this* hurt even more than a needle to the neck. Rylan struggled against her ties until her ankles and wrists were slick with blood. "Let me go, you fucking psychopath!"

"Yeah, keep squirming. Just like that," Fake Asshole Paul said, walking up and down the bed, continually snapping pics with his phone camera. "Oh, sooo good. You know, your Aunt Marla loved restraints. She was nuts for the rough stuff." He gave Rylan a wink that made her feel filthy. Then, he dropped the camera and stroked his bulging groin with his right hand.

Rylan stopped moving. She lay flat on her back and looked straight up at the ceiling, ignoring the spectacle of the grotesque monster pleasuring himself. "So, you …?"

"So, I was the boy-toy cheating douchebag you so vividly described a few hours ago." He stepped to the side of the bed and leaned over her, so she had no choice but to look into his grinning face. "Small world, isn't it?"

Rylan's heart was pounding so hard she was finding it difficult to catch her breath. In another minute, she might be in the midst of a full-fledged panic attack. She had never had one before, but she was pretty sure now she knew what it felt like. *Focus*, she admonished herself. *Don't give in. Keep him talking.* "You did all this – everything tonight – to get back at Aunt Marla?"

"No, Rylan, pay attention. I want to get back at your prick father who treated me like toilet scum and intentionally left me with a bum leg."

"My father would never –"

"Shut up, Rylan. You don't know what you're talking about. But that man you call 'Daddy' is about to get a big, nasty surprise."

Rylan bit down on her lip as tears streamed from her eyes. Paul took a picture. "That's good. That's really good. As much anguish and misery as you can dredge up, please." *Click.* "Do it for your daddy."

Rylan took a deep breath. *Stop crying*, she willed herself. *Don't give him the satisfaction.* "But why the others?" she asked. "Why did you have to kill my patients? They couldn't mean anything to you."

"Ah, that," Fake Asshole Paul said. He sat down on the edge of the bed. "That was just a bit of fun. When I caught your name in the paper, I thought, *'Wow, what potential, a whole hospital full of captive targets.'* You see, I have a little hobby. Then, I thought, *'Resident of the Year'* – or whatever the fuck you're supposed to be – *'why don't we screw up that legacy a little while we're at it.'* And voilà." He made a flourish with his arm, underscoring his vast and proud accomplishments.

"And the real Paul Bennett?"

"I picked him up in a bar, gave him the time of his life, and then we became besties. At least, you know, until I killed him."

Rylan shuddered. "And who are you really?"

"Now why would I tell you that?" he said, tilting his head to one side. He tapped an index finger on his chin. "But, then again, why not? I can confide in you, right, Rylan? It's not like you're going to be telling anyone. You can call me *Jake*. Consider that little nugget my final gift to you."

"Jake," Rylan repeated. The name felt like ground glass in her mouth.

Jake smiled. "Good, strong name, right? Much better than Paul, don't you think?"

What Rylan thought was that this "Jake" was one hundred percent certifiably insane. "And my R3?" she asked. "What happened to him?"

"A necessary elimination."

A choked cry escaped Rylan as his words registered, and she quickly parked her sorrow behind another wall. She refocused. *He likes to brag. Keep asking questions.*

"But Jane Doe? Why her? She wasn't connected to me in any way."

"Ah, Jane Doe. She was a hired decoy, someone to stir the pot while funky things went down here at Northern General tonight. She ended up being a real psycho, though, which made things a bit challenging." Jake scratched the back of his head. "It all worked out, though," he said with perverse brightness.

"All worked out?" Rylan felt dizzy. She wasn't getting enough air into her lungs. *Just hold it together. Keep him talking.*

"So, yours was the voice on the phone," Rylan said.

Jake tilted his head to one side and looked as if he was talking to a child. "Voice modulator app." He abruptly clapped his hands together and stood from the bed. "Okay, that's about all the time we have for questions today. It's time."

Rylan's heart threatened to burst through her chest wall. The phrase *It's time* swelled in her head like a sponge, leaving no space for rational thought.

As Jake made a show of preparing his syringe one final time, his eyes drifted from Rylan's face to the nightstand, and then quickly shot back to her face, the showy bravado replaced with smoldering fury. He angled his head in that peculiar new way that was so un-Paul-like then walked slowly to the bed and crouched. When he arose, he held the phone receiver in front of her face, and Rylan twisted her head away in a desperate effort to avoid the pummeling she was sure was coming.

"You sly, little bitch."

He gripped the phone receiver in one white-knuckled hand and the syringe in the other. Rylan closed her eyes and braced herself. The explosion of broken plastic that followed nearly shattered her eardrum as he slammed the receiver into its cradle.

"Adieu, Dr. Fraser," Jake said coolly.

Rylan felt his hand grab her upper arm and hold it in place. She squeezed her eyes shut, sucked in a terrified breath, and held it there, willing time to stop. She said a silent goodbye to her father, wishing she could protect him from what was to come.

A loud rap on the door made her eyes fly open. The knob jiggled roughly, and there was shouting in the hall.

Helen!

"Rylan, are you in there?" Helen was banging on the door.

Rylan opened her mouth, but Jake put an index finger to his lips in warning and made a slashing motion across his neck. His eyes practically glowed red with demon fire.

Fuck him. He's going to kill me.

Rylan wrapped every shred of indignation, terror, and anger she felt into an ear-splitting screech so powerful that it nearly snapped her vocal cords. Jake grabbed her roughly by the hair and shoved her panties back into her mouth. His face was next to hers, and she could feel his hot breath on her ear. "We are not yet done."

He pounced for the door with the speed and grace of a starved lion.

Rylan watched in horror as he held the syringe in his hand like a knife. She could hear Helen fiddling with a key in the door lock. Jake stood to the side and watched the doorknob turn, and the door swing open, the fluorescent lights of the hallway finding their way around Helen and into the room.

Rylan shook the bed with all her strength and tried to yell through the gag to warn her friend. Helen was holding the key in one hand and a Taser in the other. When they made eye contact, Rylan shifted her eyes repeatedly to look behind the door. Helen got the message, but not before Jake jumped from the shadows, inserted the needle into her shoulder, and depressed the plunger.

Helen screamed as the potassium chloride coursed painfully into her deltoid muscle, bringing on its paralytic effect. But, as she fell to the floor, with a last quake of desperate muscle contractions, she jammed the Taser into Jake's bad leg and fired off 50,000 volts of electricity. Jake's entire body went into spasm, and he released an agonized scream. He let go of the plunger as his bad leg gave out, and he fell to one knee, his face twisted in pain, his body trembling like a condemned man in an electric chair.

Helen lay still on the floor, eyes open and unmoving, her walkie-talkie crackling with status updates from her colleagues on their progress to reach her.

With a loud grunt, Jake reached for the door handle and pulled himself to a standing position. He inhaled deeply and shook his head like a wet dog trying to shake the electricity from his body, stepped clumsily over Helen, and limped through the doorway. He looked both ways down the hall then back at Rylan, giving her an overly familiar bedroom smile that made her wish the Taser had been set to kill.

"Remember, we are not yet done."

And then he was gone.

CHAPTER 38

Jake

Jake clung to the wall for support. His right leg was a screaming frenzy of muscle fasciculations and seizures, the pain extraordinary. Score one for Helen. He hadn't thought much of the old ox when he'd chatted with her on the phone a week prior, when he'd pretended to be "Joe" from Smart-Tech Security making inquiries about the hospital's closed-circuit cameras. She had blithered on about the dated system with its extensive blind spots, never once pausing to consider whether she was, in fact, speaking to a sales agent or a terrorist. So underwhelmed with her security instincts was Jake that he almost canceled the deal he'd struck with that wacko, Mantis, to rent a girl for the big night to play the role of runaway headcase.

The plan, as explained to Mantis, was that Jake *a.k.a Paul Bennett, Undercover Medical Reporter,* would be writing a piece on how lax hospital security protocols endangered vulnerable psychiatric patients. He needed an actor to play a psych patient who escaped from staff to run amok in the hospital, potentially endangering self and others in the process. Mantis ate the idea right up (undoubtedly because of the number of attached dollar signs), saying he had just the girl for the part, a real "professional."

Professional psycho, Jake now thought to himself. *No matter, though, since all's well that ends well.*

And it had ended quite well. Jane Doe's hanging herself on the D-wing was an admission of guilt in the eyes of the police, and it allowed Jake to walk off scot-free to the call room to play out naughty fantasies with doomed rising star, Dr. Rylan Fraser.

Of course, Jane Doe hadn't *actually* hung herself. Poor Jane Doe never had a snowball's chance in hell of walking out the doors of Northern Michigan General alive. It was a frame game from the start.

Things had gone off-script, however, when the duo of losers previously known as Pockface and creepy janitor dude both ended up in the wrong place at the wrong time, forcing some unwelcome improvisation upon Jake. The interruption had actually caused Jake to lose track of Jane Doe for a brief, tense time. But the "professional" had turned up again and played her part beautifully. Right to the end.

RIP, Jane Doe. And if Mantis now has a beef, he can take it up with Paul Bennett. Good luck with that.

Jake could hear Rylan's shouts from the room he'd just exited. Fortunately for him, the hallway was deserted, but those shouts were about to attract a crowd for sure – a crowd that would burst into the room to find Rylan tied to the bed naked from the waist down. It would have been more merciful if he'd given her the needle, Jake thought. At least he could find some solace in *that*.

He staggered Frankenstein-like around a corner and found a wheelie cart of dirty linens and scrubs. Until that moment, he had forgotten he, himself, was shirtless – thanks to the sheen of sweat covering his skin and white-hot sparks of electricity coursing through his nervous system. He pulled a blue scrub shirt from the pile and quickly yanked it over his head. He would not allow himself to consider what contaminants and colonies of grotesque sick-people germs were embedded in the fabric. Although it couldn't be any worse than the Armani jacket he'd left in a heap on the floor of the call room. The jacket that had been spit on, bled on, cried on, and pissed on – shame on you Jane Doe. If he made it out of this mess, he would take a Purell bath and swallow a handful of antibiotics – with a flute of champagne. It was Thanksgiving, after all.

Jake looked around and saw no one, so he started pushing the cart along the hall. It helped keep him upright as he walked. With each step, he found himself getting a little stronger, the pain dissipating. When he passed an equipment cart stocked with PPE, he helped himself to a surgical mask and head covering. A nurse pushing a vital-sign monitor crossed in front of him on her way into a room. Two security guards ran past without a glance. He kept walking.

The laundry cart was a magical talisman. It rendered him invisible. No one paid a drop of attention to a guy pushing a cart of soiled rags. As bleary-eyed residents made rounds, as food trollies stuffed with cold decaf and boiled eggs and yogurt cups began jamming up the halls, as code teams raced by on their way to the call room block, Jake walked along, gloriously ignored.

Somewhere along the way, he managed to ditch the cart and continue walking, smooth and steady. It took every ounce of effort he had, but everything depended on it. He turned left when he reached the emergency department and slipped down a wide hallway that ran behind it, ending in a retracting garage-style door that opened onto a delivery bay. The door was now open, and gusts of frigid air made the hairs on Jake's bare arms rise to attention on little goose-pimple mounds. Beyond the opening, truck engines roared, plow blades scraped, and hydraulic lifts beeped. Workers shouted conversations just to be heard over the racket. Someone laughed.

Jake squinted in the early morning sunlight, the storm over. A new day full of promise beginning. It was Thanksgiving.

CHAPTER 39

Rylan

Rylan knew Helen had only seconds before the KCL worked its lethal, dark magic, stopping her heart, and then at most a few minutes before irreversible brain damage occurred, followed swiftly by death.

She quickly spit the hastily placed gag from her mouth and yelled at the top of her lungs. "Help. Help!"

Nobody came. Either they couldn't hear her, or everyone had gone off to do morning rounds.

It was just her.

So many victims tonight. She couldn't let Helen be another.

She pulled and pushed ferociously on the bed posts with both hands and feet, her exhausted muscles bulging to their maximum capacity. The bed was old and cheap; surely, she was strong enough. At first, nothing gave, and the bed and ties held. Her strength and hope were quickly fading when she heard a creak, like wood splintering, and realized there was a chance.

I need rhythm.

She began pushing and pulling against the post in time to an inner beat, until finally some screw loosened, or some tenon released from its mortise, or maybe an old strut simply broke, and the bed collapsed to the floor. In the process, one of the bed posts cracked off, and she was able to slip her wrist from the zip tie. With her free hand, she reached over to the pocket of her lab coat, lying crumpled on the floor next to the bed, and grabbed her scissors. She cut the remaining ties, rolled out of the wreckage, quickly yanked the hem of her oversized scrub top down to her midthigh, and ran to Helen.

I can do this.

She pulled the syringe out of Helen's shoulder and noted that, in the flurry of all the Tasering, only half of the contents had been administered.

That's good.

Rylan leaned over Helen, and for the second time in the last 24 hours, began life-saving CPR. She had no concept of how much time had passed since the KCL injection, but she knew there was still a chance.

"C'mon, Helen. You can fight this. *We* can fight this."

Rylan was into the second verse of *Staying Alive*, when she heard footsteps running down the hall. It was a complete déjà vu of Mrs. Potter last evening, except Helen was her friend, and she had just saved Rylan's life.

"C'mon, Helen, please, you can do this."

A brigade of security guards arrived, Helen's posse, heavy boots thudding to a halt. Walkie-talkies squawked endlessly, and a chorus of "Can we help?" surrounded her. Rylan looked up and solemnly realized that none of them could help her. She needed medical people.

And then she saw a pair of beige Timberland boots pushing their way through the crowd.

"Make way, dammit. Move aside," the voice growled.

The strange doctor in the deerstalker hat crouched to the floor at eye level with Rylan, who continued to pump Helen's heart, bouncing rhythmically up and down.

He asked, "Potassium chloride bolus?"

Rylan simply nodded her head and wondered how he knew.

"Stop CPR."

Rylan's eyebrows became two little triangles, and she shook her head vehemently. "Not until the crash cart gets here. I'll never stop."

Dr. Upslinger produced three syringes, a big one and two small ones, from his jacket pocket and looked squarely at Rylan. "I spoke with the pathologist. Look." He held the three syringes in front of her face, fanned out like a deck of cards. "Epinephrine, calcium chloride, and sodium bicarb."

Even in Rylan's adrenaline-soaked, sweat-drenched, frenzied state, she recognized the cure for a KCL overdose. She stopped the chest compressions and backed away. "Do it."

Dr. Upslinger expertly found Helen's external jugular vein and administered the bolus of calcium chloride and sodium bicarb from the smaller syringes. He then ripped open Helen's vest and shirt and stabbed a harpoon attached to the larger syringe directly to the left of the sternum and into Helen's heart. He pushed all the fluid – the epinephrine – through the needle.

He then tilted Helen's head back, sealed his lips to hers, and blew a large breath into her lungs.

"Restart chest compressions," he said.

Rylan immediately found her rhythm again as she positioned both of her cupped hands over Helen's sternum and began pushing.

Minutes passed. With a mixture of sweat and tears accumulated in her eyes, Rylan could barely see, and she could no longer feel her hands or her arms. A searing pain had built up in her lower back. Still, she pushed on.

"Stop chest compressions," Dr. Upslinger finally said.

He then leaned over and bent his ear to Helen's mouth. He placed the pulp of his index and long finger over her carotid artery and stared off into the distance. A blanket of silence descended on the group.

"I have a faint pulse."

Helen's nostrils suddenly flared, her chest heaved outwards, and she gulped a raspy breath.

"YES!" Rylan yelled as she collapsed from a kneeled position onto her buttocks, and then slammed her back into the doorjamb. She raised her fist in the air and said it again but more quietly this time, "Yes, you did it, Helen. You did it."

A nurse arrived, running at full speed. She screeched to a halt and opened a bag at her side. She placed an oxygen mask on Helen's face and cranked open the valve on a small tank. Rylan could hear the wispy sounds of the life-preserving gas flow into Helen's lungs. The nurse then quickly started an IV and ran fluids into her veins. Rylan could now hear the wheels of the crash cart approaching along with a gurney.

Helen was going to be okay. She knew it in her gut. She wasn't going to die.

Rylan sat with her head tilted back against the doorjamb, watching from a state of complete detachment, her body numb of all the pain and anguish. Finally, Dr. Upslinger's looming figure appeared directly in front of her. He removed his winter jacket and gently placed it over her lap.

He rubbed the day-old stubble on his chin and said, "You should put some pants on, young lady."

Rylan smiled, scrunched the jacket in tighter, like a fluffy Christmas blanket, and shut her eyes.

CHAPTER 40

Rylan

Her phone rang again. It had been nonstop from the moment she escorted Helen to the ICU: from Dr. Whittaker at the ground level, rightly inquiring about all his dead patients, to the CEO of the hospital, trying to set up damage control. Not to mention the Up North Voice, the Northern Express, and a variety of internet-based news outlets. She had no idea how they'd found her cell number, but she had become quite adept at saying, "No comment." It was one thing for patients to die in a hospital and another altogether for employees to be threatened. Word had spread fast in the early hours of Thursday morning of the killing ground Northern Michigan General Hospital had become overnight. Catchy headlines like "A Thanksgiving Day Massacre" and "Snowed-in Slaughter" were all over the web. Rylan wanted desperately to turn off her phone. Yet, she needed some kind of connection to the outside world. A connection to something, anything, away from this hospital where the aura of death permeated every brick. Hospitals were where you came to be saved, not to be killed.

She had already ditched the R3 pager at the ER main desk. It had become a symbol of death, and she was quite sure she'd never be able to hear *Twinkle, Twinkle, Little Star* ever again without crumbling into a puddle of PTSD terror. In any case, it was someone else's problem now.

"Are you going to answer that?" Mike asked, indicating her cell phone as he matched her stride walking down the corridor.

Rylan gave him a narrow-eyed, sideways glance, indicating that she was still thinking about it. The phone rang again, and this time she pulled it from her lab coat pocket and punched the green button with enough force to nearly crack the screen. Mike threw up his hands in surrender and lagged a step behind to give her privacy.

Without registering the origin of the call on her screen, she huffed, "Yes, this is Dr. Fraser."

"Umm," a familiar voice said, "so is this."

There was a long, heavy pause.

"Daddy?" Her voice cracked into a thousand pieces. She stopped dead in her tracks, planted her back to the wall, and slowly slid down into a slumped sitting position on the floor. Mike stopped also, far enough away to give her space, but close enough to lend her a hand when she would need to get up. And she would need to get up very soon. The meeting was in five minutes.

"Rylan, it's good to hear your voice," Dr. Fraser senior said. "How… how are you?"

The relief in his voice was tangible. Although the hospital was keeping a tight lid on everything until proper spin could be weaved, word must have gotten to him somehow. He hadn't even wished her a "Happy Thanksgiving," a sure sign he was distracted by more pressing matters.

"I'm awful, Dad. Beyond horrible. Did you hear about everything that happened?"

"No, sweetheart. Not everything. You're going to have to fill me in. But, most importantly … you're safe?"

He sounded scared. Rylan had never heard fear like that in her father's voice. It was obvious he knew something, but she wasn't sure what. "I think I'm okay, Dad, but it was bad. I can't tell you about it right now. I have to attend a debrief meeting. How much do you know?"

"I received an email this morning. It was very upsetting."

Oh my God, Rylan thought, nauseated. *Had Jake managed to send off the pics?* "Pictures?" she asked, closing her eyes tight and practically strangling the phone beside her ear.

"No, not pictures…"

Thank God!

"… more of a threat. A very ugly, vile threat from someone I met years ago …"

Rylan had a million questions. Before she could spit any out, though, her father asked again if she was okay, obviously needing the reassurance. She'd never heard him so shaken.

I'm motherfucking far from okay, Dad.

"Rylan," Mike whispered loudly, crouching beside her, "they want us inside."

Rylan nodded her head. "Dad, I'll talk to you later. I have to go, but I have questions for you."

She terminated the call with a sharp tap on the red phone button.

What did he do all those years ago?

Rylan took Mike's outstretched hand and rose. With Mike leading the way, she was about to enter the boardroom when a voice yelled from somewhere down the corridor, "Miss Fraser! Miss Fraser! You did not have my permission to operate."

Last night was bad. Could this day be even worse?

Rylan spun and saw her diminutive staff man, Dr. Huang, walking briskly toward her. She really didn't have time for this man's ego right now.

"I specifically instructed you not to take my trauma patient to the operating room, and you disobeyed me. Not just once but twice. TWICE! You are in grave trouble, Miss Fraser."

He had caught up to her and was shaking his finger in front of her face. She wanted nothing more than to grab that finger and bite it clean off.

Rylan bowed her head and, for a moment, was prepared to cower to the person who would be evaluating her for this rotation. The person who held all the power and could literally sink her entire career with a few nasty sentences.

"Do you know," he was yelling at her now, "while you were pretending to be a surgeon, I was trapped in a snowbank almost freezing to death before the police rescued me this morning?"

He holds all the power.

"I could have died!" he cried out.

Oh, how she just didn't care anything about how this misogynistic asshole's night had gone.

"And you … you were here experimenting on my patients without my consent!"

He owns my career.

She suddenly decided it wasn't worth it. Nothing was worth this. She'd had enough. Enough of all of it. It took every scrap of remaining energy in her body, but she brought herself to her full height and targeted Dr. Huang, like a rogue missile.

"It's *Dr. Fraser*. And, I don't know what you've heard so far, but while you were lounging about in your car in some snowbank, I was saving limbs and lives. That trauma patient would have died if I hadn't intervened. That kid in the ER would've lost his arm or worse if I hadn't been there. So, you can take your condescending horseshit and shove it straight up your very tight ass."

Dr. Huang took a step back, pure shock usurping the anger on his face. He stuttered, "You, you, you … will regret this."

"Wrong, Dr. Huang. I will never regret saving lives." She huffed the word "*Prick*" and turned toward the conference room.

·   ·   ·   ·   ·

It was 10AM. Bright sunshine, partially blocked by the shades, illuminated the room, casting a grim shadow that suited the mood inside just right. Looking outside, it was like last night never happened, perhaps a trick of the mind brought on by sleep deprivation.

They were sitting in plush seats around a large conference table in the boardroom, gathered for a small preliminary debriefing with only the key players of the debacle present: Dr. Greyson, the pathologist; Dr. Rylan Fraser, fifth-year orthopedic resident on call; Dr. Mike Curran, emergency room staff; Dr. Reggie Upslinger, locum internist; and, finally, a disheveled administrator sent by her CEO who was clearly here against her will on a major holiday and way out of her depth. Coffee, tea, and various juices were scattered over the table along with fresh donuts and muffins, but Rylan had no thirst and no appetite.

"You look like shit, Rylan."

"Thanks, Mike. You don't look so hot yourself."

"I'll bet. I must have run a dozen codes last night in every corner of the hospital. It was like everyone wanted to die on the same night."

"Yeah," Rylan responded absently, her gaze focused on a window, thinking, *God, I need some sunshine.* "Well, I, alone, must have been responsible for the deaths of a dozen people last night in every corner of the hospital."

She felt a tug on the sleeve of her lab coat but ignored it.

Mike's voice became louder. "What the hell are you talking about? Those deaths had nothing to do with you. They were the actions of a psychopath. A serial killer."

"He specifically targeted my patients, Mike." She was still staring outside, wishing she were there rather than here. "If my name was attached to your chart last night, it was a death sentence. Once word gets out, I'll be lucky if anyone ever wants to be my patient again."

Rylan's gut turned to lead as her own words hit home and some degree of realization of what the night's events could mean for her career sank in. Eighteen hours earlier, the world was her oyster. Now, *she* was the oyster about to be gobbled up by gluttonous higher-ups like Dr. Huang and the CEO looking for a scapegoat. It wasn't fair.

"Regardless," she turned to look at Mike and continued, "after what I just said to Huang, I'm sure my career here at Northern Michigan

General Hospital is very much over." She pushed her chair back from the table and crouched over, elbows on knees, fingers clenched into tight fists on which she rested her forehead. She then swallowed a number of deep staccato breaths in an effort to ward off creeping panic.

Mike placed a hand on her shoulder. "That guy's an imbecile and deserved every word. And the rest of it wasn't your fault, Rylan. Not your fault at all."

"Still, I'm totally fucked." She dropped her voice. "And when the media finds out I slept with him, I'll be crucified."

"Well, you saved Helen. You saved that kid's arm. You did emergency, lifesaving surgery that you'd never done before on your own, saving that trauma guy. That was all you."

"Well, he's not out of the woods yet," Rylan said, "but Todd has made it his life's mission to keep him alive, and he is stable now. Chalk one up for the good guys. You know, I've decided Todd's not such a turkey after all."

"Who are you kidding? He's still Todd the Dickwad." Mike smirked.

Rylan laughed out loud. She then covered her mouth with her hand. "You're right. Must be the sleep dep talking."

•   •   •   •   •

"This is what we know so far." The detective, wearing a well-fitting grey suit with an open collar and no tie, shuffled through papers splayed out on the conference table before picking out a particular one. He held it up to the light and adjusted his black-framed glasses before beginning.

"Paul Bennett, the real psychiatrist, was found dead in his apartment late last night. Preliminary toxicology is consistent with that of the patients brought to the morgue over the last eighteen hours." The detective looked to Dr. Greyson who nodded his head, his mop-top hairstyle messy and flattened, as if suffering the weight of the night's events.

"Dr. James Redfield, the third-year resident who was supposed to be on call with Dr. Fraser this weekend, was found dead in a vehicle parked in front of his apartment. It's presumed he was murdered as well, although his body was just discovered, and toxicology is still pending."

Hearing this, and despite already knowing it, Rylan couldn't help but tear up. She had worked with James intermittently over the past three years, and although she didn't like him very much, he was a good resident and would have made an excellent surgeon. She could only imagine how his fiancée would take the news. And then, the reality penetrated more deeply as she realized that if he hadn't been working with her on this rotation, on this long weekend, he would still be alive. It was her fault he was dead. She just wanted to curl up in some corner and shut her eyes forever.

The detective continued. "In addition, six patients and one employee were killed bringing the total to nine homicides, which makes this one of the most prolific serial killings in a single night ever."

A series of groans spewed from everyone at the table as the full degree of devastation registered. Rylan sunk her face deeper into her hands. This was not a wiki entry she wanted any part of.

"And we are not counting the near death of the head of security, who owes her life to the quick thinking of Dr. Upslinger." At this, everyone turned to look at Dr. Upslinger, who appeared exhausted on the verge of collapse and was staring with empty eyes at a coffee mug on the table in front of him. He had talked with Rylan after they had saved Helen's life, and Rylan knew he was thinking about his recently departed wife and the strange series of connections that led to his realizing Paul Bennett wasn't the real Paul Bennett. Had he come to this conclusion sooner, he might have saved even more lives. Still, under the circumstances, Rylan would take it as a win. Certainly, Helen would. Dr. Upslinger slowly turned his head, looked at Rylan, and gave her a tired, sympathetic smile.

"The *Modus Operandi* of the killer seems to have been a dose of a drug called propofol, a heavy sedative, followed by potassium chloride to stop the heart. This is one drug shy of the cocktail used for state executions. Based on the descriptions you've provided, the perp fits the profile of a serial killer known as "The Executioner."

Everyone's eyes widened as the words hit home, and a quiet, tense reverie descended even deeper upon the room.

"As bad as everything was, it could have been worse. Much worse. This man has been wanted by the FBI for many years and is exceptionally cunning and dangerous."

"No shit, Sherlock," Rylan whispered to Mike.

"The good news is we do not believe the killer is still in the hospital."

Rylan released a heavy sigh. Although deep down she knew he was long gone, it still felt good to hear someone say it.

"We identified footprints in the snow outside of the loading docks. We were able to follow them to the parking lot. Unfortunately, the CCTV recordings aimed at this area of the parking lot were blank." Mike and Rylan exchanged knowing glances. "We presume the killer was driving a very large truck since he pushed through four feet of snow in the parking lot to gain access to the highway. APBs have been released and roadblocks are being set up; however, given the current situation after the storm, the fact that we have no idea what his truck looks like, and that we really have nothing to go on other than some grainy in-hospital CCTV video and your physical descriptions – something easily altered with the simplest of disguises – we are doubtful he will be apprehended any time soon. In fact, given the time delay, he is likely far, far away at this point."

A random, burning question popped into Rylan's mind, and she raised her hand.

"Yes, Dr. Fraser."

"Do we know his real name?"

"He goes by many aliases, but we think his actual name is Jake Alastor."

•   •   •   •   •

Rylan walked slowly down the corridor towards the exit, her mind spinning with the detective's information. As she zipped up her parka, she noticed the red blood stain – the blood bullet – on her blouse collar.

She sighed, thinking back to the moment it occurred, a harbinger of things to come. And when Paul noticed it. Or Jake. Or whatever his name is. How could she have been so easily duped?

She was adjusting her backpack over her shoulder when she passed Helen's security desk. A new security guard she didn't recognize was perched there. He looked up from his paperwork and smiled at her. Perhaps a thank you for saving his boss's life? Word had spread faster than a virus.

Rylan had gone to the ICU to check on both Helen and Brad, the trauma victim, after the debrief. Both were doing surprisingly well. Neither was awake enough to carry on a conversation, but they looked better, and their numbers were all on the mend. It was as if Jake Alastor's mere presence had cast a veil of darkness over the isolated northern hospital which his departure had now lifted.

She continued her walk down the hallway and glanced into the ER where she saw Mike at the main desk talking to a colleague, presumably signing out his patients. He looked exhausted. He caught her eye, smiled, and gave her a slow nod, a sign of respect, much as Dr. English had done in the OR.

Respect.

That's all she'd ever wanted. From her resident colleagues, her staff, the nurses, the administrators, her patients, her father. Respect. And a belief that she could do the job as well – or better – than anyone else. She had proved that in spades tonight. At least to herself.

Rylan returned the same nod of respect to Mike – how many lives had *he* saved last night? She then stepped through the sliding doors of the ER where she'd entered some eighteen hours earlier, walked to the end of the portico and into daylight. Police vehicles were parked haphazardly everywhere with cops walking back and forth. It was a comforting sight. Even more so because she knew the detective had sent patrolmen to check her apartment and stand watch.

Remember, we are not yet done.

A shiver that had nothing to do with the freezing temperatures ran through her body. She shook it off, planted both running shoes to ground herself, and inhaled a gigantic breath of freedom. There was nothing so good as fresh air after a long hospital shift. For an eternal moment, she stood there stock still, bathing in the vitamin D, and then she pulled the hood of her parka over her head to ward off the cold. She watched her misty breath float off toward the sky as she exhaled, hoping the evil humors of the evening were being carried away with it.

Rylan's father had called several more times, anxious to speak with her. She'd let the calls go to voicemail. She guessed that Jake had promised some major-motion-picture-worthy version of death and dismemberment for Patrick's one and only daughter, payback for whatever slight, real or imagined, Patrick had inflicted on him years ago. Was it possible that the great Patrick Fraser had made some mistakes? Rylan knew it was. He was, after all, a human being just like her, and not the infallible superhero she'd believed him to be her entire life. She would call him back when she settled in at home, and she would hear everything.

Rylan slogged through the heavy snow, trying to make a path to her car. She was depleted and spent, but with each step into the knee-high snow, she discovered a spark deep within her that wasn't there when the night began. A spark that seemed ready to ignite her confidence to a whole new level. She was ready to play in the big leagues now. And she was ready to step out from under her father's wing. To fly her own path. To blaze her own trail.

It was time.

EPILOGUE

South of Traverse City, there was barely a dusting of snow on the ground. Mother Nature was funny that way. Jake rolled to a stop before the small cabin he'd rented for a song in the off-season near Fife Lake, nothing more than a dilapidated shack begging for a tear-down. The lure had been the recently-built 30 x 40-foot pole garage on the property with twelve-foot overhead doors and a concrete floor. *Bring your camper or motorhome and enjoy all Northern Michigan has to offer!* Jake climbed from the cab of his truck, opened an overhead door, and parked the truck inside. Once the engine was off, he allowed his eyes to adjust to the dim lighting and gave the place a quick inspection. A metal shelving unit against a wall held various bric-a-brac, and parts of a broken Skidoo were strewn across the floor. Otherwise, the space was wide-open and empty – except for a dated Nissan Sentra in the corner.

Jake stretched and rubbed his sore leg. The adrenalin keeping him going was leeching from his system, and, for a moment, he contemplated crawling back into the truck for forty winks. But he quickly brushed the notion aside. He wasn't in the clear yet, and there was still much to do and miles to cover.

He pulled a screwdriver from the glove box and removed the truck's plates. Next, he wiped for prints. Finally, he tossed the truck's keys onto the front seat and slammed the door. When the owner of the garage returned, he'd think Santa had paid a visit.

He walked over to the Nissan and felt for a key box near the rear wheel. He popped the trunk and was relieved to find his go-bag where he left it. He peeled off his skeevy scrubs and splashed some bottled water over his chest, then changed into a pair of canvas cargo pants, flannel shirt, and baseball cap. He felt a ripple of elation when he tossed aside the black Crocs he'd worn in the call room back at the hospital and slipped into thick wool socks and a pair of broken-in work boots. Much better.

Jake slid behind the wheel of the Nissan and rooted around under the passenger seat. A crisp manila envelope held an ID for a certain "William Monroe," a handsome (he looked *exactly* like Jake) upstate New York real estate agent and owner of a popular craft beer brewery. Jake knew as much about brewing beer as he did about psychiatry, but he had managed to become sufficiently educated about the latter over an afternoon on his laptop at Starbucks, studying Medline Plus, so he wasn't overly concerned about the former. He'd find a podcast on the subject to listen to on his way to Lexington.

He turned on the cell phone he retrieved from the envelope and was pleasantly shocked to see one bar of service. Jake wasted no time logging into the dating app. He grinned as he perused the string of messages from Courtney, the last an eager, "I can't believe we are finally meeting!" followed by a smiley face emoji and a two-glasses-clinking-in-celebration emoji. Jake and Courtney had been messaging for months now. While Jake didn't find her profile picture particularly attractive – middle-aged, thickening a bit in the hips and thinning a little in the hairline – he was most certainly attracted by her position as CEO for a much-respected chemical supply company in Lexington, Kentucky. An online search revealed a plump salary, limited social life, and a handful of considerable assets including a tasteful, spacious home just outside the city.

He put the key into the ignition and started the car. He consulted an old-fashioned road atlas from the center console to figure out where he'd be able to pick up route 131 South to Grand Rapids (after a quick pitstop at the lake to dump some incriminating trash.) It looked like he would then need to cut east on I-96. He traced the route with a finger and frowned. It was going to be a long day. He pulled an energy drink from his bag and downed three Advil, then tapped out a quick message to Courtney, "On my way!" He hoped she'd have a turkey dinner and a bottle of bourbon waiting. He added a turkey emoji and a drink emoji to drop the hint.

Jake stepped on the gas and eased out onto the road. With each mile he put between himself and Northern Michigan General Hospital, he should have been feeling a little lighter. He was getting away. It had been touch-and-go there for a while, but he was getting away. Just like he did after "mischief-making" at that beach resort a few years back (three unexplained casualties in one weekend). Just like he did after wreaking quiet devastation on that college campus in Missouri (the papers called it a spate of suicides). Each time he'd achieved such unrefuted power over life and death in the past, he'd felt a drunken euphoria that lasted for days, weeks even. So … why was the phantom of regret riding beside him in the passenger seat now?

Easy.

He had failed to kill Rylan Fraser.

He had failed to fully and adequately punish Patrick Fraser.

He had come *this* close to almost getting caught.

Such things had never happened before. Jake considered where he'd gone wrong. He blamed the green eyes, the ones he'd seen brim with compassion and sparkle with mischief during their hours together. On some unconscious level, they must have gotten to him, made him stupid. He could have had his way with Rylan in the call room, killed her, photographed her dead, naked body, and Fed-Ex'ed the pics to Patrick first thing in the morning, just as he'd promised in the scheduled email that Patrick awoke to in his inbox. *Happy Thanksgiving, Motherfucker.* But instead, he had wanted just a little more of Rylan Fraser, a little more time to explore her body and swim in the depths of those eyes. An error of weakness. Never again would he make the same mistake.

His failure left those eyes spared to open on many a new day. He was quite sure, however, that something of the sparkle would be gone. Jake knew that, now and forever, a film of fear would coat those pretty corneas. Rylan would never be rid of it, always looking over her shoulder for the man who could return any time to finish what he started. And she would be right to worry.

Remember, Rylan, we are not yet done.

The End

ACKNOWLEDGMENTS

It has taken us ten years to get to this point through literally thousands of pages of first, second, third, and umpteenth drafts of chapter after chapter and book after book, learning with every sentence. None of it would have been possible without help. In the case of *Call Game*, we'd like to thank these beta readers whose contributions and recommendations are everywhere in this novel: Brian Cody, Andrea Reibmayr, Dr. Emily Elder, Dr. Brynlea Barbeau, Caro Robson, Amy Reich, and Frederick Dios.

We'd also like to offer a special thanks to Dr. Gary Gerlacher, author of the *AJ Docker* medical thriller series, who opened the door to Black Rose Writing publishing house for us. We are grateful for the support and expertise of the Black Rose Writing Team in bringing our book into the world.

Laura Cody would particularly like to shout out her husband, Brian Cody, for his patience, his ability to wield a red pen like a grade school grammar teacher, and, most importantly, for his unwavering support and all-around awesomeness.

ABOUT THE AUTHORS

Dr. Graham Elder runs a busy surgical practice in Northern Ontario. He is the author of the bestselling medical fiction series A Covid Odyssey. Very outdoorsy, he enjoys Nordic skiing, snowshoeing, kayaking, biking, and hiking with his two massive dogs. Graham has been married thirty-four years and has two wonderful children.

Dr. Laura Downs Cody is a forensic psychiatrist, fiction writer, and lover of books. Her short fiction has appeared in numerous publications. She is happiest hiking and adoring beautiful vistas and gorgeous sunsets. She loves chocolate (addiction-level), puttering around the kitchen, and long afternoon runs. Laura lives in New York with her three children, two cats, and one husband.

Laura and Graham met over a cadaver in the anatomy lab their first week of medical school and have been friends ever since. In 2015, they joined forces and twodocswriting.com was born. A forensic psychiatrist writing with an orthopedic surgeon? What devilish harm could come of that?

NOTE FROM
GRAHAM ELDER AND LAURA CODY

Word-of-mouth is crucial for any author to succeed. If you enjoyed *Call Game*, please leave a review online—anywhere you are able. Even if it's just a sentence or two. It would make all the difference and would be very much appreciated.

Thanks!
Graham Elder and Laura Cody

We hope you enjoyed reading this title from:

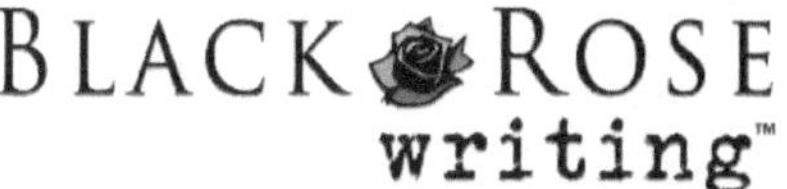

www.blackrosewriting.com

Subscribe to our mailing list – *The Rosevine* – and receive **FREE** books, daily deals, and stay current with news about upcoming releases and our hottest authors.
Scan the QR code below to sign up.

Already a subscriber? Please accept a sincere thank you for being a fan of Black Rose Writing authors.

View other Black Rose Writing titles at www.blackrosewriting.com/books and use promo code **PRINT** to receive a **20% discount** when purchasing.

9 781685 136673